Unfinished Business

Janet Kay

PRAISE FOR UNFINISHED BUSINESS

I would give **Unfinished Business** a "must read" rating! It's a perfect fit for anyone interested in suspense within a setting of our beautiful north country. I especially enjoyed her inclusion of real people she's met and real places she's visited. Her references to Native American culture are perfect and help tie it all together. Five stars for Janet Kay!

~Mike Williams, author of *Life at Kettle Falls*

Unfinished Business is a captivating novel about a young woman searching for the truth about her maternal grandparents. Beautifully set in the woods and lakes of Northeastern Minnesota, she is aided in her search by the "journal" of the legendary Justine Kerfoot.

~Sue Kerfoot, Justine Kerfoot's family

Readers will find love, mystery and intrigue as they enter a spirit world connecting generations in Janet Kay's newest novel, **Unfinished Business.** Her creative story interweaves settings of Northland cities with authentic treasures including the remote Isle Royale National Park, Voyageur's National Park, the charming town of Grand Marais and historic Gunflint Lodge. Janet Kay challenges you to think beyond the present as her characters complete their unfinished business, connecting with the past and looking forward to a future in the next world.

~Debra Raye King,
author of *Gravedigger's Daughter – Growing Up Rural*

With a title like **Unfinished Business** the reader in me is hooked from the start. Readers will enjoy an up north feel and will relish this read as it takes you into the characters' lives and the history of remote cabin living, along with a little romance as the embers of the fire burn. Janet Kay has woven a fun story.

~Jim Bishop, author of *Orton*

Janet Kay is a gifted storyteller who enthralls her readers with her brilliant imagination and alluring plots.

~Stacie Theis, Beachbound Book Reviewer

Other Books by Janet Kay

www.novelsbyjanetkay.com

Waters of The Dancing Sky

Amelia 1868

The Sisters

Rainy Lake Rendezvous

It is the secret of the world
That all things subsist
And do not die,
But retire a little from sight
And afterwards return again.

Ralph Waldo Emerson

CHAPTER ONE

Run! Run faster!

I run barefoot through the woods, shivering beneath a silver moon that is pulsating, sending angry spikes of energy through my soul. Trying to catch my breath, I stumble over rocky outcrops and rotted tree limbs strewn amongst massive oaks and ancient pines reaching high into the night sky. I try to hide in the shadows of mighty trees bending low to the ground as the wild wind howls eerily through the dense forest.

I hear the pounding waves of Lake Superior crashing against the rocky shoreline below. I run harder, faster, trying to escape from an evil force crashing through the brush behind me. Angry trees swirl around me in distorted shapes, reaching out to grab me. I feel a sense of evil seeping from the bark of the trees as their twisted branches scrape my arms and my legs.

"Help! Help me!" I scream into the night as heavy footsteps from behind seem to be closing in on me.

"Angelique..." A hauntingly familiar voice thunders throughout the woods as snowflakes begin to fall, dancing around me, obscuring my vision. Oh my God, he has found me!

"Angelique..." More voices join the chorus, chanting louder and louder.

"Leave me alone. Please leave me alone." I run harder, faster, but the voices continue to follow, taunting me.

A massive oak bends low to the ground, its gnarled branches reaching out of the shadows, trying to ensnare me in its limbs. Trying to smother the life out of me. Trying to hold me until the monster pursuing me catches up.

Exhausted, shaking in fear, I begin to sob uncontrollably. "Where am I? What am I doing here?" I begin to wail as I stumble through the forest, terrified to look behind me. I can't bear to see his face.

A bolt of lightning flashes through the night sky, illuminating the path before me. It leads to a rocky cliff looming high over the raging waters of the great lake. I am trapped with nowhere to go.

"Angelique!" his voice roars from behind me. "You have no place to go. No place to hide."

He's getting closer, closer yet. "Why? Why are you doing this to me?" I whimper as I trip over a tree stump and fall to the ground. Trembling in fear, I curl into a ball beneath a tree. Trying to hide. Trying to protect myself from his fury. I can no longer feel my limbs. I can no longer think clearly.

Suddenly the forest grows eerily still. I can no longer hear his heavy footsteps crunching through the forest. The trees have frozen in place. The snow and fierce winds have ceased, leaving behind a gentle breeze. I cautiously open my eyes, listening for any signs of danger. There is nothing. Is this just a bad dream?

Finally, I dare to move. I cautiously rise, trying to figure out where I am and where I need to go...until a gunshot shatters the stillness of the forest and my world goes black.

....

"Angela, wake up! Angela." My mother's voice woke me from another nightmare. Was I alive after all? Drenched in sweat, I opened my eyes to see Emily, my mother, sitting on the bed beside me, a worried expression on her face. She gently stroked my forehead. "It's all right, Angela. It's only a dream."

It took a few minutes for me to come back, to reorient myself to the real world. I darted my eyes around the room, seeking safety, listening for footsteps and the sound of a gunshot. Searching for angry trees. There were none. Instead, I found myself gazing out my bedroom window as the early morning sunlight broke through a bank of fog hovering over Lake Superior. I heard the waves crashing against the rocky shoreline below my mother's house. *I'm home and I'm okay,* I tried to reassure myself. *Yes, I'm okay...or I will be. Someday.*

I was back home at my mother's historic mansion north of Duluth, Minnesota, where I'd grown up. I'd returned several weeks ago after escaping from an abusive marriage. I was thirty years old and my life was a mess. Not much to brag about. Maybe I was lost in the woods, trying to figure out where I was going and what I was supposed to be doing with my life. But why was I having these horrible nightmares about Angelique?

"Angela," Emily said softly, "you keep having these dreams." A far-away look transformed the features of her aging face as if she was lost in the past. She nervously twisted a lock of gray hair around her finger before asking me, "Why do you keep talking about Angelique in your dreams? Angelique, of all people?" There was an edge to her voice and a flicker of anger burning in her blue eyes.

It was common knowledge that the subject of Angelique was not a welcome topic of conversation in this household. It had been that way since I was a little girl seeking answers to my endless questions about my maternal grandmother, Angelique, who had mysteriously disappeared long ago before I was even born. For some reason I had become obsessed with learning more about her. Where had she gone? And why? Why must it remain a family secret that nobody would share with me?

Pulling myself back to the present, I finally met my mother's lingering gaze. She was anxiously waiting for an answer.

"I don't know. I only wish I did. I know you don't like to hear about her, and I'm sorry if I've upset you. I don't know why I dream about her. I just don't know what to say."

"Something is not right, Angela. Maybe we should think about setting up an appointment for you with a good psychiatrist."

A wave of anger and resentment rose within me. "Let's just forget this ever happened, okay? Let's forget everything—like the fact that I'm trying to recover from what Jeff did to me. Like the fact that my whole life has been turned upside down. So maybe I'm not myself these days? Maybe I have some bizarre nightmares? Maybe I can't meet your lofty expectations? I'm sorry about that. Maybe I just need some time. Some space. Maybe I just need to get away-"

"You are away," her voice was stern and gravelly. "You're here with me. You have a wonderful place to stay. What more do you want?"

"I'm sorry. I simply can't discuss this with you anymore, Emily. I need some fresh air." With that, I stomped into my bathroom and closed the door. A twinge of guilt flickered through my anger. Maybe my mother didn't deserve my harsh words. It wasn't her fault that I had never been able to meet her expectations. It wasn't her fault that I'd messed up my life and had to move back home with my tail between my legs as she would say.

Still, I needed to find a way to make it on my own. Being here in this house where I'd grown up, where I'd never really been exposed to the real world, simply wasn't going to work anymore. It reminded me of what a failure I was.

I could sense my mother waiting on the other side of the bathroom door as I stripped off my sweat-drenched pajamas, turned on the taps of the old claw foot bathtub that had been retrofitted with jacuzzi jets.

As I climbed into the tub, I caught a glimpse of myself in the antique mirror. My emerald green eyes reminded me of my father's eyes. They seemed to glow through the rising layers of mist and steam. My long, dark hair hung limply over my bare shoulders. I was still trim and fit and able to fit into size six clothing. I'd always taken care of myself, hiked and exercised almost every day. After all, my primary marital obligation had been to serve as my husband's "showpiece" at his fancy dinners and conferences. That no longer mattered.

As I immersed myself into the bubbles swirling around me, I wondered what did matter at this stage of my life. What would it be like to simply slip beneath the water and end it all? What did I have to look forward to?

As my racing heartbeat began to stabilize, my eyelids fluttered and closed in exhaustion. I suddenly bolted from my reverie as a transparent image glowed above the faucets. Angelique! I'd not seen a vision of my grandmother in several years. But she was here now, sending soothing energy my way. Encouraging me to move forward, to fulfill my destiny. Letting me know she was and always would be with me. Somehow our lives seemed to have become intertwined, as if we were on a journey together, a journey that transcended time and place.

What I needed to know was why I was having nightmares about her. What did they mean? Was she trying to warn me about something? Why did I feel a growing sense of urgency, as if we were running out of time?

Basking in the warmth of her presence, I was suddenly startled by a loud knocking on my bathroom door. My mother, of course, checking up on me. Angelique magically disappeared at that precise moment, leaving behind a glimmer of hope that I would cling to as I made my own way in this world

"Angela? Is everything all right in there? Do you want to talk?"

"I'm fine," I finally replied as I heard her footsteps retreating. I sensed a note of sadness in her voice. Maybe she was hoping I would come out and spend some time with her. Maybe we could even try to resolve the differences that had consumed our lives for so many years. I didn't fully understand what those differences were. All I knew was that they seemed to be linked to the mysterious Angelique.

CHAPTER TWO

$\mathcal{I}$t's going to be a great day...well, maybe a good day, I tried to convince myself as I urged myself to climb out of my comfortable Victorian style bed with its lacy white canopy and heavy, carved wooden headboard and finials.

Growing up here, I'd always rush to my window seat as soon I got up each morning. Cuddling up with my favorite blanket, I could gaze down across our massive garden with its fountain and gazebo to watch the waves of Lake Superior gently lapping, sometimes leaping, across the shoreline. I'd spent many hours there sketching in my notebook. Sometimes images seemed to come to me out of nowhere. Sometimes I was surprised to see what I'd drawn. And sometimes those sketches got me into trouble with my mother—especially the one I'd drawn of Angelique. But that was another story for another time, one I didn't need to dwell on this morning.

Yes, it was going to be a good day. What I needed was to get out into nature, to hike through one of my favorite places in Duluth—the Leif Erickson Park Rose Garden and Lakewalk. Besides, I had nothing else to do. Not yet. No job anymore, not since I'd left my soon-to-be ex-husband two weeks ago in Chicago. It wasn't safe to stay there, not with all of Jeff's threats and continual harassment. Maybe that's why I was dreaming about being chased through the woods...and killed? But why was Angelique the focus of my nightmares?

Stop it, I scolded myself. Quit thinking about Jeff and your nightmares!

I threw on a pair of jeans, my favorite well-worn sweatshirt, and hiking shoes, brushed my hair and teeth, and headed downstairs for breakfast. I knew that Beth, Emily's devoted housekeeper and cook of many years, would have something good waiting for me. If I hurried, maybe I'd be done eating and on my way before Emily was even out of bed.

That wasn't nice. I should be grateful that she'd taken me in, given me a place to call home until I was ready to move back into the world. Besides, she was my mother, even if I'd called her Emily instead of Mother for many years. The distance between us seemed to be the result of family secrets she'd always withheld from me. Secrets about her past. About our family history.

All I knew was that Emily had been adopted by a wealthy prominent Duluth family at the age of three after her father had drowned in a shipwreck on Lake Superior. Her mother, Angelique, had disappeared. Emily had grown up as an only child since her adoptive parents had been unable to have children of their own. She'd spent her entire life in this mansion on Congdon Boulevard that she now owned after their deaths.

Maybe losing her birth parents and being adopted at such a young age had somehow traumatized her, making it impossible for her to process what had happened to them? Maybe she still carried scars deep within herself that she refused to acknowledge or deal with? Feelings of having been abandoned? Maybe I should have more compassion for her.

I walked down the winding wooden staircase, marveling again at the sunlight streaming in through the stained glass window rising above the landing. At the bottom of the stairs, the long hallway leading to the sitting room was lined with old-fashioned portraits of Emily's adoptive parents and their ancestors. A cozy fire blazed in the sitting room which was filled with antique Victorian furniture, a baby grand piano, and shelves of first edition rare books. Huge windows overlooked the gardens and rocky shoreline.

Beyond the sitting room, the breakfast nook was filled with ferns and vines, an antique table and buffet. The views of the great lake and its waves lapping against the shoreline had always inspired and calmed me. As a child, I had always preferred eating here instead of the massive formal dining room where I'd suffered through so many formal dinners with important people, trying to mind my manners.

This morning, I found Emily already seated at the little table in the breakfast nook, reading the *Duluth Tribune*. "Good morning," she greeted me warmly. "I hope you slept better last night?"

As usual, my mother was already dressed for the day, having

selected an elegant blue pantsuit today. It matched her eyes that were framed in an oversized pair of black-rimmed glasses. Her short, gray hair, which she had done at a beauty salon every week, was fashionably curled and styled. Still fit and trim as she approached seventy years of age, she took good care of herself.

"I did." I smiled back at her, slipping into my chair as Beth, the housekeeper and cook, brought out a plate of Eggs Benedict with hash brown potatoes, orange juice and a cup of coffee for me. I thanked her warmly before turning my attention back to my mother.

"I'm going to head out for a walk at the Rose Garden after breakfast," I informed her. "I need some exercise, I think, and just to get out."

"That's a great idea. No matter what problems a person has in life, there's something about that lake that heals and takes those troubles away."

At least she wasn't preaching to me about seeing a psychiatrist this morning. I sipped my coffee and dug into the delicious Eggs Benedict, one of Beth's specialties. "Speaking of healing, I need to apologize for my behavior yesterday...."

"It's okay." She attempted a weak smile.

"No, it's not. I was rude and ungrateful, caught up in my own trauma. Yes, I have some things to work out. I need to find a new job and get on with my life. For now, I do appreciate being able to stay with you."

Emily wiped away a stray tear as she replied, "Thank you for that, Angela. You will do just fine, and in the meantime, I am here for you. Maybe we can learn to understand each other a little better in the process."

Suddenly her demeanor changed and she tensed up, as if she was afraid of revealing too much, perhaps of becoming vulnerable. Typical Emily. She had rigid boundaries; always had, even with her own family.

Emily quickly changed the subject. "I hope you'll be home for dinner?"

While I'd actually been planning to spend the entire day out and about, including dinner by myself at Sir Ben's or another of my favorite places around Canal Park, I had second thoughts. Emily sounded hopeful, like she really wanted to have dinner together. After all, since my father died several years ago, she'd lived alone in this house. Alone except for her staff which consisted of Beth and Charlie, the gardener/handyman who lived in a cottage on the property. They were like family to her. And she still had lady friends, book club groups, church friends. She was involved in community projects. For someone her age, I thought she was very energetic. But still...

I hesitated long enough for Emily to continue. "Unless you have other plans, of course. I was thinking you may enjoy going out for dinner actually, maybe to one of your favorite places where we used to go, one of your father's favorite places?"

I almost teared up, touched at her offer, remembering how much my father had loved Sir Ben's. The three of us had spent some fun times there, listening to and singing along with the piano, watching sunsets over Lake Superior from the patio. "I'd love to go to Sir Ben's with you." I found myself reaching out and patting her hand.

So it was settled. After my day wandering around the Lakewalk, I'd come home, change clothes, and we would head out to Sir Ben's.

I pulled my long, dark hair into a ponytail, plunked an old baseball cap on my head, one that I'd bought years ago up on the North Shore, and donned an oversized pair of dark sunglasses before heading out to my classic Corvette convertible. I used to love that car, a gift from Jeff shortly after we'd married. That was before I discovered who he really was and what he was capable of. Now, I hated it and was anxious to get rid of it as soon as possible. Besides, I needed something like an SUV with 4-wheel drive if I was going to survive winters up here. I was no longer a wealthy resident of one of Chicago's exclusive suburbs. I needed the money to support myself until I could find a decent job, hopefully in the information technology or marketing fields which I'd previously worked in. For now, any job would do, perhaps something in the hospitality field up the North Shore? Or could I possibly make a living selling my photographs or art work?

Charlie was trimming the rose bushes as I drove down the long winding driveway toward the stone pillars marking the entrance gate. He smiled warmly as he walked towards my car. "Welcome home, Angela."

Good old Charlie. He'd been here forever, as long as I could remember. Always keeping an eye on things, on people coming and going. He lived alone in the little stone cottage nestled amongst massive trees. Although he was probably in his sixties, he was in good shape. It felt good, and safe, to know that Charlie was around...in case I had any unwanted visitors.

I climbed out of the car and gave him a hug. "So good to see you."

"Likewise, Miss Angela." He beamed at me. "I see you're off today. Where are you headed?"

"The Lakewalk. I need to get out there, smell the roses in the garden, and take a long walk."

He frowned. "Just be careful. You've got my new phone number, right?"

I nodded.

Charlie knew, and he had my back. I was also aware that he packed a pistol. He'd run several burglars off the property some years ago. He didn't mess around if he thought any of us, his extended family, was in any kind of danger.

"Thanks, Charlie. That means a lot to me."

His frown deepened.

"What?"

"That car. Yeah, she's a beauty. But...if anyone is looking for you, you'd be really easy to find. It's the only one like that anywhere around here, you know."

He was right. I needed to get rid of it as soon as possible. Hopefully, Jeff was too busy making money and having affairs with women to even think about me. But I never knew what he was capable of, especially if he thought I'd get any of his precious money in our upcoming divorce settlement.

"I have an idea. How'd you like to take my old truck today instead?"

And so, it was settled. I hid my fancy car in one of the garages on the property and climbed into Charlie's trusty old Ford 150 pickup. At least it had an automatic shift and good tires. Charlie also agreed to try to find a buyer for my car and perhaps a good SUV that I could purchase.

I was off on my adventures of the day disguised in my sloppy old clothes, baseball cap, and sunglasses-driving a beat-up old truck! What more could a girl want?

CHAPTER THREE

$\mathcal{C}$ raving solitude, I was a little disappointed when I arrived at the parking lot by the Rose Garden. Too many cars. Something must be going on this morning. Still, I should be able to hike around the gardens, away from the crowd, and head out along the Lakewalk. I could get some exercise and find a secluded bench overlooking the big lake. I grabbed my bottle of water and my camera and climbed out of the old truck.

The sound of heavenly music drifted through the air as I got closer to the Rose Garden—a violin playing classical music. Turning the corner, I stopped dead in my tracks. A wedding was taking place at the old-fashioned gazebo. It was beautifully decorated with white floral arrangements. A dark-haired bride dressed in a long white dress and her groom in a black tuxedo gazed lovingly into each other's eyes.

I hung back, trying to be respectful, my heart heavy with sadness instead of joy. Remembering my own wedding, how much in love I'd been as we'd traded vows at the altar of one of Chicago's historic churches. It had been like a fairy tale coming true. I'd finally met the man of my dreams. We loved the same things—traveling, Italian food, sushi, good wine, long walks beside the lake. We had such a wonderful future planned. And he treated me like a queen in those days. Breakfast in bed on lazy Sunday mornings.

I also remembered, and would never forget, how all my dreams had been cruelly shattered. My heart still ached, although I knew there was no hope anymore for Jeff and me. He wasn't the man I thought he was, to say the least. Had I been so blindly in love that I didn't notice the occasional bursts of anger blazing in his eyes for no apparent reason? He'd quickly turn away, take a deep breath, and that would be the end of it. Maybe I'd done something to annoy him? Maybe I needed to try harder to be a good wife to this man who worked so hard, and such long hours, to support me and our lavish lifestyle.

Despite my efforts to stay focused on the present, my mind flashed back to another time, another place...

I'd worked as a consultant for a large marketing business, making frequent business trips. That particular day my business trip had ended sooner than expected. I was anxious to get home to Jeff. I knew he would be in court all day so I took a taxi from the airport. I planned to surprise him with a special dinner when he got home from work after defending one of his high-profile clients in court. I'd light the candles, open a bottle of vintage wine, put on soft music. When he walked in the door, I'd be standing there in the beautiful negligee he'd given me years ago.

It was going to be a romantic evening, finally. He'd been so busy and consumed with work lately that we seemed to be drifting apart after three years of marriage. Jeff had no interest whatsoever in having children, something he never revealed to me before we were married. I did. I felt my life would never be complete without children.

Strange. His car was parked in the driveway, I saw, when the taxi dropped me off. I let myself in.

"Jeff?" I called out. No response. I walked through the lower level of the house, from room to room, calling his name. Still no response. Had something happened to him? Where was he?

As I entered the kitchen, I heard strange sounds coming from upstairs. Heart pounding, I tiptoed up the massive curved stairway to our bedroom, following the sounds. Flinging the door open, I discovered my husband in bed with another woman!

"Oh my God. What in the hell is going on here?" I cried out as a furious, naked Jeff jumped out of the rumpled bed, charging towards me.

"What the hell are you doing here?" He backed me into the corner as a frantic slender blond woman grabbed clothes off the floor and ran out the door. She tried to hide her face but I recognized her. It was none other than his secretary, Julie! I had known her fairly well, or so I thought. Jeff and I had enjoyed dinners out at some of Chicago's finest restaurants with Julie and her husband, Tom. Oh my God!

Jeff was furious, his eyes blazing as he crushed me into the wall with all his weight. I was sobbing uncontrollably, unable to say anything, unable to understand what was happening.

"If you ever tell anyone, you will be sorry," he growled. "Do you understand? It would ruin my career. Just shut the hell up and it will be okay." With that he reached out and slapped me hard across the face. He glared at me with hatred in his eyes as I slumped to the ground, covering my face against any more blows.

"I said, do you understand?" He kicked me hard as I cowered on the floor.

"Stop!" I pleaded. "What do you want from me?"

"I told you! Keep your mouth shut. And quit interfering in my life. If I want to screw other women, that's up to me. What do you think I've been doing for years? Do you really think you could satisfy a man like me? Hell no! You're pathetic, Angela. Pathetic. If you don't like it, just leave. Get the hell out of my life so I can be free. You're nothing but a weight around my neck, spending my hard-earned money."

With that, he turned away, threw his clothes on and stormed out of the bedroom.

I huddled on the floor in the corner, in shock, terrified until I heard the heavy front door slam shut. I started to get up when I heard the door open again and heavy footsteps slowly climbing back up the stairs. I cowered in the corner, heart pounding, as he entered the room.

Jeff stood there in the doorway, breathing hard, glaring at me. Finally, he spoke. "This never happened, you know. Remember that. When I return, life will be back to normal. And..." He leaned in closer, his eyes blazing. "Don't even think about leaving. You have responsibilities here and a reputation to uphold. You will resume your duties here, do you understand?"

All I could do was nod in agreement. This was not the time to protest.

"Good. But just in case you even think about leaving, know that I will find you. You will be sorry. So sorry. You've seen nothing yet. Trust me. Now get up and clean yourself up. You look disgusting."

With that, he was gone. I heard his car roaring out of the driveway. I finally managed to get up off the floor. Looking into the mirror above my dressing table, I could see a purplish color beginning to bloom around my swelling eye. After gulping down a few pain pills, I stumbled downstairs where I found an ice pack in the refrigerator which I applied to my face for a few minutes. It wasn't long before I decided I'd better throw a few things in my car and leave. Forever...

That was the last time I saw Jeff—three weeks ago. I'd escaped to stay with an old friend, Pam, whom Jeff did not know. She got me to a doctor and steered me to a good lawyer, one who could actually stand up to Jeff in court. I filed for divorce before heading north to my mother's house.

Only three weeks ago. Yet it seemed much longer.

I shuddered, waves of fear washing over me at the thought of what Jeff could do to me if he found me. He would stop at nothing if he thought he had to pay me a decent divorce settlement, or if he thought I may tarnish his reputation during divorce proceedings. He would come looking for me to ensure that I would not talk, nor would I ask for much of anything. I had to get away—farther away—before he came looking for me.

A chill in the air brought me back to the present. I had to get out of here. I quickly walked past the fountain and through the back of the garden, barely noticing the vast variety of fragrant roses of every color that surrounded me. The colorful leaves swirling through the air and drifting to the ground reminded me that before long the roses and fall colors would be gone—as I would be. Gone someplace. Someplace far away. I just didn't know where.

I hiked down the stairway onto the Lakewalk and took off at a brisk pace, trying to clear my head. Any other day I'd be mesmerized by the sights and sounds of Lake Superior lapping or crashing against the rocky shoreline. Any other day, I'd stop to admire the big ships and freighters sailing toward the aerial lift bridge that would rise into the air to allow them to pass through into the harbor. There, they would load their cargo consisting of iron ore, coal, limestone, and grain. I used to love standing by the old lighthouse watching the ships come through. Ships coming and going to and from destinations around the world.

I had to remember that there still was a big world out there. There was and could be so much more to life than what I thought I had with Jeff. With that thought in mind, and after a fast three-mile hike, I found myself a secluded bench nestled in a grove of trees overlooking the lake and aerial bridge.

Breathing deeply, I inhaled the scent and the magic of this special place. There was something about water that always calmed my soul as

14

I gazed into the depths of Lake Superior.

I barely moved as a seagull soared through the air and landed on a rocky ledge beside me. He seemed to gaze into my eyes as I felt a comforting sense of peace wash over me. I don't know how long we stared into each other's eyes. This was not your ordinary seagull. Finally, he soared into the air, circled around me several times and disappeared.

I will be okay.

Still, I would never again trust or love another man.

I lingered, enjoying the solitude and the magical healing powers of this great lake shimmering around me. The past was over. All I needed to do now was put it behind me and plan a future for myself.

CHAPTER FOUR

" *S*...I haven't been here since..." Emily stammered in a hushed tone as we entered Sir Benedict's Tavern on the Lake, a classic English style pub overlooking Lake Superior. "Not since your father and I..."

"Are you sure you want to eat here? We could do Pickwick's or Grandma's or another place down by Canal Park," I offered, touching her shoulder.

She straightened, a determined look upon her face. "I want to stay here. He loved it here, you know, and he'd want...the two of us...to do this." She marched into the cozy candlelit restaurant ahead of me toward the ordering desk by the wooden antique bar. Someone was playing classical tunes on the piano. A jazz band would be performing shortly.

"Inside or out?" I asked her after we'd ordered our appetizers, gourmet sandwiches, and cups of their homemade French Onion soup. One of our favorites, it had a rich broth with a hint of sweetness, chunks of caramelized onions, croutons, and melted cheese.

"It's not that cold yet. Let's dine out on the patio, as long as we can still hear the music."

We settled beneath an umbrella table with a clear view of the lake. Flaming torches and heat lamps surrounded us as we ate and enjoyed our glasses of wine. I'd ordered a bottle, figuring that I could use a few glasses of wine tonight. And perhaps it would even loosen Emily up enough to do some reminiscing about my father, her beloved husband.

I often wondered if she'd been able to let her boundaries down enough to have a real relationship with him all those years. Had he ever known whatever secrets she carried in her heart? Yet, they did appear to have been happy together, in the more formal way that some wealthy dignified couples seemed to live their lives. Always busy with business or entertaining clients. Not a lot of time for having fun with family like some of my friends' families did.

I was surprised to see her quickly finish her first glass of wine. She sighed deeply, settled back in her chair, her eyes drifting back to memories of days gone by. I waited, not wanting to ruin her mood.

She finally smiled, gazing out toward the lake. "Oh, how your father loved to come here. You know he loved to sing and he had such a lovely soft, tenor voice. He'd get up there by the piano, after a few martinis, and belt out his favorite tunes. The audience loved him."

I did remember. And yes, he was very good. As a child, however, I'd been embarrassed that my father was up there on the stage. He wasn't being very prim and proper, the way I was always supposed to be. Now, I'd give anything to be sitting here listening to his amazing voice, seeing the light dancing in his eyes. He'd been happy then, especially after taking an early retirement to escape from the stress of his career as a prominent attorney.

"Maybe he's here with us tonight, watching over us, happy that we're here together remembering him," I said.

She cocked her head, a slight frown almost concealing the glimmer of hope in her eyes. "Do you really think that's possible?"

"I do." I stared into her eyes. "I believe that Dad lives on in another time and place, yes. But he's still with us in some way, still a part of our lives. And he always will be. We just need to cherish our memories together and be open to signs from him."

"Hmm...you've always had some interesting but rather strange ideas, Angela, about things beyond this world. I just don't know what to think, as much as I'd like to believe some of that."

"Of course, you need to believe what you want to believe."

She grew quiet again as we sipped our wine, watching the sun slink down into the lake, casting golden reflections over dancing waters.

When we got home, I encouraged her to take a walk out to our vintage gazebo in the garden where we'd enjoy a night cap, as she called it. I grabbed a bottle of wine and two glasses before we headed out along the brick walkway framed by solar lights. We curled up in the comfortable wicker rocking chairs, a small table between us for a candle and our wine. I lit the candle and we settled into a comfortable silence.

Once she'd quietly consumed a couple of glasses of wine, seemingly lost in thought, I broke the silence. She seemed a little tipsy. Perhaps a perfect opportunity for me to ask a few questions and finally get some answers.

"I love this gazebo." I smiled at her. "Did you come down here when you were little and just read or sketch or think about things? What was it like for you growing up here? You've never shared much about those early years, and I'd really like to know more."

She hesitated, tensing up a bit, leaning forward in her chair before continuing. Through the flickering candlelight, I could see the anger burning in her eyes. "What was it like?" she exploded in a totally uncharacteristic Emily fashion, a slight slur in her voice.

"What was it like to grow up knowing that you'd been discarded like a piece of trash by your own mother? How could anyone just walk away and leave a three-year-old daughter alone, especially after her father had just drowned at sea? What was it like, you want to know? Well, it wasn't easy, no matter how nice my adoptive parents were. I will never forgive my mother, do you understand? Wherever she is, I hope she rots in hell!"

Never in my life had I heard my mother swear or utter such harsh words. Never. I could not even respond.

"So now you know why I cringe when you have your nightmares and talk about visits from Angelique! That makes no sense at all! Now you know why I don't want her name mentioned in my home, not after what she did to me. Why do you continue to dream about this horrid woman, the grandmother you never met?"

"I'm sorry for what you went through. And I'm sorry about my nightmares and all of that. I have no idea why this is happening to me, why she pops up in my dreams sometimes. But now that we are finally discussing this taboo subject, I have one more question for you."

"What's that?" She quieted down, taking a big gulp of her wine.

"Why did you name me Angela?"

"What??"

"I said, why did you name me Angela? It's about as close to Angelique, the mother you hated, as you can get."

Emily broke down and began to sob. In between her tears, she whimpered, "Because...because somehow I hoped...that by doing so...maybe...maybe my mother would still be with me somehow...or maybe...she would come back to me...someday."

18

By then I was also in tears, feeling the pain that my poor mother had buried deep within herself for so many years. I impulsively rose and took her into my arms, holding her close, stroking her back, trying to comfort her. Trying to understand how the caring Angelique of my dreams could have abandoned her own daughter.

It almost sounded like a part of Emily had actually loved the mother she hated, wishing for her return someday. How was that possible? Perhaps hate was nothing more than a twisted version of love...a reaction to the perception of being unloved. On the other hand, apathy or a lack of caring was all about the absence of love itself. I could certainly relate to that.

As an eerie layer of fog drifted in off the lake, I blew out the candle and gently escorted my semi-intoxicated mother back to the house. As we approached the door, she stopped and looked me in the eye. "One more thing I want you to know. If I was hard on you growing up, expecting too much of you, it was because I wanted so much more for you. I didn't want you to be hurt or discarded like a piece of trash, the way I was. Yes, I know you're having a tough time right now, but you will be fine. You have a strong spirit, Angela, and I am proud of you."

"Thanks, Mother." I found myself blurting out the word I hadn't used since I was little and began calling her Emily.

She stopped abruptly, a shocked look upon her face. Tears welled in her eyes once more as she grabbed my hand. "Mother...I like that. Please call me that from now on, will you?"

I held out my arms, tears in my own eyes, as she fell into them. We shared a long overdue hug, feeling closer than we had in many years.

Beth greeted us at the door and helped my mother to bed.

I collapsed on the window seat in my bedroom, finally putting some of the mysterious pieces of our lives together. I drifted back in time to a day I'd never forget. I was about five years old. One of my favorite things to do was sketching in my notebook. Most of my sketches were of my beloved Lake Superior in her many moods, boats on the lake, people on the shore. I spent hours sketching while propped up on my favorite Barbie pillows on this window seat in the old-fashioned turret in my bedroom. I seemed to find inspiration there.

I'd graduated to sketching facial profiles of my mother, my father and my playmates. My parents had been amazed at the lifelike sketches I was able to draw at such a young age. They assured me that I was talented and would grow up to be a famous artist someday.

But one day I was somehow compelled to sketch a portrait of the nice lady who frequently visited me at night in my dreams. She would stand at the foot of my canopy bed smiling at me, inserting her thoughts into my head. She always seemed to be watching out for me, trying to help me, trying to be my friend. I felt special when she came to visit. At the end of her visits, she would blow me a kiss before she magically disappeared.

I was so excited when I finished the sketch of my lady friend. Running down the spiral staircase, I found my mother in the parlor preparing for a visit from her book club members. The scent of lilacs arranged in an antique crystal vase, filled the air. The housekeeper had already arranged fresh blueberry scones and tea on the buffet.

"Mommy, look!" I'd proudly thrust my work of art into her face, waiting for the usual accolades. I knew she'd love this sketch even more than all the others. It was the best one I'd ever drawn.

But Mommy's reaction was not at all what I'd expected. "What in the name of heaven is this? Who is this?" she cried out as she collapsed into a chair by the massive stone fireplace. It looked like she was going to faint. Her skin grew pale. Her hands trembled. She seemed to gasp for air as she clutched the arms of the chair for support.

"Mommy?" I whispered. "Mommy, what's wrong?"

Beth came running in with a glass of water for Emily, trying to soothe her as I looked on, terrified. Finally, she turned to me. I was still clutching my sketch to my little chest, tears running down my face.

"It's okay, Angela. Your mother will be okay. That's a nice drawing." She smiled at me. "Who is the lady in your sketch?"

"It's...it's..." I began to stammer. "It's the nice lady who comes to see me sometimes when I'm sleeping."

"Angelique! Oh my God. Angelique!" Mommy muttered, shaking her head in disbelief. "How can this be?"

Once she regained her composure, Emily, hands clenched in her lap, began questioning me. Had I ever seen a picture of this woman before?

The answer was no, of course not. Did I have any idea who this woman was? No. What was she like when she came to visit? Did she try to hurt me? No. No. And no.

"She's just a nice lady who cares about me," I informed my mother.

With that, Emily rose from her chair, eyes blazing. "You are not to ever again mention this...this person, this Angelique, do you hear me? Never again!" She grabbed the sketch from my hands and ripped it into pieces before storming out of the room.

I'd collapsed in tears, sobbing as Beth scooped me up and settled me into her lap in the rocking chair. She wiped the tears from my eyes, rocking gently back and forth, back and forth, while humming a lullaby.

When Daddy got home from his law office, earlier than usual that day, he took over. He explained to me that Mommy was upset because this "nice lady" looked so much like Mommy's real mother, the one who had deserted her and left her an orphan at the age of three. Her name had been Angelique. The grandmother I would never know.

It had been difficult for me to understand any of this at my young age, but I learned to never discuss Angelique or her night time visits with anyone ever again.

My mother later apologized for her actions that day, for hurting my feelings. She held me close as if she would never let go. I'd forgiven her, I thought. But that was the last time I'd called her Mommy. She became Emily to me, until now, until tonight when she finally opened up to me and became my "Mother" again.

I could hear the waves crashing against the rocky shoreline beneath my window seat as the lonely wail of one of the ship's horns echoed across the lake. I could see nothing. The whole world seemed to be shrouded in fog but I had faith that the fog would lift and the full moon would cast its beams across the waters once again. Life was like that. Sometimes.

CHAPTER FIVE

Fall was creating a spectacular show this year around Duluth and up the North Shore. Brilliant shades of gold and red contrasted sharply with the evergreens and stark white birch. Fall had always been my favorite time of year. I loved hiking the trails through the many parks along Lake Superior. This year was no exception. Although I was busy with divorce preparation and exploring options for my future, I made time for a daily hike. I loved crunching through the fallen leaves, stopping to admire the lake shimmering in the sunlight. It was therapeutic.

My travels took me from Gooseberry Falls to Tettegouche State Park and Split Rock Lighthouse. I loved the North Shore and felt compelled to go farther north. Something pulled me in that direction, something I couldn't explain.

I began dreaming of living in a cozy cabin in the woods, living a simpler life, finding time to write, to sketch again, and to paint in my spare time. The money from the sale of my car should tide me over until I got my divorce settlement. Or I could find a job of some kind up there.

Mother would probably not approve of such a lifestyle, but I had to follow my own dreams. Besides, it would be safer for me to move on. If Jeff wanted to find me, he could easily contact my mother or, heaven forbid, show up at her house. Of course, Charlie was on high alert and would run him off. Still...I needed a fresh start and a place of my own.

My dreams became more and more vivid, more urgent. Sometimes Jeff was chasing me, threatening to kill me, bursting into my bedroom in the middle of the night. I was always running away. My destination was always the same—a rustic log cabin tucked away in a forest somewhere near Grand Marais. It was on a lake surrounded by massive pine and oak trees. The small cabin had a stone fireplace, a bearskin rug on the wall, shelves of books, and an antique desk in the corner of the living room. There was a little deck on the lakeside with a nice view of a pristine lake surrounded by forest.

I had vivid dreams of sitting at that little desk writing a novel, one of my childhood dreams; of hiking around taking photos which I could perhaps sell at a local art gallery in Grand Marais, and of finally getting back to my sketching and painting. My future was perhaps unfolding before my eyes through my dreams. I longed to find that cabin in the woods—if it actually existed. Of course, that was a crazy idea. Still, I began planning a trip up the North Shore to Grand Marais.

Winter would be setting in soon. I couldn't wait forever to make my move. I began researching places to stay. That would be a start. I had enough money in my personal account to rent a place and make it through the winter, especially now that Charlie had sold my fancy car which I'd replaced with a perfectly fine 4-wheel drive SUV. Maybe I'd find a job up there. And maybe I'd even find that cabin.

At least I could hope, right?

Maybe I'd even get a half-way decent divorce settlement. Oddly enough, Jeff had not insisted on a prenuptial agreement when we married. Did he think I wouldn't be around long enough to claim any of his wealth? Or that I'd be too intimidated to dare to leave him? Any divorce settlement he agreed to would be more like hush money, I realized, to keep me from exposing what he'd done to me. Anything to save his lucrative business and access to his wealthy women clients.

My divorce seemed to be on track so far. Surprisingly, no news from Jeff. Maybe he wouldn't be trying to find me after all? While that was a big relief, it was also an indication of how little I had meant to him. How could I have been so blind? As much as he loved his money, I began to wonder why he'd married me. Had he thought that he could tap into my mother's wealth someday?

All I knew was that I was through with men. I didn't need a man in my life. It would be so much simpler to be on my own, make my own decisions, run my own life. Never again, although I still desperately wanted to have children someday. I'd have to figure out a way to make that happen before I was too old to get down on the ground and play with my kids.

Sometimes I'd get a little teary, I had to admit, thinking about the times we once shared. Times when he acted like he loved me. Times when he did nice things for me. But those days were gone. Every morning when I woke up now, I told myself, "You are so much better off without him. You have a wonderful life to look forward to. You can make it whatever you want it to be."

I began to make plans to move. I started preparing Mother for my departure, aware that she wouldn't approve. But she surprised me, being more supportive than I had expected.

"Angela, if that's what you need to do, do it. You can always come home anytime you want to, you know." She smiled wistfully. "Just so you can find yourself a nice safe place..."

"I will, Mother, and since I'll just be moving someplace up the North Shore, perhaps near Grand Marais, I'll be closer than when I lived in Chicago. I can even come home for Christmas this year."

"That would be wonderful! I was hoping you could still come with me, before you leave, to the Fitzgerald beacon lighting ceremony at Split Rock Lighthouse?"

My mother had gone to this somber event almost every year of her life, in honor of her father, Jonathan, who had gone down with his ship in one of Lake Superior's tragic storms years ago. His body, like all of his crew members, had never been recovered. While he hadn't been on the *Edmond Fitzgerald*, this ceremony at Split Rock honored all the brave heroes who had lost their lives in one of the many shipwrecks for which Lake Superior was famous. An estimated 550 ships had disappeared in the depths of this lake. It was therefore known as the largest and most treacherous of the Great Lakes.

"I'd love to go with you. After that, I'll be ready to hit the road."

....

November tenth dawned as an appropriately gloomy day, fitting for an event memorializing those who had lost their lives at sea. Until I'd married and moved away, I'd participated in this tradition every year with my parents. It was a relatively short drive up the North Shore. We always took the scenic route along Lake Superior, stopping at Brighton Beach to skip a few stones into the lake. Then on to the charming town of Two Harbors where we'd hike out to the lighthouse, weather permitting, before stopping at Vanilla Bean, one of our favorite restaurants, for brunch.

Today was no exception. Mother actually decided to wait in the car this year while I hiked down to Brighton Beach. She hated the cold and was a little concerned about slipping on the ice-covered rocks that lined the beach. I promised to skip a stone for her, in memory of her beloved father. Although she'd been only three years old when he drowned, she cherished the few memories she had of him. He'd become a hero in her mind, growing larger than life.

Hiking along the rocky shoreline into the wind beneath a bank of fog, I found several smooth skipping stones and stood silently on a rocky outcropping. As I skipped each stone into the lake, I sent silent messages to the deceased grandfather I'd never known. Sending him love and hugs from my mother and me.

It was hard to comprehend that he'd disappeared in a raging storm and his body had never been found. Breathing deeply, closing my eyes as the wind whipped my hair into a frenzy, I let the eerie images flow through me—images of corpses forever entombed on a deteriorating ship at the bottom of the lake. I could envision skeletons scattered around a sunken ship that was partially buried beneath the floor of Lake Superior, now covered with moss and debris.

I tried hard to focus on finding my grandfather amongst the remains of the crew, as I had for years. Ever since I realized that I seemed to have some strange powers that somehow allowed me to see things that others could not see. I never shared these perceptions with others, certainly not my parents. Years ago, I had tried to share some of my strange dreams and insights with them only to be reprimanded for having an overly active imagination.

I knew beyond a doubt that this ship that I was seeing in my mind, lying on the lake's floor some 1,000 feet beneath the lake's surface was the *Americana II*. It was the last ship my grandfather had sailed on. I knew that because I'd researched images of sunken ships on line and found this one that was a perfect match for the ship that I saw in my mind every year.

It bothered me that I could not find my grandfather amongst the bodies that I could see strewn around the sunken ship. Surely, I'd recognize him from Emily's cherished photo of him. An important piece of this puzzle remained missing.

The closure I needed was not to be found. I finally skipped the last stone I was holding tightly in my hand, silently saying a prayer for the spirit of my grandfather, wherever he was. Was he in heaven? Or perhaps already reincarnated upon this earth—or another planet? These were thoughts I didn't dare share with others, certainly not my mother.

Mother was anxiously waiting when I returned to the car, worried that I'd been gone so long. A bittersweet smile spread across her face as she wiped away a tear. "Daddy always called me his little princess." She began to reminisce as she did every year. "And he gave me a big brown teddy bear for Christmas that I slept with for many years even after he...after he..." She couldn't continue.

"I know. It's okay, Mother." I reached out to hold her hand. "He's still up there somewhere, you know, still loving you. He must have been a wonderful man. Tell me more about him.

"Oh, he was that, Angela. I wish you had known him. So different from that woman, that Angelique, who called herself a mother and deserted me. My father was the one good thing in my life during those early years. Except... except he wasn't home much. He was always at sea or gone someplace..." Her eyes clouded over.

It was all so mysterious. Nobody seemed to know or remember much about my grandfather. His only claim to fame seemed to be his tragic death. As a result, he'd become a hero. Had he really been a wonderful man? I needed to find out more about him and who he really was.

We drove in silence to the Vanilla Bean for a late lunch as we'd done every year. It was her favorite restaurant in Two Harbors, mine as well. Delicious homemade food included their famous chicken wild rice soup and sandwiches made with their cranberry wild rice bread.

Her mood improved once she was settled into a little table by the window overlooking the main street. Sipping her coffee, she began sharing more old stories with me, some of which I'd never before heard. None that shed any light on my mysterious grandfather.

After a leisurely lunch, we got back into the car and continued up the North Shore towards Split Rock Lighthouse which was perched on a massive rocky cliff. Waves crashed against the cliffs, sending spray high into the air when we arrived. We hiked up the stairs to the lighthouse, as we'd done for many years, to get the best view of the lake, the wind and waves, and the ceremony.

We sipped coffee to keep warm while waiting quietly for the annual Muster of the Last Watch ceremony to begin. At precisely four thirty p.m., the tolling of a ship's bell echoed through the fog as the program began. The names of all twenty-nine crew members who had gone down with the *Edmond Fitzgerald*, an American Great Lakes freighter, on November 10, 1975, were read. The bell tolled mournfully after each name was read. Although the names of those, like my grandfather, who had drowned on other ships at sea were not read, they were all recognized and honored.

Total silence, and more than a few tears, penetrated the gloom of the evening as the Navy hymn was sung and, finally, the iconic memorial beacon at the top of the lighthouse was lit. The revolving light cast rotating rays of gold through the dark skies, reflecting upon the waves below. This light once guided ships safely home. Now, in the age of technology, it was no longer needed and was lit just once each year to commemorate and memorialize those who had been guided safely home.

Mother and I sat silently after the ceremony while others hurried to their cars and drove away. Finally, we climbed back down the stairs and headed to our car. By then, we were shivering as the cold winds seemed to penetrate our very being.

"I'm not sure how many more years I will be doing this," my mother said.

"I can take you anytime you like, you know, now that I will be closer."

"That would be lovely, Angela, but I'm getting older. And I tire more easily these days. I can't do all the things I used to do. And sometimes I even forget things."

"We all do, you know. It's a part of life. I think you're doing amazingly well for your age. Just remember that you need to let me know anytime you need help. Maybe..." The words slipped out before I had a chance to think them through. "Maybe it's not a good idea for me to move away?"

Oh no, I should never have said that. I needed to get away. I needed to rebuild my life. I cautiously peered at her, afraid to hear her response.

"Thank you, Angela. That means a lot to me. But..." She took a deep breath. "As much as I enjoy your company, I'm also fine with some down time. And I keep busy, as you know. I want you to follow your dreams and build a new life for yourself. If that means moving up the North Shore, I support that. It is a lovely place and I have memories up there also, you know."

I breathed a huge sigh of relief, grateful for my mother's words and her approval of my plan.

"Yes, we did have some fun times exploring the parks together when I was growing up."

"It's more than that, my dear. That's where I was born and where I spent the first few years of my life. Maybe I never told you that?"

"What?" I gripped the steering wheel tightly, shocked. My mother had always been secretive about her early life. She'd always led me to believe she'd been born and spent her early years someplace around Duluth.

"I guess it never really mattered. It was a part of my life I wanted to forget, I guess. But as I get older, I'm thinking that you should probably know some things."

"Yes! I want to know, Mother. Where were you born? Where did you live when you were little?"

"Someplace around Grand Marais, I think. It's a lovely town, you know, one your father and I used to take you to. Sometimes I remember living around there, near a big lake...but I was so little. I don't remember much anymore."

"Grand Marais? Really? That's where I'm hoping to settle, if I can find a place and a job and everything."

"Really? You said North Shore, but I had no idea where. Why Grand Marais?"

Why indeed? Why was some strange force urging me to relocate there? I had no idea. Why was I dreaming of a cabin on a lake in the woods located someplace around Grand Marais? Of course, I couldn't tell my mother any of this. It made no sense, not even to me.

"It just sounds like a lovely place to live," I finally said to assure her. "I did some research and liked it. The charming town nestled around the harbor. Artist's Point. Artists and writers seem to be drawn to the area. And the local history is intriguing."

And that was all true. But there was more—more that I did not yet understand. And now, knowing that my mother had actually lived there, I was all the more intrigued and determined to learn more.

CHAPTER SIX

*F*arewells had always been bittersweet for me. Twinges of guilt and apprehension seeped through me as I waved goodbye to my mother, Beth, and Charlie. They stood on the wraparound porch by the driveway waving back at me as I drove down the long driveway, through the stone pillar arches framing the wrought iron gate and out onto the highway.

Heading north on Highway 61, I opened the windows and breathed in the air that blew in from Lake Superior. The farther north I got, I found myself releasing my sorrow over what I was leaving behind and focusing instead on what lay ahead. A new beginning for me. A chance to pursue my passions in life. Freedom from the abuse of my soon-to-be ex-husband. And perhaps an opportunity to learn more about my mother's biological ancestors. Maybe I was fulfilling my destiny at last.

There was something about the North Shore that calmed my soul. It was more than the great lake lapping or crashing along the rocky shoreline and the magnificent colors of fall spreading through the woods. I passed through little towns with cozy cabins for rent, charming restaurants to dine in, parks to explore, trails to hike, artist galleries to visit.

I'd rented a cabin at the historic Cascade Lodge & Restaurant south of Grand Marais and was anxious to get settled in. I felt at home the moment I entered the lodge, admiring the massive sitting room with an old stone fireplace, a library full of books, comfortable chairs, and floor to ceiling windows overlooking Lake Superior just across the road. There was even a piano, and guests were invited to spend time relaxing here.

My historic log cabin was a short walk from the lodge, nestled at the edge of the Cascade River State Park. To get there, I walked across an old wooden bridge, gazing down at the river flowing beneath me and out into Lake Superior. My cabin had a tiny deck with a view of the lake and a fireplace. It was perfect—aside from the fact that it was advertised as "the honeymoon cottage!"

After checking in, I began unpacking. My car was loaded everything I'd managed to take with me when I escaped from Chicago and a few items I'd taken from my childhood home. Hopefully I'd be able to retrieve some of the important things I'd left behind someday, especially my art work and attempts at writing. For now, less was more, and I had all that I needed.

Tomorrow I'd stock up on a few groceries so I could cook meals in my mini-kitchen. But tonight, I decided to dine out at the Cascade Restaurant. The sun was sinking low in the sky as I headed out into the chill of the evening. First, I followed a path across a little bridge and discovered a rustic outdoor chapel in the woods with a large wooden cross and several log benches. It was so peaceful that I sat a while, thinking positive thoughts into the universe. *I can do this! I will do this! I will create a better life for myself, much better than the one I left behind in Chicago.*

Shivering in the early evening chill, I was about to rise and hike down to the restaurant when a bald eagle swooped over my head and landed in a nearby giant pine tree. He seemed to stare into my eyes as I watched him, feeling as though we were somehow connecting with each other. A strange sense of peace and comfort washed over me as I basked in the eagle's majestic presence. Was he trying to tell me something? If so, what was it?

Finally, he flew back up into the sky after swooping over my head once again. Shivering, but consumed with a feeling that I was perhaps on the right track of something important, I made my way down the path towards the restaurant.

My dinner, at a cozy little table beside a blazing fire in the old stone fireplace was delicious. I enjoyed the warm atmosphere accented with deer horn chandeliers. Afterwards, I ordered a second glass of red wine to go, zipped up my warm jacket, and crossed the highway to a bench overlooking Lake Superior. A full moon cast golden reflections across the waves that lapped gently across the shoreline.

"Cheers! Here's to a new beginning!" I toasted myself and sipped my wine before heading back to my cabin.

Janet Kay

Tomorrow I'd begin scouting out a permanent place to live. But for now, I was perfectly content as I slipped beneath my down comforter and was lulled to sleep by the sound of the river flowing beneath my cabin. It wasn't long, however, before my fears came bubbling to the surface. What if Jeff found me? Was he even looking for me? I shuddered and tried to assure myself that I was indeed safe here.

Just in case, I got up and shoved a heavy chair in front of the locked door.

CHAPTER SEVEN

The Grand Marais harbor, where I hoped to capture a few sunrise photos, was shrouded in a cloak of fog when I arrived early the next morning. I thought that a visit to Artist's Point before breakfast would be a good precursor to getting down to the business of finding a permanent place to live.

As I wound around the harbor, I could hear—but not see—the honking of a flock of Canadian geese. It was time for them to gather together in formation before flying south for the winter. I always enjoyed seeing them lift off the ground together, honking loudly, sometimes jockeying for position as they flew away.

The fog was beginning to recede when I arrived at Artist's Point, parked my car, and hiked down to the lake with my camera. Shivering in the cold breeze, I climbed up onto the rocky point and waited. Just when I was tempted to leave, lured by the thought of a warm restaurant and hot cup of coffee, the fog lifted and the clouds parted enough to reveal soft pastel shades of pink swirling through the sky. I held my breath, focusing my camera, as the colors became more vivid and the sun rose over the horizon, casting shadows of gold across the dancing waves.

A new day was dawning, I reminded myself as I shot a series of photos that I hoped might be saleable. There was something about a sunrise that promised hope and new beginnings. That was what I desperately needed.

I walked out to the lighthouse carefully, fighting the wind and the cold. I was alone, and it felt good. Alone except for the flock of Canadian geese which I could now see. There had to be at least a hundred of them! The honking became louder and louder as they begin to lift up into the sky, somehow organizing themselves into formation. I zoomed my telephoto lens in and began shooting as they took flight, leaving Grand Marais behind—until next spring. Perfect timing, I congratulated myself, as I went back to my car, my fingers numb.

Starving by now, I headed for the Blue Water Cafe, a family-run business that had been here forever, or so it seemed. They were famous for their homemade pies, also their breakfasts. I found a two-seater table by the window looking out over the main street and warmed up with a cup of coffee before diving into their Swedish pancakes complete with lingonberry sauce.

Afterwards I strolled around this charming town nestled between the Sawtooth Mountains and Lake Superior. I felt like I was stepping back in time. There was an old blacksmith shop, an old-fashioned trading post, historical homes and wrought iron street lamps that adorned the streets.

I couldn't help remembering visits here some years ago with my family. Daddy had loved spending time here fishing, hiking, exploring. My mother had enjoyed shopping, eating out, just sitting by the lake watching the seagulls and the boats.

Why, on our visits, had Mother never mentioned the fact that she had lived somewhere in this area for the first three years of her life? Now that I knew, I was intrigued with finding out exactly where she had lived.

I found a number of art galleries and other shops where I could hopefully sell my photos and art work someday. I saw posters about a Grand Marais Art Colony and decided I needed to join that group. But I was getting ahead of myself. It was time to head for the library and settle in with local newspapers, maybe find a local real estate agent. I found a corner table and began poring through the For Sale and For Rent ads, making notes in my notebook. Nothing seemed to catch my eye. I didn't need a big, fancy, expensive house. As much as I loved Grand Marais, I wanted to live farther out in the wilderness on a pristine lake. Maybe it would help to just drive around and get my bearings first.

I decided to ask the librarian for advice about finding a cabin in the woods.

"Have you considered one of the lakes out on the Gunflint Trail?" she asked me. "If you want to be close to nature, away from the crowds, there are some beautiful lakes out there—Gunflint Lake for one. You sometimes see moose, bear and wolves, if you like wildlife."

I started researching the Gunflint Trail and couldn't quit. Its history was fascinating, including a pioneer woman named Justine Kerfoot who once owned and operated Gunflint Lodge on Gunflint Lake. Justine sounded fascinating, a woman ahead of her time, a writer as well. I discovered a book she'd written *Woman of the Boundary Waters* and checked out a copy.

Glancing through the book, I was intrigued with her descriptive writing. "The tall dark pines, like figures in a black and white etching, stand draped in capes of snow. They flank the Gunflint Trail in elegant silence, their frosty caps tilted at stylish angles," she wrote.

I was hooked and ready to head out along the Gunflint Trail, until I looked out the window and realized the day had slipped by way too quickly and the sun was already sinking low over the horizon. Given that the Trail was fifty-seven miles long, ending at Saganaga Lake in the remote Boundary Waters Wilderness, I decided my trip would have to wait until tomorrow.

I curled up that night in my cabin with Justine's book, a cup of hot chocolate, and a glowing fire in my fireplace. I could hear ice beginning to form, tinkling against the rocks in the stream beneath my cabin. I needed to find a long-term rental or home to buy before winter set in.

Although I was exhausted after a long day, I could not sleep for long. My dreams kept waking me up—dreams of that little cabin in the woods. It was a good dream in that I loved that special place and felt at peace there. But strange voices kept badgering me.

"Into the forest you must go, to lose your mind and find your soul," a loud voice echoed through the forest, repeating a version of John Muir's famous lines. Another voice joined the chorus. They grew louder and louder, closing in on me. Was I dreaming? I was now running through the woods once again as the voices followed me, urging me on to an unknown destination.

"Secrets, secrets, so many secrets," a soft voice whispered in my ear. "Follow me and you will discover the truth. It is time."

Jumping up in bed, my eyes wide open, I caught a glimpse of a luminous figure disappearing into the night. Angelique! I could feel her lingering presence and a familiar sense of comfort. Yet, she also seemed to convey a sense of urgency. Was she trying to lead me to discovering secrets from long ago? Or was it more than that?

All I knew was that my dreams and visions had become much more intense since I left Chicago—and they all revolved around my mysterious grandmother.

Why me? If she had some kind of unfinished business, why was I was the one she'd chosen to solve this mystery? Or was I the only one she knew with the ability to connect with spirits from the past?

CHAPTER EIGHT

Since sleep was no longer an option, I decided to climb out of bed and caffeinate myself. Gazing out through the frosty window pane while my coffee brewed, I marveled at the full moon glowing over Lake Superior. It reigned proudly over a star-studded sky, sprinkling diamonds of hope that glittered across the gently rolling waves.

After throwing on a pair of jeans and hooded sweatshirt, quickly brushing my teeth and hair, I donned a warm jacket and went out to sit on my deck, enjoying the view as I sipped my coffee.

I settled into the rocking chair, deep in thought about my recurring dreams and what they could possibly mean. Why was I always being chased through the woods, and who was chasing me? Jeff? Or was I running from myself, perhaps away from my past and into an uncertain future that I feared? But why was my grandmother always there, comforting me, yet guiding me, with more of a sense of urgency than ever before?

*Secrets, secrets, so many secrets...*her whispered words lingered in my mind. And what truths did she need me to discover?

The only sound to be heard in the stillness of the wintery night was that of the stream rushing beneath the deck on its way to the big lake. Shards of ice clinked against the rocky boulders which were covered with Icicles glistening beneath the light of the moon.

Before long I decided to head out early, in the dark. Back to Grand Marais where I'd drive out along the Gunflint Trail. Maybe get some sunrise photos along the way. Dawn was beginning to break by the time I arrived at the entrance to the Gunflint Trail and began the drive up into the Sawtooth Mountains.

Surrounded by dense forest, I kept a tight grip on the steering wheel. Rounding a corner, I suddenly came face to face with a moving object blocking the road. Slamming on my brakes, heart pounding, I soon realized it was a large moose standing directly in front of my car. Grabbing my camera, I rolled down the window and got a few shots of him ambling back into the forest. My first encounter with a moose!

I drove slowly, absorbing the wonders of nature surrounding me. A sense of peace and tranquility engulfed me. It was a different world out here, away from the rat race and stress that consumed so much of our lives these days. I suddenly realized that this was where I was meant to be.

My mind drifted back to some of the things I'd learned in Justine's book about the history of this place. Yes, Justine! I was already calling her by her first name. Somehow, I felt a strange connection with this soul who had died in 2001. I needed to learn more about her and her life up here in the wilderness that she had loved and written about so passionately.

Perhaps there were some similarities between the two of us. She had made a radical change in her life and ended up finding a lifestyle that she was passionate about, that she wrote about. It hadn't always been an easy life out here in the wilderness in those days. But she had found the courage and passion to pursue her dreams and make a difference.

As for me, I was leaving behind an abusive marriage and a good job. But Justine's words inspired me to dig deep and find the courage and strength I needed to pursue my new passions in life.

The Gunflint Trail was paved these days although that wasn't always the case. In the early 1800s the Chippewa Indians established a village on the shores of Gunflint Lake. Although they lived a nomadic lifestyle, they built rustic camps here. The women made beautiful beaded moccasins. They gathered and preserved enough food and supplies to survive the harsh winters. By 1870, the rugged dirt trail leading from Lake Superior up into the Boundary Waters wilderness near the Canadian border became more heavily traveled with fur trappers and miners venturing into the area.

In 1927, Justine's family bought the rustic Gunflint Lodge on the shores of Gunflint Lake. An intelligent woman of unusual strength and character, she'd left behind her medical school and former dreams of becoming a doctor to pursue her real mission in life. She ended up running her family's lodge, mushing her own dog sled team, guiding fishing expeditions, interacting with her Ojibwe Indian friends and eventually writing a weekly column for the Grand Marais newspaper.

Justine followed her dreams. I could do the same. I felt compelled to learn more about her and her life up here in the wilderness. Although Justine had died in 2001, she had left a legacy behind. For some strange reason, I felt a connection between her life and the mysteries buried within my own family's history.

Breathing a deep sigh, I refocused my energy upon the scenery. Rustic signs along the road directed tourists to various resorts hidden in the woods. Before long, I noticed a large moose replica guarding a tranquil lake at the entrance to Poplar Haus. I needed a break so I pulled in to scope out the place. It was charming—especially an old log cabin perched along the shoreline of Poplar Lake. It reminded me of the cabin of my dreams. Almost. But this one did not speak to my soul.

Getting out of the car, I stretched and hiked around for a bit, snapping a few photos as snowflakes began to fall and the wind picked up. While I was tempted to stop at the restaurant on the premises, I decided I had miles to go...and promises to keep? So, I got back into my SUV and headed farther down the trail towards Gunflint Lake and Justine's Gunflint Lodge. Only ten miles, according to the next sign along the trail.

CHAPTER NINE

I was hungry by the time I turned off the Gunflint Trail and followed the winding road toward the historic Gunflint Lodge which was perched along the shore of Gunflint Lake. Waves crashed against the shoreline as ice-covered rocks gleamed beneath the rays of the sun peeking out through the clouds. Snowflakes swirled around me as I hurried to the entrance, through an old-fashioned wooden door and into a charming gift shop. It was filled with books, Northern Lights jewelry, stuffed moose toys, and much more. Someday I'd come back and do a little shopping. But for now, I wandered into the dining room for lunch.

I passed through the main room where a fire blazed in the stone fireplace which dominated the room. A couple sat together on a comfortable leather sofa, reading by the warmth of the fire as they gazed out through floor to ceiling windows overlooking the lake. Knotty pine paneling held mounts of big fish, a fox, a wolf, and a bearskin. What a perfect place to relax and watch the snow fall, listen to the soft music playing in the background while enjoying the scent of the vanilla candles.

I would love nothing more than to spend some time here, but my growling stomach led me to the dining room instead. I stopped dead in my tracks when I saw a large portrait of Justine Kerfoot hanging over the entrance to the dining room—which was called "Justine's Restaurant."

Why did I feel so much at home here as I slid into an old wooden chair at a table for two by the windows overlooking the lake? How I'd love to find a cabin nearby...but what were the chances of that?

Gazing around the dining room, I was intrigued with the antique buffet and an old birch bark canoe hanging from the ceiling. A pair of vintage wood-framed snowshoes with rawhide webbing and leather binding were mounted on one wall. I couldn't help wondering if Justine had once worn them. I was also intrigued with a large moose head mount and black bear hide that dominated another wall, along with old photos from long ago.

Gazing out the windows, I watched seagulls hovering over the lake, probably getting ready to head south for the winter. Adirondak chairs, now blanketed with a thin coat of snow, and several umbrella tables were arranged on a large deck outside. Another old-fashioned stone fireplace dominated one of the walls in the dining room. Stacks of white birch logs sat near the hearth, ready to keep the crackling fire going.

It wasn't long before a waitress with long, dark hair and a friendly smile appeared to take my order. I hadn't even opened the menu yet.

"This place is fascinating," I said. "I've just been reading about Justine Kerfoot, and it's awesome to see the place where she lived."

"Oh yes." The waitress beamed. "She truly was a legend, and I'm proud to say that Justine was my great-grandmother. This place has been in our family for generations."

I could hardly believe my luck. "I'd love to visit with you someday and learn more about her. Somehow, I feel almost connected to this place. It's very strange."

She smiled patiently, waiting for me to continue, to come back from my reverie. I immediately liked this young woman and felt a connection with her. She was probably about my age. Sabrina was her name, according to her nametag. Sabrina. A very interesting name.

"So, what do you recommend, Sabrina?" I finally glanced at the menu.

"If you like fish, the walleye chowder with wild rice is one of our house specialties, and our hot chocolate with peppermint is a big hit this time of the year if you'd like something to warm you up on a day like this."

I took her advice and had one of the most delicious meals ever.

Sabrina stopped to chat while I ate. "It won't be long before we start decorating for Christmas. This place is transformed into a winter wonderland that attracts people come from all over. They come for the Christmas smorgasbord of traditional foods. But they also come for the sleigh rides and dog sled adventures. Or for the kids to meet Santa Claus. We know how to do Christmas out here on the Gunflint!"

I assured her that I would be back. But first, I needed to find a place to live, hopefully not far away from this lodge. She was not aware of any places for sale nearby but suggested I take a drive around the lake, which was exactly what I'd planned to do.

"Be sure to come on back." Sabrina smiled warmly as I was leaving. "I'd love to chat with you more about my great-grandmother or anything else. You're welcome just to stop in for a drink, sit by the fire, and read a book. Some of our neighbors do that, along with guests staying in our cabins."

I ventured out into the snow. Thankfully, it was a light snow, not enough to curtail my drive around the lake. Not yet, anyway. I cleared the accumulation of snow from my windshield, climbed into my car, and headed out to find my little cabin in the woods. I almost had to laugh at myself. What were my chances of finding a place like the one in my dreams? Still...

Which way to go? Although my initial inclination was to take a right back toward the Gunflint Trail, something compelled me to turn left instead. This was probably a mistake, as the road soon became narrower, winding through the tall, stately white pines. I could barely see the lake from here—just a few driveways with fire numbers on them. No For Sale or For Rent signs. I probably should have simply connected with a real estate agent instead of driving around back roads by myself in what could easily become a snowstorm. At least I should be able to find my way back to the safety of the lodge.

As the world around me began to turn into a winter wonderland and I was ready to give up my search for a home today, I discovered a homemade sign along a driveway on the lake side of the road about two miles from the lodge. Covered with a dusting of snow and leaning against an old mailbox, it was difficult to read. But something made me stop and get out. My heart raced as I brushed the snow off the sign which read "For Sale by Owner" along with a phone number.

Could this possibly be what I was looking for? I parked my car on the road and cautiously trudged down the driveway which was framed with stately evergreens and towering white birch trees. I warned myself not to expect anything like the cabin in my dreams. But maybe, just maybe, it would be a place that I could call home. I already knew I loved this area and felt that I belonged here. It didn't have to be perfect. I could afford to fix it up after all once my divorce settlement was finalized. I couldn't help smiling as I envisioned Jeff stewing over the fact that he'd have to provide me with a decent settlement simply to hide his secretive evil side from the rest of the world. Maybe I had won after all.

As I got closer, I stopped dead in my tracks. There before my eyes stood a rustic log cabin that was almost identical to the one in my dreams. Tucked away in the woods, the cabin had a little deck on the backside that overlooked a path winding down to Gunflint Lake. I circled it, peeking in through the frosted window panes. What I saw took my breath away—an old stone fireplace framed by shelves filled with books, a bearskin rug on the wall, and what looked like an antique desk in the corner of the living room.

How could this be? Was this real, or was I dreaming? I shook my head as I stood mesmerized outside the cabin. Was it possible that Angelique had led me here? That was crazy, but...

As the snow continued to fall, I decided it was time to head back to my rental cabin before it got any worse. I had a long drive ahead of me back to Grand Marais and then south to the Cascade Lodge. I scribbled down the phone number on the For Sale sign and left.

As the snowfall became heavier, I was tempted to turn around and check into the Gunflint Lodge for the night. But I didn't have my pajamas or anything with me, so I white-knuckled it back down Highway 61 until I finally arrived back at the Cascade Lodge.

Parking my car as close to my cabin as possible, I stomped my way through the snowdrifts that now covered the little bridge leading to my door. Breathing a sigh of relief at having made it back, I took a hot shower and climbed into bed after making myself a peanut butter sandwich for dinner. Thankfully, I had picked up a few things at the Grand Marais grocery store the other day. If I was going to live up here, I would have to be more prepared for weather events like this one. I'd call the owner of that little cabin first thing in the morning. Hopefully, the snow would let up enough that I could get out there tomorrow.

The wind howled throughout the night as snow pelted my cabin. I pulled up the weather report on my smart phone and saw that we could be in for ten to fifteen inches of heavy, wet snow. A travel advisory had been issued for the entire North Shore and out onto the Gunflint Trail.

Janet Kay

I was jolted from a fitful sleep by the sound of a large tree crashing to the ground outside my window. My nightlight suddenly went out. I crept out of bed and flipped on the light switch. Nothing. The electricity was out. I managed to find a flashlight and made my way to the fireplace where I lit a fire to try to keep the place warm until the electricity came back on again. Grabbing the blankets off my bed, I settled on the sofa by the fireplace for the rest of the night. Morning couldn't come soon enough.

CHAPTER TEN

"Angela, are you all right?" My mother's voice startled me out of my bizarre dreams when I answered my phone early the next morning. "They say there's a winter blizzard all the way up the North Shore. No travel advised."

Trying to clear my head, I sat up on the sofa. Thankfully, the electricity was back on and the room was warm. I shuffled in my well-worn slippers to the kitchenette to start coffee. Peering out the window, all I could see was white—a world covered with fluffy down blowing and drifting in every direction. She was right. But I desperately needed to get back up the Gunflint and check on my future home. Would that be possible today? The first step would be calling the owner.

"Angela? Are you there?"

"Sorry, Mother. I'm just waking up. But yes, it does look like I may be stranded here today...although I really hoped to get out to the Gunflint Trail to check out the most amazing little log cabin..."

"What on earth for?" She sounded horrified to me. "I had hoped you would have come to your senses by now. Why would you want to live way out there in the middle of nowhere? Away from a doctor or stores or people? There must be places for you to rent closer to Grand Marais— or Duluth, of course. You'd be much safer here, you know."

"I know, Mother." I tried to be patient. "But from what I could see, this little cabin is the perfect place for me and I'm hoping I could buy it at a good price. I feel like I belong here."

"You belong *there*?"

"Well, so to speak, I guess." This wasn't the time to tell her about my visionary dreams. Perhaps I never would. She meant well, after all. "There's a delightful lodge and restaurant just a few miles down the road. Very nice people. It's not like I'd be alone in the wilderness, you know. I thought you'd encouraged me to follow my dreams?"

"Well, yes, but I thought you'd at least choose to live in a civilized place, not out in the wilderness on the Gunflint Trail. You need to give this more thought, Angela." She hesitated for a moment. "This isn't the time to make a big decision like this when you're still in the midst of a divorce and stressed out about life in general. I mean...your nightmares and everything..."

"Maybe my nightmares would end if I could escape to a beautiful place like this. It feels so good just to be away from the hustle and bustle of a big city. And I don't have to look over my shoulder to be sure I'm not being followed up here. Jeff would have no clue where I am."

"I understand, but..." Her voice trailed off. "But, once you've recovered from your divorce and spent some time hiding out up there, you may well decide to move back to Duluth. You could get a good job here. There are so many things to do, places and performances to see. Restaurants..."

"I know, Mother. But I can always come down and visit anytime. Besides, I'm safer up here where Jeff has no idea where I am. I don't mean to alarm you, but if he finds me...well, it's not going to be good."

There was silence on the other end of the line which was beginning to crackle, probably interference from the snowstorm raging outside.

"Mother?"

"I worry about you and just want you to be safe." She sighed dramatically as she always did when she felt she was losing the battle with me. She had changed her tune from when she supported my move. "If you are safer there, then so be it. For now, anyway. At least stay put until the weather clears. And if you really are determined to live out there in the middle of nowhere, at least think about renting so you can get out of there after the divorce when it is safer."

"I'm not a child anymore." My annoyance grew. "You need to understand that. Maybe I march to a different drummer than you do. Maybe I always have. You need to respect my right to decide what is right for me. Can you understand that? Please...I don't want to argue about this any longer."

"Sometimes I just don't understand you, but there's nothing I can do about that, apparently. If I didn't care about you, I wouldn't be upset over this. I do understand this is your decision. All I ask is that you stay safe. Is that enough?"

"Thanks. I appreciate your concern and I'll be careful. Is everything okay at home?"

"Everything's fine. I do need to run. My book club is coming over this morning. Just be careful and let me know what you decide. You know I love you, Angela."

"Love you too, Mother. I'll stay in touch."

I started the coffee and threw on a pair of jeans and warm sweatshirt before poking my head out the door. A gust of wind blew a heavy shower of snow into my face. Stepping out onto the deck, I discovered that the snow was up to my knees and still falling. My car, at the end of the bridge, was buried in so much snow that it was hard to see. I'd been told that the lodge staff would plow and shovel my walk later after the storm ended. Hopefully in time to hike down to the Cascade Lodge Restaurant for dinner.

Not a good day to go out, I reluctantly admitted as I retreated into my cabin. But I could at least call the owner of the cabin and arrange to see it soon.

The phone rang quite a while before a gentleman finally answered. His voice sounded like he was elderly, and I detected a faint Scandinavian accent. Not surprising since there were quite a few Swedish Americans in this area. I was also proud to have some Swedish blood since my seafaring grandfather who had gone down with his ship was part Swedish. In his honor, my mother had always made traditional Swedish dishes during the Christmas holidays. Swedish meatballs. Pickled herring. Swedish rice pudding. Even lutefisk.

The cabin owner's name was Karl Olsson. He was a friendly, slow-talking man who was happy to tell me all about his home and the times he'd shared there with his family over the years. This place had obviously meant a great deal to him. Now, at eighty years of age, he was no longer able to take care of it properly, and his wife had died last year, leaving him alone.

"I'm so sorry, Mr. Olsson."

"Call me Karl," he said. "Lots of wonderful memories there on Gunflint Lake. I still plan to drive out and stay at the lodge nearby anytime I can do so. They're such nice, caring people. You would like them."

"I've met them. And I need to tell you that I fell in love with your little log cabin the minute I saw it. I'd love to meet you there and take a look inside—after the storm is over, of course."

He was silent for a moment before cautiously responding, "I would like to know more about you and your plans for my cabin—if I should decide to sell it to you."

I told him about my writing, sketching, and photography, my love of nature and the lake. That I'd be the only occupant and a full-time resident. That I wanted to maintain the historical integrity of the place and didn't plan to make any major changes.

"And you have no plans to resell it to a developer, add more cabins or develop it into some kind of resort?"

"Absolutely not! I want to maintain it as it is, a special place where I can create and just absorb the beauty around me—the lake, the woods."

He chuckled. "Sorry to ask so many questions, but, you know, as much as this place means to me, I need to find the right buyer. I don't need a damn developer trying to commercialize this place. Young lady, I would like to meet you there to discuss this further. I think we may be able to make a good deal for both of us."

I was elated and couldn't wait for the storm to end. Karl sounded like a nice man. For now, I built a fire in the fireplace, made myself scrambled eggs and toast for breakfast and settled down on the sofa with a cup of coffee and a psychological thriller set in the Northwoods.

By early evening, the sound of a plow broke my concentration. I looked out the window to see the plow heading back to the lodge, the driveway and parking lot open. Someone had shoveled my little bridge and removed the heavy blanket of snow concealing my car.

Gazing down at Lake Superior, I could see welcoming lights glowing through the windows of the cozy Cascade Lodge restaurant. I put on my boots and parka and hiked out through a surreal winter wonderland to the restaurant.

Breathing deeply, I felt safe here and more relaxed than I'd been in a very long time. The only sound to be heard was gentle waves lapping against the shoreline beneath a star-studded sky. What a difference from living in a congested, noisy city like Chicago where you could not even see the stars much less enjoy a lake like this one.

But shortly after I fell asleep about midnight, I was awakened by a flash of light at the end of my bed. A transparent image of Angelique shimmered in the dark, an intense and troubled look upon her pale face.

"We have work to do, my dear, and we are running out of time...out of time...time..." she whispered softly.

CHAPTER ELEVEN

$\mathcal{N}$ow that the storm had retreated and the roads were plowed, I could hardly wait to meet Karl. He called to tell me he would be at the cabin for a few days and invited me for coffee and cinnamon rolls he'd picked up at the bakery in Grand Marais.

After a two-hour drive along partially snow-covered roads, I drove down Karl's long, winding driveway, which had been plowed. I was surrounded by tall pine and birch trees decked out in their winter finery. I trudged along the shoveled path and knocked on the door. Visions of my dreams danced in my head.

"Come in, young lady." A slim, elderly man with thick gray hair and old-fashioned rimless glasses welcomed me warmly. He extended his hand in a gentlemanly fashion. "I'm Karl, and I'm pleased to meet you, Angela." His eyes twinkled.

My mouth dropped open as I gazed around the room. How could this be possible? Was I dreaming? My head was reeling as I steadied myself, leaning against a vintage rocking chair. The identical chair I had dreamed of, right down to the floral design on the embroidered cushion.

This was most definitely the cabin of my dreams, down to the finest details. The stone fireplace that now housed a crackling fire. The bearskin rug on the wall. The vintage rollaway desk. Shelves of books framing the fireplace, and an antique hutch filled with the loon dishes and old glassware that I'd seen in my dreams. The little round table in the kitchen with two old-fashioned chairs. My dream had come to life!

I realized that Karl was watching me, a look of concern spreading across his face. "Is this not what you had expected?"

"I'm sorry if I'm being rude, but I am overwhelmed. This is exactly what I was looking for. I can't believe this," I shook my head. "Every little detail. It's perfect!"

"I'm pleased that you like it. Come, I'll show you around."

We walked slowly up the stairs to the loft where the bedroom was located. Again, it was exactly what I had expected, including the view of the lake through the window over "my" bed, and the ornate oak vintage dressing table with carved legs and a cloudy tri-fold mirror. There were two doors on the far wall. One was the closet. The other, as I had anticipated, led to a cozy office with an old rolltop desk and wood chair. My writing alcove and workroom.

After a tour of the cabin, we put on our boots and made our way down the shoveled path to Gunflint Lake. Karl stopped several times to rest along the way. Once we finally reached the lake, he brushed off the bench overlooking the lake with his glove and took a seat.

He seemed to be lost in thought, as I sat quietly beside him. "Lots of special memories here, I will miss this place," he finally said.

Knowing that he now lived about forty-five miles away in Grand Marais, I suggested, "If you should decide to sell to me, know that you will be welcome to come visit me anytime, Karl."

His eyes brightened. "I'd like that very much."

"Tell me more about this place. How long have you lived here? What was it like when you first came?"

He began sharing stories from the past, his eyes misty, as snowflakes fluttered around us. I listened intently, instantly liking this man. We both enjoyed the same things—nature, the woods, the lake, the magical history surrounding this place. He was as intrigued with Justine Kerfoot as I was. He was a writer, like me, although he specialized in poetry. And he was also an amateur photographer. I felt like I'd found a new friend.

I knew beyond a doubt that I simply must convince Karl to sell this place to me. Whatever it took. I belonged in this cabin in the woods on Gunflint Lake. I desperately needed to be here. There had to be a reason why I had been led to this place, and I was determined to find out what that was.

"I think we have a lot in common," he concluded with a warm smile. "I'd like to get to know you better, Angela."

"I'd like that very much." I paused, brushing a light dusting of snowflakes off my lap before continuing. "So how many years have you owned this place?" For some reason, that was important to me. I guess I always liked to know the history behind various places. The past seemed to bring the present to life.

"Minnie and I just stumbled upon this cabin one summer, the summer of 1980, when we made our annual trip to Grand Marais, a place she loved so much..." His voice trailed off as he wiped a tear from his eye.

"I'm sorry," I found myself reaching out to touch his gloved hand. He squeezed my hand back.

"Anyway..." He cleared his throat. "We always loved to come on out to the Gunflint Lodge for a good dinner and sometimes rented a cabin there. I remember the two of us sitting by the fireplace in the lodge one chilly late summer day. The locals were talking about a strange event just a few miles down the road... a neighbor who had disappeared without a trace, leaving everything behind. Apparently, they'd been renting this cabin, so the landlord decided he would sell it. We just happened to be there at the right time, before anyone else had a chance to buy it. You see, property on Gunflint Lake is much sought after. Almost impossible to buy anything around here."

I suddenly felt a gentle, invisible nudge from beyond, urging me to make an offer, assuring me that this is where I needed to be.

"I very much want to buy this place, Karl." I looked directly into his eyes. "It speaks to me. Somehow, I know beyond a doubt that I belong here. If I can afford it..."

"And I would very much like to sell it to you, as long as you respect my wish to keep it pretty much as it is. No developers. No big fancy house."

"I'm willing to put that into writing, in a sales contract, if we can come up with a price..."

Karl rose slowly from the bench, deep in thought, as he began the slow hike back to the cabin and the warmth of the fire. I followed, holding my breath.

Finally, he stopped, a wistful smile spreading across his face. "What can you afford?"

"How much do you want? I am willing and able to pay a fair price. What is the assessed valuation?"

He shook his head. "That doesn't matter, my dear. I don't need the money. All I want is for someone like you to love this place and take care of it, in memory of my wife, and of me someday, when it's my time to join her on the other side of life."

A tear slid down my cheek as I gazed into his tear-filled eyes. He gently wrapped his arm around my shoulders. "It's yours, my dear..." And he then quoted me an unbelievably affordable price.

I gasped. "That's not enough!"

"Angela," he replied firmly, "I will be insulted if you do not take me up on my offer. You are the one I want to live here."

So, the deal was struck. I could feel my grandmother smiling down upon me. I could hardly believe my good fortune. Not only had I found and purchased the cabin of my dreams...but I'd also found a new friend, one I looked forward to spending some time with in the future.

CHAPTER TWELVE

$\mathcal{G}$t took a little while to negotiate all the details of the sale as I worked with my attorney, my bank, and a real estate agent who drafted a sales contract after the title was cleared. Finally, closing day arrived. It didn't take me long then to settle into my new home since I hadn't taken many personal belongings with me when I fled from Jeff. My new place was completely and comfortably furnished, and Karl had left most of his personal property behind after choosing several important items that had special meaning for him. Someday, I would hang some of my own framed photos on the walls. Maybe a few decorative pillows and a cozy afghan to enjoy while cuddling up on the davenport before the fireplace.

I stocked up on groceries in Grand Marais and picked up a bottle of wine at the liquor store to celebrate the first night in my new home.

The sun was sinking low in the sky as I trudged along the snow-covered path down to the lake, balancing my glass of Merlot in my gloved hand. I let out a long sigh as I settled on the bench overlooking Gunflint Lake. My new home! My new world! My new beginning!

Still, I had to admit that I was a little lonely. I was alone. All alone. As I slipped into a bit of a funk, I felt an invisible but calming presence wrap its arms around me, soothing me and taking the chill out of the air. I was already making some new friends. I had a wonderful future ahead, I decided, as I basked in the warmth of the setting sun. Shades of pink and gold began to swirl through the sky. No, I didn't need the big house we had in Chicago, the money, the stressful job—nor the cheating and abusive husband that I'd now left behind.

Well...almost left behind, I had to admit. I'd successfully pushed Jeff and my upcoming divorce from my mind for a while, choosing to focus on the new life I was creating for myself. I still hadn't answered the last call from my attorney. I just wanted it over as soon as possible. Thankfully, I'd heard nothing at all from Jeff. I was feeling safer every day and began to believe that things would be all right as long as I didn't demand an unreasonable settlement or expose him for who he truly was.

Someday, I'd have one of my Chicago friends pick up my personal belongings. I was not about to return to the place that now haunted me in my dreams as I replayed that final ugly scene over and over again in my mind.

How could I have been blind enough not to see who Jeff really was—and what he was doing behind my back? How could I have loved a man like that? He was all about power, control and money. A workaholic, he was obsessed with making a name for himself. And he had no problem lying about any and everything if his lies could help him achieve his endless goals. Yes, he was a narcissist with a sadistic and violent streak that he usually managed to hide from others.

As for me, I really didn't need a fancy house and lavish lifestyle like he did. I had not enjoyed all the glamorous parties and having to plaster a smile upon my face. I was more than content with the simple life I'd now chosen for myself. Needless to say, I absolutely loved my little cabin—more so than that monstrous million-dollar mansion I left behind in Chicago. I didn't need a beautiful house like the one I'd grown up in, the one where my mother still lived.

Still, I had to think about my future in the Northwoods. While I should have enough money to survive and lead a simple life with the settlement I expected to receive, I was not content to sit and do nothing. All I really wanted was an opportunity to sketch again, to paint, write novels and take photos. My lifelong dreams that I'd put on a shelf since I met Jeff. Maybe it was time to pursue those dreams. What better time and place to do that than right here, right now, on Gunflint Lake?

Lost in thought, I finally looked up to see a sliver of a moon rising over the snow-covered lake, shimmering across the icy trails. It was time to head back to my cozy cabin. Maybe I'd light a fire and read one of the many books Karl had left for me on the shelves of his library.

Tomorrow I would get out my good camera (thank God I'd thrown that into my car when I escaped!) and I'd set out on my first photo shoot along the Gunflint Trail. I hoped to get some photos that were good enough for me to enlarge and perhaps sell at one of the local art galleries or the Lake Superior Trading Post in Grand Marais.

I also planned to spend time hiking or snowshoeing along these trails or sitting on my bench by the lake, drawing inspiration from nature and forces beyond this world to start plotting my debut novel.

Yes, I had a good life to look forward to. No sense in spending any more time licking my wounds over a man I had probably not loved as much as I thought. How can you love someone you don't really know?

It did hurt, however, when I envisioned myself as a victim of his abuse. But I had to admit that I felt a sense of relief and control over my own life now. And I no longer had to tiptoe around Jeff, trying to anticipate his changing moods.

Enough already. I made my way back to the house with my flashlight and empty wine glass. Stars were coming out, twinkling at me through a pitch-black sky.

As I opened the back door and passed the little antique desk in the corner of the room, I noticed a book prominently displayed in the middle of the desk. That was strange. I hadn't left a book there. I hadn't had time yet to check out the books on the library shelves.

After taking off my boots and parka, I put on my fleece-lined mukluks and walked over to check it out. As I did so, a strange chill swept through the air, floating around the open book. I felt a distinct presence that I could not see. Angelique? Suddenly it disappeared, whatever or whoever it was.

Picking up the book, I was surprised to see that it was a hard cover copy of *Woman of the Boundary Waters* by Justine Kerfoot! Yes, I was intrigued with her and her books, but I didn't have my own copy. Something didn't feel right about this.

Although I had my suspicions, I had to check out any rational explanations before jumping to irrational conclusions. Had someone been here in my home while I was down by the lake? Why would they have left a book, especially this book, for me? Also, my doors had been locked- a precaution I now took just in case Jeff somehow figured out where I was and wanted to cause trouble.

Could Karl have stopped in and left this for me? I couldn't resist calling him right away. He sounded puzzled. "That is strange, Angela. Yes, I had that book on my shelves there...but, to be honest, that is one of the books I took with me. You see, my dear wife Minnie loved that book. She'd spend evenings reading it by the fire."

"I'm glad you took it, Karl. I'm just trying to figure out how this book mysteriously showed up here on the desk."

After a quick dinner of frozen pizza, I settled down by a crackling fire with Justine's book. I was all the more fascinated with her and her life. I felt compelled to find out more. Sabrina, Justine's great-granddaughter, should be able to tell me more. Maybe I'd pay her a visit tomorrow at the Gunflint Lodge.

As I climbed the stairs to spend the first night in my four-poster bed, I once again felt a familiar and presence around me.

Angelique? Why are you here? What are you trying to tell me?

*There are no secrets that time does not reveal...*her unspoken words infiltrated my mind. *But time is of the essence. We are running out of time.*

What secrets? I pleaded silently. *And why are we running out of time?* But her presence suddenly disappeared as quickly as it had appeared.

I couldn't help wondering if I was imagining things again, as my mother always accused me of doing. Or if Angelique was actually hovering around, trying to lure me into solving a mystery of some kind. If so, why did she have to be so secretive?

CHAPTER THIRTEEN

*E*arly the next morning, I awoke to thoughts simmering in my subconscious mind. *Timing is everything...timing is everything...*

Okay, I got it... I sighed impatiently as I climbed out from beneath my down comforter and into my slippers. Gazing out my bedroom window, I admired the star-studded sky casting glimmers of hope over the world below. It was comforting to realize that I was just a tiny speck in this gigantic universe.

I wondered how many planets were up there. How many people living out there somewhere.

Was God up there in the heavens? And were Angelique and my other ancestors also enjoying an afterlife in heaven, a place where the bad things on this earth did not exist? Hopefully, a place where people like Jeff could not prey on others.

But if heaven was all that it was made out to be, why did some deceased spirits, like my grandmother, insist on visiting us here on Earth?

Unfinished business, perhaps? Whatever it was, it was beginning to feel like my grandmother had chosen me to resolve an issue, whatever it was. Why me? Maybe because of my openness to things beyond this world, the strange insights I'd always had. Maybe because we had similar abilities to see things that other people didn't.

I suddenly remembered overhearing a conversation between my parents years ago when I was young, after they had chastised me for talking about what they called "my imaginary friends." After I'd told my mother about my nighttime visits from that nice lady (who turned out to be my grandmother). And after I'd drawn that sketch of the grandmother I'd never known.

Hiding at the top of the winding staircase in my long flannel nightgown late that night, I'd heard them arguing while having a cocktail in the living room.

"I am not overreacting, James!" My mother had raised her usually calm voice.

"The hell you're not! So let her have her imaginary friends. She's just a little girl and she has a creative streak. We need to nurture that."

"So, tell me how she knew about and was able to draw that sketch of my biological mother, of all people? You heard her talk about Angelique visiting her. That's crazy, and you know it. What if...what if..." Her voice began to break as if she were starting to cry.

"What if what, Emily?" My father's voice became softer, more caring, as I heard the creak of his chair.

"What if she's...like Angelique?"

"I don't understand how anything Angela has done would make you think she would someday desert her child the way your mother abandoned you."

"There's more."

"Well, it's about time you told me, don't you think? After all these years of your refusing to talk about your past?"

After a brief silence, my mother began to talk in a hushed tone. I tiptoed a little closer to the staircase, careful that they still couldn't see me. I had to hear more.

"Angelique was descended from French Voyageurs and Ojibwe Indians. She grew up someplace in the woods near the Gunflint Trail where she lived a wild and adventurous life. I've been told that she had an overactive imagination. She even talked to ghosts. Some said she had psychic abilities. And some went so far as to claim she was actually a witch..."

Then I heard sobbing sounds coming from my mother along with comforting sounds from my father. "And her eyes..." My mother gasped. "I will never forget those piercing green eyes. Exactly like Angela's..."

Finally, my father broke the silence. "Emily, that's all hearsay. You can't believe all of that nonsense, can you? Ghosts? A witch? Maybe she marched to a different drummer, but this is a stretch, you know. And it's crazy to even think that Angela is anything like your mother!"

My mother's voice bristled as I heard her rise from her chair and leave the room. "And now you know why I never told you."

My father pleaded with her. "Emily."

"That's enough, James. I refuse to discuss this any longer. All I care about is making sure that our daughter doesn't grow up to be like...like her!"

End of conversation. I heard the sound of my mother's retreating footsteps and ice cubes clunking in a glass. My father had apparently been in need of a good, stiff drink.

Bringing myself back to the present, I padded down the stairs to make coffee. Bluejays cawed outside my window as I decided to go outside to watch the sunrise from the deck overlooking the lake. I put on my jacket, hat, and gloves over my pajamas; grabbed my steaming cup of coffee and a warm cushion to place on the wooden rocker. The memory of my parents' conversation made me realize the idea of the Gunflint Trail must have been planted already back then.

Streaks of pink began to swirl through the early morning sky as I rocked in my chair, sipping my coffee, admiring the winter wonderland surrounding me. A thin layer of frost covered the trees in the forest and several inches of fresh snow blanketed my new world. My new life.

I still couldn't help wondering...did I have psychic abilities like Angelique may have had? Was it wrong that I also "talked to ghosts" as my mother had claimed? Or was all of this just my overactive imagination?

Whatever it was, this was not the time to dwell upon it. It was time to get dressed and venture out to enjoy my day taking photos along with a stop to see Sabrina at the Gunflint Lodge.

CHAPTER FOURTEEN

How long had it been since I had taken the time to head out on a solo photo shoot, something I'd always loved to do? Too long, I decided, as I hiked down my driveway. The lighting was perfect with the sun reflecting upon the frost-covered pines. I adjusted my camera settings and angles as I shot what would hopefully be some impressive photos. Perhaps they'd be good enough to reproduce on metal or canvas. Maybe I'd even set up a studio of my own to sell my prints someday.

Afterward, I warmed up in my car and drove farther down the Gunflint Trail to discover more great photo ops. And I did—a moose standing at the side of the road, the sunlight casting reflections upon his face. He looked directly at me as if posing for me, instead of fleeing back into the woods.

I felt like I was the only person in the world this morning as I made fresh tracks through the recently fallen layer of snow. So different from the hustle and bustle and insane traffic I'd had to deal with in Chicago.

I made it all the way to the end of the Gunflint with photo shoot stops at Saganaga Lake and the Chick-Wauk Museum. At the end of the trail, I got out of my car to peer across the lake into Canada.

Pleased with the amazing photo opportunities, I gave in to my rumbling stomach and decided it was time for lunch at the Gunflint Lodge. Hopefully Sabrina would be there. I wanted to talk with her about Justine. But I also hoped she would become my friend. Despite my introverted tendencies and desire to escape from people, I still appreciated having a few good friends in my world. I'd had to leave the only ones I had behind in Chicago. Hopefully we could reconnect someday.

When I entered the gift shop at the entrance to the Gunflint Lodge, I found Sabrina behind the desk waiting on customers. She smiled warmly when she recognized me.

"Hey, Angela. I was just thinking about you. Karl tells me that you're going to be my neighbor!"

"I am, and I'm thrilled about it."

"Awesome! Hey, I'd love to chat with you if you have time. I have a break here in half an hour or so?"

"Sounds good. Maybe I'll take a look around the shop here and grab some lunch first."

As I began to browse through the jewelry section, admiring some gorgeous Northern Lights jewelry, I became aware of a man standing across from me, his back to me. A strange sensation began to stir deep within my soul. I was having trouble breathing and had to hold on to the counter to try to calm myself. I wasn't afraid. I didn't know what I was feeling or what was wrong with me. I couldn't keep my eyes off of him.

Suddenly he turned around and started to walk away, until he glanced my way and stopped abruptly. He was tall with a muscular build and broad shoulders, dark wavy hair, and a strong jaw. Despite the casual worn jeans and tee-shirt that he was wearing, he had a classic, almost distinguished look about him.

His mouth gaped as he shook his head in bewilderment. I, too, was stunned and speechless. Somehow, I felt like I knew this man, like I'd always known him. But how was that possible? I couldn't figure it out. All I knew was that I felt a strong connection to this stranger.

"Is it really you?" he gasped, still shaking his head. "Do you know how long I have been searching to find you again, my lovely?" He seemed to be in a trance as the words slipped out of his mouth.

My lovely? Who talked that way in today's world? Yet, somehow, this old-fashioned expression rang a bell, a bell from the past. It drowned out everything around me—except this strikingly handsome gentleman standing before me.

I made the mistake of looking into his deep brown eyes. Waves of familiarity washed through me as I recognized an old soul that I had somehow once known, known extremely well in fact. Weren't the eyes the window to the soul? Could that be true? Or was I totally losing it?

"My apologies." He backed off a little, sensing my discomfort. "I...I don't know what to say, and I'm sorry. It's just that...somehow you seem so familiar, like I've known you forever. I don't mean to be rude."

"It's okay," I assured him. "I must admit that I am also a little stunned, feeling like I know you from somewhere. But where? I am really confused right now. I'm sorry. I just don't remember..."

He breathed a sigh of relief and was silent for a long moment before responding. "Perhaps it's best not to try to remember the past, not yet. But I do feel like I owe you a drink, or lunch perhaps? I was just about to find a table in the restaurant. And I would enjoy your company."

Something compelled me to take him up on his offer. I had to figure out who this man was although I realized I needed to be very careful. I was certainly not ready to have a relationship with anyone, not after what Jeff did to me. But I had to figure out why I was drawn to this man. He seemed to be a perfect gentleman. Perhaps a little old-fashioned. But that was all right with me.

My heart was fluttering wildly as he led me to a table, gallantly pulled a chair out to seat me, and settled into the seat across from me. His warm smile almost made me melt, releasing some strangely conflicted feelings within me, including one of devastating loss. A strange vision crept into my mind. I was wandering alone through cobblestoned streets beneath a lamplight as a horse-drawn carriage crossed my path.

"I hope our meeting like this is not disturbing you?"

I shook my head and gave him an uneasy smile in return. Trying to pull myself together, I extended my hand across the table. "My name is Angela and I've just moved up here into a log cabin to pursue my dreams of writing and photography." Why was I sharing this information with a total stranger? Yet, somehow, I felt comfortable doing so.

"And I'm Thomas." He held my hand a moment longer than necessary, looking deeply into my eyes before suddenly turning away. "Let's not worry about how or if we once knew each other, all right? I'd just like to get to know you—again—I'm sorry. Forget the 'again' part."

I had to laugh at that as I began to relax. I was beginning to feel comfortable with this stranger and I definitely wanted to get to know him also. We began to chat as if we'd known each other forever. I was pleased to learn that he was a resident of nearby Grand Marais where he owned and operated several businesses including guided fishing and dog sledding excursions. He obviously loved what he did, but I sensed that something was missing in his life.

Finally, he hesitantly asked me if I was married or had children. For some reason, my mouth began blurting out personal information about my divorce. Things I should certainly not be telling a man I'd just met. "I swear I will never marry again," I concluded my rant.

Thomas played with his napkin a moment, as if he knew something that I did not know. Clearing his throat, he told me that he had never married because he'd never found the woman he was seeking. Maybe someday, but certainly not unless and until the woman of his dreams was ready. He left it at that.

I changed the subject. "So, what brings you to the Gunflint Lodge?"

"This place is my home away from home," he confessed. "I love Grand Marais, but sometimes I need to get away from people. I love to simply absorb nature, take my camera out for a long hike, sit by Gunflint Lake with a glass of wine or two."

Leaning across the table toward each other, we were soon eagerly discussing photography and the best places to capture various shots. We even decided it would be fun to spend a day together taking photos. He could show me some wonderful places.

"Hey, there. I see you've met Thomas." Sabrina sidled up to our table where we'd been chatting for almost an hour already as we devoured our lunches.

I'd completely forgotten about meeting with her in half an hour ago. "Yes. Oh, I'm so sorry, Sabrina. Time just seemed to fly. Do you still have time for a chat?"

"I do unless you're busy now and want to meet tomorrow instead?"

I didn't miss the twinkle in her eye. With that, Thomas rose from the table, grabbing the check and excused himself. "It was lovely to meet you, Angela, and I look forward to seeing you again."

"Likewise, Thomas. Wait, I can pay for my own lunch.," I reached out for the check that he held tightly in his hand.

"Absolutely not. It's the least a gentleman can do for a lady like you, after having such a delightful conversation. I hope to see you again soon." With that, he bowed toward me, our eyes connecting. And then he was gone. I couldn't help noticing a puzzled look upon Sabrina's face as she watched him leave.

My heart fluttering, I tried to calm myself before turning back to her.

She had one of those looks upon her face, as if she was thinking that something was happening between Thomas and me.

"He's a very nice man, Angela, one of our regulars here. Almost like family. It's just that...well, I've never seen him act quite so gentlemanly in such an old-fashioned way. Like he just stepped out of the last century or something."

Or something, I thought.

Changing the subject, she went on. "How about a glass of wine by the fireplace to celebrate your move into our neighborhood?"

I was certainly up for that. Maybe it would help to make sense of what had just happened, and why I felt this insanely strong connection to a man I'd just met. Or why I kept drowning in those eyes of his. Eyes that I'd somehow always known.

CHAPTER FIFTEEN

"Cheers! Here's to my new neighbor and new friend." Sabrina clinked her glass of wine against mine and we each took a sip. She was settled on one end of the leather sofa, her long legs stretched out on the old wood coffee table, while I was curled up on the other end of the sofa. Almost like old friends already. It felt good—being there with her by the warmth of a fire crackling in the old stone fireplace that Justine's family had built many years ago.

Sabrina had grown up at the lodge, loved the area, and never wanted to leave. It was her family's legacy, she told me, one that she was proud to carry on. Someday she hoped to marry and have children who would carry on this family tradition "for at least another hundred years." She laughed. First, she had to find a good man who also loved this lifestyle.

"It was 1927, almost a hundred years ago, when Justine's family bought this Gunflint Lodge. Imagine what it was like then. No roads like they have today. Indian friends. Harsh winters. Justine had been in medical school before they moved up here. She left her upcoming career as a doctor behind and never looked back. Fell in love with this country."

"Yes, I've been reading her book and am totally intrigued. She certainly was a woman of incredible strength and character—and very smart."

"You got that right." Sabrina refilled our wine glasses. "Imagine her guiding fishermen, mushing her own dog sled team, cutting firewood to keep the lodge warm, surviving winters here in the wilderness where she and her family were essentially cut off from the rest of the world."

"Pretty amazing all right. I see that later in life she wrote a newspaper column called On the Gunflint Trail for the Grand Marais newspaper?"

"That's right...you've obviously been doing some research about my great-grandmother."

"I must admit I'm fascinated with her and the life she led. Maybe because I'd love to live a similar life. At least to understand what it was like for her. I already love it up here, maybe almost as much as she did, and you do—"

"Now I know why I liked you right away and wanted to be your friend." Sabrina giggled as she sipped her wine.

"Likewise. I must confess that I'm also a writer—or will be someday, now that I finally have time to write. And I'd love to set a novel right here, Sabrina."

"That would be wonderful. We could sell copies here in our gift shop. I'd be happy to help any way I can. Any questions you have or information you need about this place, just ask."

"For some reason, I feel like the more I can immerse myself in your great-grandmother's life, I will be able to recreate the right historical context. If that makes any sense."

I watched her swirl the wine in her glass thoughtfully before she answered. Flickers of flames from the fireplace cast reflections that seemed to dance within her glass. "Actually, we have recently discovered some of Justine's old journals and are very excited about reading them. Maybe I could share some of that with you?"

"That would be wonderful. How exciting to find a treasure like that! I'd love to learn more, whenever you are ready to share."

"I'll let you know. You see, I do need to clear this with my mother, Annette, first. She wants to be the first to read it all. Maybe she's concerned that Justine wrote some entries about my mother's growing-up years here. You see, Justine, my mother's grandmother, was almost like a mother to her after her own mother passed away. Annette was actually a lot like Justine—independent and strong. Sometimes people clash if they're too much alike, too independent and strong-willed, you know."

"Makes sense to me," I assured her. "Is your mother still involved here at the lodge?"

Sabrina shook her head sadly. "Not as much as she used to be. She's been diagnosed with early onset dementia and is not quite herself these days. It's very sad to see this strong dynamic woman..." She shook her head sadly, taking a deep breath. "Anyway," she continued, "We've kind of had to take over here."

"I hear you." I reached out to touch her hand. She clung to mine for a moment. "My mother is pushing seventy and sometimes forgets things. Nothing serious, and I guess we all forget some things. Maybe that's a part of aging. Still...I'm so sorry your mother is dealing with this."

I decided it was time to change the subject. "Actually, my mother spent the first few years of her life in this area before she was adopted by a nice family in Duluth."

"Really?" Sabrina's eyes widened. "That's very interesting. Any idea where she lived up here?"

"No, but I'd love to find out. She was only three years old when her father drowned in a shipwreck on Lake Superior and her mother mysteriously disappeared. It's kind of a mystery that has haunted my mother her entire life."

Just as Sabrina opened her mouth to respond. the door blew open and several men hauling big boxes and a large Christmas tree burst into the room. "Hey, Sabrina. We're ready to put the tree up so you all can start decorating. Where do you want it?"

Sabrina showed them where to put the tree, then turned back to me. "We start decorating early up here and we do it up right. It's a lot of fun if you want to stop in and join us, usually in the morning about ten o'clock." Sabrina then excused herself to get back to work after giving me a hug and tapping her personal phone number into my phone. "Stay in touch, Angela. I'm sorry I have to get back to work."

It was dark by the time I got back to my cabin and lit a fire in the fireplace. I took a hot shower and got into my pajamas before settling down at the antique desk. I lit the kerosene lamp, more because of its historical ambiance than necessity, and settled down to write in my journal. Sometimes that helped to sort out my thoughts and feelings, to find meaning in things that made no sense at all.

I was trying hard to summarize what was happening to me. It wasn't easy. But the main themes seemed to be the fact that someone or something had guided me to this cabin in the middle of nowhere. Some force was also trying to connect me with Justine Kerfoot and her family. My grandmother, Angelique, also seemed to be hanging around, trying to guide me to discover some family secrets. And then there was my recurring nightmare about "Angelique" being chased through the woods.

To top it all off, I'd just met a man whom I felt an incredibly strong connection with—as if I'd known him forever. As if karma or destiny or some strange force had drawn us together again. None of this made any sense. I knew that. Frustrated, I closed my journal and went to bed. Maybe I could focus better tomorrow.

In the middle of the night, I was awakened by surreal dreams that seemed to surface from another time and another place.

I am dressed in an elegant old-fashioned dress and sitting in a horsedrawn carriage ambling down the dirt paths of an old western town. Passing taverns, cowboys, and ladies of the night gathering along the boardwalk. A street fight is developing between two dudes who are positioning themselves on the road.

I'm not alone. Beside me sits a gentleman who is protectively holding my hand. His eyes are focused on the activities surrounding us as if trying to gauge our safety. When he turns to look at me, trying to reassure me of our safety, I look into his eyes and recognize Thomas! Our eyes connect so deeply on a level that only soulmates would understand. I know in my heart that this man is the love of my life, perhaps many lives.

Suddenly a shot rings out. I am horrified as my love slumps down in his seat, blood spurting through his overcoat. "Julia, my lovely, I will always love you," he whispers. His last words.

Clinging to him, I sob, trying to revive him, as he takes his last breath. "Oh, David, please don't leave me. I need you. I love you. Please, David. Please..."

Trembling and drenched in sweat, I awakened from my dream. A dream that didn't seem to be a dream at all.

CHAPTER SIXTEEN

*D*espite my weird dreams and everything else that was going on, I knew I needed to focus on moving beyond my old life and creating a new one. I spent the next few weeks poring over my journal entries that documented everything Jeff had done to me. After consulting with my attorney, however, I had decided not to pursue any criminal actions against him. It wasn't worth the stress and invoking his wrath against me. And I had no intentions of returning to Chicago or ever having to face Jeff again. Maybe a no contest divorce was the best option. All I wanted was to get this over peacefully and to get him out of my life forever.

Somehow his betrayal and abuse didn't hurt nearly as much anymore. My self-confidence and self-esteem were slowly returning. Why? Maybe because I was living my dream life far away from the big city. But, if I was honest with myself, I had to admit that Thomas played a role in my desire to move on. He helped me feel better about myself and life in general. All of this despite the fact that we'd just met and I really didn't know him. Or did I?

Yes, Thomas. I sighed as I took a break from reviewing the settlement documents that my lawyer had just emailed me.

While Thomas was careful to respect the boundaries I had set between us, knowing I was going through a divorce, I could not deny that there was something magical, almost spiritual, between us. We spent time hanging out at the lodge or going on photo shoots together. I'd never felt so connected to another human being. It was almost as if we read each other's minds. And it felt so good to be able to just be me instead of pretending to be the person that Jeff insisted I must be in order to present well to his clients.

Thomas was quite impressed with my photography, as I was with his. He introduced me to several art gallery and gift shop owners in Grand Marais who were happy to handle my canvas and metal prints. Once I had the time, I would get involved with the Art Colony there, attend a few classes, meet other artists, participate in some of their exhibits and events. It was interesting that so many artists and writers seemed to flock to this beautiful Northwoods country along the shores of Lake Superior. I got it...totally got it. How could one not be inspired when immersed in a setting like this? It seemed to make your creative juices flow freely. And, I reminded myself, that would help a great deal when I was ready to start working on my debut novel.

Yes, I had so much to look forward to. My glass was now half full instead of half empty, as my mother would say. I had hoped to bring her up here to my cabin for Christmas, but she insisted that I come down to spend the holiday with her in Duluth. I gave in.

Christmas was only a few weeks away, and I was enjoying spending time decorating for Christmas at the lodge with Sabrina, her staff, and several other neighbors and friends. Of course, Thomas was also there when he wasn't busy with his dog sledding business. And Karl also stopped in now and then.

The Gunflint Lodge was being transformed into a winter wonderland. It included outdoor displays lit up with twinkling white lights. Inside, fresh evergreen trees and boughs were adorned with sparkling lights, pinecones, and antique ornaments. Christmas candles were everywhere and soft Christmas music played in the background as we decorated or sat by the fire sipping hot chocolate with peppermint sticks.

Everything was going so well until just a week before Christmas when I came down with a bad cold and cough. I isolated myself at home resting, drinking lots of fluids, and trying to get better before Christmas. Thomas called every day to check up on me.

Early one morning my phone rang. I grabbed it from the nightstand and sleepily answered it. It was Sabrina. "Hey, Angela, we miss you over here. Just wondering how you are feeling...any better?"

"I'm getting there but not ready to go out or expose anyone else yet," I responded.

"You don't sound so good. Listen, we just made a big kettle of chicken noodle soup, and I'm going to bring some over and drop it off for you. My grandmother always told me that was the secret to getting over being sick."

"You don't have to do that, but thanks so much, Sabrina."

"Okay, I'm on my way. If you unlock the door, I can just come in and leave it on your kitchen table. I won't stay. I'll have my mother with me since we're on our way to her doctor's appointment."

I padded down the stairs in my slippers, unlocked the door, and headed back up to bed after taking a good dose of cold medicine. Before long I heard a car in the driveway and the sound of my front door opening.

"It's just me," Sabrina called out up the stairs. "Enjoy the soup and I hope you feel better soon."

"Thanks so much, Sabrina."

"Mother? What are you doing out of the car?" an exasperated Sabrina exclaimed as the door opened and closed again. After a lingering moment she continued, a hint of worry in her voice, "Mother? What is it?"

"I remember this place," a quiet elderly voice replied slowly. "Yes, I used to come here and play with my friend. We played with our dolls right there by that fireplace. And sometimes her mother would read us a story. My friend was a little younger than me. Yes, I remember..." Her voice trailed off.

"What do you remember, Mother? What was her name?"

The very questions I wanted to ask!

"Hmm...no, I don't remember her name anymore. It was so long ago. But I remember that she and her mother just left one day and never came back. I was sad."

Sabrina's mother sounded excited now as she drifted back in time, remembering details from long ago despite the fact that she often didn't remember what she had for dinner last night.

"Oh my, yes." She sighed. "She had the most beautiful baby doll I'd ever seen. The doll's eyes followed you around the room. She wore a lovely pink dress and bonnet with frilly white lace trim. Oh my, how my little friend loved her little Susan. She slept with her every night."

"The doll's name was Susan?" Sabrina asked. "Do you remember anything else about your friend?"

"Hmm...she had the most beautiful eyes and pretty, long black hair—just like her mother's."

"Do you remember anything else about your friend?"

"What friend? What are you talking about?"

End of conversation. I could hear Sabrina escorting her mother from the house and locking the door behind her.

I bolted upright in bed, my heart pounding almost as much as my throbbing head. Could it possibly be? Could that little girl who disappeared from this cabin years ago possibly be my mother, Emily? And if Emily and Angelique disappeared together, how did Emily end up alone and placed for adoption? What happened to Angelique?

Maybe this was nothing but wishful thinking due to my obsession with trying to discover family secrets from the past. I had to find out where my mother lived up here the first three years of her life. I needed to talk to her soon—just in case this new information jogged any old memories in her mind. Perhaps it would be best to wait until my visit with her over Christmas.

Could Angelique have guided me here, to the very home where she had lived with her husband and my mother, Emily? If so, why? I needed to learn more from Sabrina's mother, and perhaps from Justine's journals.

CHAPTER SEVENTEEN

Mother always did the holidays up right, and this year was no exception. As I drove through the black wrought iron entry gates, I rolled down the windows so I could hear the Christmas carols playing softly in the background. The driveway was lined with glowing lanterns and evergreen boughs tied with red velvet ribbons. The exterior of the house twinkled with an assortment of lights that Mother's holiday decorating company installed for her every year.

She greeted me with a warm hug when I stepped into the foyer before leading me to the great room. A massive Christmas tree dominated the wood-paneled room, its twinkling white lights casting reflections upon the floor-to-ceiling windows overlooking Lake Superior below.

Several large tables were set up on both sides of the fireplace, filled with her vast collection of Department 56 Snow Village pieces which she'd collected over the years. She excitedly showed me several she'd just added to her collection. While she used to set this up herself in past years, she now had to rely on Beth who was delighted to help her out.

Growing up, I remember being entranced with her collection which included Victorian houses, quaint shops and restaurants, an ornate church, rustic lodge, and so much more—all lit up from within and casting a warm glow throughout the great room. We would shut the lights off at night, light a fire in the fireplace, and enjoy it all sipping glasses of hot apple cider. Wine for the adults.

Christmas carols played in the background. I had loved arranging, and rearranging, all the ceramic figurines—children sledding down the hills my mother had created from soft cotton, carolers, ice skaters. Christmas puppies and horse drawn carriages. It was like stepping back into another time and place.

This evening, we settled down on the ornate loveseat, enjoying the warmth of the crackling fire. Beth soon came in, proudly displaying a tray of hors d'oeuvres that she'd prepared for this special occasion. She'd tried out a few new recipes this year, she told us. Crab cake bites. Spinach artichoke dip wrapped in pastry puffs. And sausage stuffing bites with cranberry sauce. Of course, there were also several glasses of wine.

"Beth, this looks and smells delicious. Thanks so much." I gave her a hug before settling back down with my glass of wine. Thank God for dear Beth who was much more than Mother's long-time maid. She'd become a part of our extended family.

"Cheers!" I toasted my mother. "This is lovely as always. I'm so glad to be home with you for Christmas again."

"I wouldn't have it any other way. I missed you the last few years...you know, when Jeff refused to come home with you, or even let you come yourself." An icy tone crept into her voice. I hadn't realized back then how much she'd disliked my ex-husband.

"I'm sorry about that. It won't happen again. I'm proud to let you know that he is officially history as of yesterday!"

"That's wonderful news, Angela. Are you doing all right? This has to be hard for you. I hope you at least got a decent settlement...after all he did to you?"

"I feel better than I have since I married that man," I confessed, "and I did get a good enough settlement, thank God. I could have gone for more but I just wanted him out of my life as soon as possible. And he didn't want to be exposed for what he'd done to me, obviously. That could have damaged his high and mighty reputation. Whatever."

"I'm so glad it's over and that it went well. I knew you could get through this and move on with your life. Maybe a new job. Maybe even one here in Duluth..."

"Mother," I said. "I really love it where I am. It feels like a fresh start and I've already made some nice friends. I'm not alone, and I can still come see you as often as you'd like."

She sighed heavily. "That's fine, but always know you have a place here. I'm glad you have new friends up there. Just remember that you don't need a man in your life, you know. Well, maybe someday, but I sure wouldn't rush into anything."

I couldn't help giggling at her advice as thoughts of Thomas flashed through my mind. I hoped I wasn't blushing at the mere thought of him.

This was no time to even mention his name to my mother, much less the strange connection Thomas and I had with each other.

I quickly changed the subject, asking about her life and the plans she'd made for the holidays. Of course, I already knew she would have her traditional holiday party complete with a small orchestra and a grand buffet.

This year she suggested visiting the historic Glensheen Mansion on the shores of Lake Superior. There was to be a special fundraising event that included wine, cheese, and music.

The mansion was always decorated beautifully for Christmas with elegant trees displayed in most of the rooms, including the bedrooms. I was up for that and hoping to explore the grounds and get some good photos.

While I was anxious to ask her about her early childhood, I managed to control myself until just after our Christmas celebrations. Just in case my questions triggered any unpleasant memories. I didn't want to spoil the holidays for her. She loved Christmas more than any other event of the year.

It was a lovely Christmas and I felt more connected to Mother than ever. She seemed to be letting her hair down in some respects. I felt like I was getting to know my real mother—finally. Maybe it took getting older to make that happen. I wasn't sure. Whatever it was, it made me happy. Hopefully she would open up more someday soon.

Finally, the day before I was scheduled to return home to my cabin, I broached the subject of her childhood over coffee and pastries that morning. Holding my breath, I began to tell her about Annette, Sabrina's mother's, visit to my cabin. I wasn't sure how much to reveal, especially the part about the little girl who had lived there, in my cabin, with her mother before they suddenly disappeared one day.

Mother was listening intently, trying to take it all in, as if trying to remember her past. When I mentioned the doll, Susan, her mouth dropped open. Tears filled her eyes and her hands began to tremble.

"Susan?" her voice croaked. "Did you say Susan? Oh, my goodness, Angela. I had a doll named Susan when I was very little. I lost her when I went away. I was so sad. She was so beautiful and her eyes followed me everywhere. I had forgotten about her until now."

I put my arm around her as she leaned into me.

"Do you remember a beautiful yellow dress that she wore?" I lied, holding my breath, trying to test her memory.

"No, no, no!" She shook her head. "Susan always wore a lovely pink dress and bonnet with lacy white trim!"

"Sorry if I was wrong about that." I had to take a deep breath before moving on. My mother's memories appeared to be surfacing and confirming much of what Sabrina's mother had revealed.

"I'm sorry, Mother, if this upset you. I'm just trying to figure some things out. I know it seems strange, but it is possible that my cabin is the one in which you spent the first three years of your life. I want to show it to you someday."

I was trembling inside, trying hard not to show it as I tried to reassure and comfort her.

"No, no, it's all right. I can't hide from the past any longer. Who knows how many years I have left? And you have a right to know some of these things about your family history. I finally understand that. Maybe I need to face the past, as much as I have dreaded doing so for my entire life. But what are the chances of you somehow ending up in the cabin where I was born? That is unbelievable, Angela."

"You're right about that, but strange things happen sometimes. Maybe there's a reason. That's what I need to find out."

I wasn't about to share my opinion that it was, in fact, my mysterious deceased grandmother, Angelique, who seemed to have guided me to that place.

I gazed into her blue eyes, perhaps a shade duller than those that Sabrina's mother had described. Aging did that to a person. While Mother's hair was now gray, I remembered the long dark hair she had years ago.

"You don't remember your friend's name, do you? The one you used to play dolls with?"

I watched her staring into the past, a frown of deep concentration upon her face. I waited patiently.

Finally, she looked at me, a wistful look spreading across her face. "Annette," she whispered. "I think her name was Annette... Yes, yes,

Annette!" She smiled softly with that warm remembrance."

It was my turn to become speechless as I shook my head in disbelief.

Perhaps the missing pieces of our past were finally starting to come together.

CHAPTER EIGHTEEN

Two days before New Years, I drove back home, reveling in the fact that I was now officially divorced. I was free! I was looking forward to spending New Year's Eve with Thomas. Now, I was finally able to pursue a relationship with him—if I chose to do so. As I navigated my way up Highway 61, my mind was also spinning with possibilities about how I could find out more about my family's past. Where had Angelique gone? I also needed to find out more about her father, Jonathan, who had drowned at sea shortly before his wife and child mysteriously disappeared.

I was beginning to understand why I'd been compelled to find this little cabin in the woods. Thanks, Angelique, I thought. But why now?

*Because timing is everything...*a silent voice inserted itself into my subconscious. *It is time. We need to do this now...*

I was felt a growing sense of urgency flowing from my grandmother. Why now? For some unknown reason, I had established a relationship with my deceased grandmother. Perhaps she'd been there all my life from the first time she'd visited me at night when I was just a little girl. Then she'd disappeared for a few years...or maybe I was too busy with my life to open myself up to her visits. It was time to pay more attention. I was more convinced than ever that she had unfinished business she wanted me to take care of for her. Things that I somehow also needed to know about my past.

Deep in thought, I almost missed seeing a moose standing in my driveway as I pulled in. Illuminated by my headlights, it stared at me. Grabbing my camera, I carefully rolled down the window and snapped a few shots before he lumbered into the woods.

It was pitch-dark and I was both surprised and relieved to see the porch lights were on when I arrived at the cabin. Thomas or Sabrina must have stopped by. Beneath the lights, in front of the door, I found a beautifully wrapped Christmas present. What? Where did that come from?

Unlocking the door, I lugged my suitcase along with the generous gifts my mother had given me for Christmas. Then I scooped up the mysterious present, somehow knowing that it had to be from Thomas. And I was right. A note was attached to the package.

"Merry Christmas, my dear Angela, and welcome home," I read. "I have missed you and am anxious to see you again soon. For now, please accept this gift, a token of my esteem for you. Hopefully it will bring back memories of long ago—or of what life was like once upon a time. Something that photographers like the two of us can appreciate.

"Speaking of which, I have arranged to take you on a horse-drawn sleigh ride on New Year's Eve if you are interested," his note continued. "I will pick you up at six o'clock and we can have dinner at the Lodge before we embark. Yours truly, Thomas."

I read, and reread, his note several times. Rubbing my finger gently over his handwritten words, I could feel his warmth seeping into my very being. I wasn't sure what was happening here, to say the least, but I was enchanted and unable to step back from what appeared to be my destiny.

Thomas was charming, in a very old-fashioned way. Even his language, his gallantry, seemed to speak of another time, another place. Sabrina had also noticed this and teased me that I seemed to have some kind of magical power to draw Thomas back in time. What if she was right?

I finally placed Thomas's note on the coffee table and opened the package. I peeled off layers of vintage Christmas wrap dominated by angels floating through a cloudy universe before pulling out an ornate antique photo frame.

As I peeled the covering tissue off the framed photo, I almost dropped it onto the floor. How could this be?

My mind reeled as I recalled my recent dream about a murder in days long past. This vintage black and white photo perfectly depicted the opening scene in my dream—before gun shots were fired. A couple was seated in a horse-drawn carriage in the midst of an old western town. I couldn't see their faces, only the backs of their heads. But, somehow, I felt like I was there in that carriage! Cowboys and ladies of the night clustered along the board-walk near a ramshackle tavern with hitching posts in the background.

What was happening to me? And how could Thomas have found this photo that perfectly depicted my dreams? Who were these people? In my dream, they called each other David and Julia. I distinctly remembered that. Or I thought I did. And I distinctly remembered David's eyes because they were identical to Thomas's eyes, They evoked the same soulful response within me.

I desperately needed some fresh air and a glass of wine. I needed to clear my head, to try to understand what was happening. I grabbed a flashlight, put on my parka, boots, gloves, and hat, and headed down the trail to the lake.

Settled on my log bench by the lake, I took some deep breaths as I tried to focus on the brilliant stars glowing above me, lighting up the black sky. I reminded myself that I was just a tiny speck in a gigantic universe. While my problems may seem to be overwhelming at times, they should be of little concern in the big picture of life and death. Now if only I could convince myself of that.

Angelique, where are you now? Help me figure this out please...

No response. Not surprising. There would be no reason for her to be involved in my relationship with Thomas. Or was there? Could this have anything to do with whatever Angelique wanted from me? I couldn't help wondering how much spirits from beyond saw and knew about their loved ones who were still here on this earth. Especially spirits like Angelique who managed to muster up enough energy to visit us here. Did she know what was happening between Thomas and me? If so, it would be nice if she could shed some light upon this unusual relationship.

In the meantime, I needed some sleep. Tomorrow was New Year's Eve and I had plans with Thomas. I wasn't sure how much I'd tell him about my dream and the fact that it perfectly depicted the scene in the antique photo he'd given me. Things seemed to flow so comfortably between us that I felt like I could just be me and let it all out if I chose to do so. I wasn't worried that he would think I was crazy.

CHAPTER NINETEEN

At precisely six o'clock on New Year's Eve, Thomas knocked on my door. Heart fluttering, I opened the door and invited him in. It was so good to see him again. I couldn't quit smiling, nor could he wipe a huge grin off his face.

"I've missed you, my lovely," he whispered as he took my hand in his, brought it to his lips and kissed it.

"As I have you, Thomas." My eyes melted into his once again. Then, impulsively, I held out my arms towards him, indicating I was finally ready to be hugged.

He immediately gathered me in his strong arms and held me close. Neither of us spoke. The only sound to be heard was the pounding of our hearts. I felt like I'd suddenly come home after spending a lifetime apart.

I brushed a tear from my eye. Gazing up at him, I saw tears in his eyes as well.

"Finally. You'll never know how long I've waited for this day, Angela. Waited to find you, to hold you in my arms."

"I don't know what to say, not yet..."

"That's perfectly fine." He changed the subject. "So how was your Christmas with your mother?"

He always seemed to know when I needed some space and time to process things.

"It was lovely," I said, beginning to tell him all about our holiday together, "although I missed you."

"And I missed you."

"Wonderful news, however. My divorce is final and the settlement not bad. It's over, Thomas, and I am finally free."

He scooped me up into his arms once again.

It was like a reunion when we arrived at the lodge. Sabrina, her staff, Karl, and other neighbors whom I'd met were there to enjoy the lodge's specialty New Year's Eve prime rib dinner.

Sabrina re-introduced me to her mother, Annette, who I now knew was Mother's toddlerhood friend. I couldn't wait for an opportunity to talk with her someday when the time was right. What would she remember about my mother? Annette was the one controlling access to her deceased grandmother Justine's journals. How I hoped to be able to access those, or any possible excerpts pertaining to my family. It was possible that Justine knew more about my mother and grandmother than Annette did. Annette was just a young child when my mother and grandmother disappeared.

As always, Justine Kerfoot's portrait greeted us as we walked into the beautifully decorated dining room. I couldn't help smiling up at her as we passed through. Sabrina seated us at a table for two in a relatively private area nestled between the stone fireplace and the window wall overlooking the lake. I wasn't surprised. Very romantic. Or perhaps Thomas had requested this seating? Either way, it was perfect.

"Here's to a wonderful year ahead, Angela. To spending time together creating more wonderful memories." Thomas clinked his champagne glass against mine as our eyes met across the table.

"To us." I smiled at this amazing man, thanking God for bringing him into my life.

I sipped slowly, not exactly a fan of champagne, while he watched me with a twinkle in his eyes. "How about an Old-Fashioned instead?"

How did he know that had always been my favorite cocktail? And why was this triggering something in me, perhaps a memory from long ago? Something I couldn't quite remember...

"Topped off with two maraschino cherries, right?"

I could only shake my head in amazement, finally muttering, "Yes, but how..."

He took my hand across the table and held it gently, our eyes locking together, going deeper and deeper into the past.

"Because that was always your favorite drink, and you always wanted an extra cherry."

I shook my head, bewildered. What was happening between us? How did he know so much about me and what I liked?

After a delicious dinner and bidding our friends a Happy New Year, complete with hugs all around, Thomas and I retreated to his car where

Janet Kay

we put on our winter jackets and pants over our dinner clothing. I exchanged my high heels for snow boots. Then we walked across the road to the stable where a horse-drawn sleigh and driver were waiting for us. Just the two of us.

"My lady?" Thomas bowed and extended his hand to help me into the carriage. Always the perfect gentleman.

As the horse began to slowly trot along the snowy trail, surrounded by forest on both sides, I found myself cuddling up close to Thomas, lost in the magic of the moment. He put his arm around me and pulled me close.

Gazing into each other's eyes, going deeper and deeper, it felt as if our souls were bonding together and becoming one.

"Oh, my lovely, my Julia." The words escaped from his mouth, followed by a look of shock upon his face as he shook his head in bewilderment.

"David?" I gushed, almost unaware of what I was saying or where my words were coming from.

Julia and David? Like the characters in my dream?

"I know this is very confusing for you, for both of us actually, Angela. I've had years to figure it out, to try to find you again. I don't want to frighten you away...so I'm not sure how much I should tell you, or when. Help me out here, okay?"

"Confused is an understatement, Thomas. I can tell you that I had a dream about a Julia and David in a horse-drawn carriage, long ago, in an old western town. And..." I shook my head, unable to continue for a moment.

"You don't need to tell me anymore than you are comfortable with. I can wait."

"No, I need to try to figure this out. You know that beautiful antique photo you gave me? Well, first of all, I want to thank you. It's beautiful..."

"You are more than welcome."

"But that photo is identical to what I saw in my dreams. How can that be?"

"Do you really want to know? Now?"

"I do."

"I found that photo when I was researching my past life. Now, don't

84

think I'm crazy, please. But I've always known that I've lived before, that my life ended abruptly, and that I had some unfinished business on this earth. I needed to come back and find the love of my life, the one I left behind on the streets of Virginia City, Montana in 1865."

He gazed into my eyes again as if to make sure he hadn't said too much, to make sure he wasn't scaring me away.

"Are you trying to tell me that is you, David, in that photo? And that the woman is me, or Julia?"

"Yes, I am. We were to be wed soon and had taken a carriage ride through town. One of my friends was a photographer and I'd asked him to capture this photo of the evening you agreed to become my wife. Somehow the photo survived and I found it in the archives of a museum out there."

"Unbelievable." I sighed. "Why did you leave me then, Thomas, or David...?" I had to ask, hoping that the tragic ending in my dream was not true.

"Not by choice, my lovely. That's for sure. I was gunned down, accidently, in a shooting duel outside the tavern in that photo. My last memory is of you holding me, begging me not to die, not to leave you. That's why I had to come back. Why I had to find you."

Tears began to stream down my face as I fell into his arms. He held me close. While none of this made sense to me, I somehow believed it with all my heart and soul. Perhaps I'd also spent much of this lifetime trying to find him, my soulmate, once again.

"If that's true, we are together again, and I feel whole, finally."

"As do I." He sighed deeply.

I had one more nagging question that I simply had to ask. "So how did you find me? That sounds almost impossible, Thomas. How would you have known that Julia's soul had been reincarnated into the body of an Angela who could have lived anywhere in this world?"

He grinned that grin that had always made my heart melt, even back in the days when he was David. "It's a long story but to keep it short, I started off with some past life regression therapy where I discovered our past life together, where we lived, the photo I sent you."

"But how would you know that I was now Angela and where to find me?"

"I still don't quite understand that part of it. It was like a mysterious spirit was whispering in my ear, guiding me to you. Guiding me up here to Grand Marais and ultimately, Gunflint Lake."

"Can you tell me anything more about this spirit?" My suspicions were suddenly aroused, knowing that the spirit of my grandmother, Angelique, had certainly guided me to this place. But that, of course, was to discover my family history.

"All I know is that she called herself Angelique."

"What did you say?" I could barely speak.

"She said her name was Angelique."

"Oh my God. That's my grandmother, Angelique, the one who guided me to this place also. But why? Why would she be trying to get us together?"

"Maybe because she loves you and wants you to be happy? Maybe because you and I also have some unfinished business to take care of in this lifetime?"

Thank God for Angelique, I thought, as I tried to absorb this surreal situation along with her involvement in it.

We fell into silence for the remainder of our sleigh ride, losing ourselves in the magical winter wonderland surrounding us. Thanking God, and Angelique, for bringing us together again. Drifting back into memories of a shared past.

After he brought me home, he stood at the door, apparently waiting for an invitation to come in, which I was quick to deliver. We belonged together. After all these years, it was finally time to be with the man whom I now realized was, and probably always had been, the love of my life.

He made a fire in the fireplace and I lit several candles on the coffee table before we shut off the lights and settled comfortably on the sofa. And we began to talk, reminiscing about memories we shared from that other lifetime. The more we talked, the more we remembered. The more we remembered, the stronger the bond between us grew. There was no doubt in either of our minds that we were soulmates. That this was meant to be.

I cuddled up against him, getting sleepy, and he held me close. I guess I drifted off to sleep because I finally awakened as he was carrying me up the stairs to my bedroom. He settled me comfortably on the bed and covered me with a blanket before leaning down to kiss me goodnight.

"Good night, my lovely. We can talk more tomorrow."

"Please stay." I found myself reaching out for him. He sighed as he settled down on the bed beside me, obviously relieved that I had been the one to make the first move. It wasn't long before we were naked beneath the covers, finally consummating a relationship we'd begun more than a century ago. Somehow, it felt like we'd always been together across time and space.

CHAPTER TWENTY

$\mathcal{I}$ awoke the next morning to the tantalizing smell of bacon frying and coffee brewing. The other side of my bed was empty. Throwing on my robe, I padded down the stairs to find Thomas busily making us breakfast. Jeff had certainly never bothered to make me a cup of coffee, let alone breakfast.

"Good morning, my love." I wrapped my arms around him from behind. He spun, dropping the spatula, as he scooped me up into his arms and swung me around the room.

"You are amazing, Thomas, and I am one very lucky lady," I purred as our lips met.

"As are you, Angela. This is the happiest day of my life. Together again after so long. I will never let you go this time around. I promise."

"And I won't let you go either." I stroked his arm as he got back to frying the eggs and bacon before they burned.

We had a leisurely breakfast together, hopefully the first of many more to come. As we talked about our respective plans for the day, I told him about my search for information about my family, especially my mother and grandmother who once lived in this house.

The more I shared, the more intrigued he became. "You know I have some expertise in genealogical research and some experience in finding things out about the past. I have a membership with the larger genealogy networks and access to a number of online sites. I really want to help you. We can work on this together, if you show me the information you've already gathered."

"That would be wonderful!"

He had to leave after breakfast since he had customers to take on a dog sled adventure that afternoon. He was also busy working with a contractor to renovate one of his fishing boats.

I kissed him goodbye and decided to wander over to the lodge. Just in case there were any new developments about Justine's journals or anything else. It was New Year's Day, but life went on as usual up here on the Gunflint Trail if you worked in the hospitality or sporting industries. Tourists still flocked to the restaurants and scheduled dog sledding adventures.

I couldn't help grinning as I hiked through the snow to the lodge. I couldn't remember ever being so happy, certainly not so much in love. The whole world had become more beautiful overnight. With Thomas in it, I was convinced that everything would go well. Perhaps, working together, we could even solve the mystery that Angelique had created with her disappearance.

Stomping the snow off my boots as I stepped into the gift shop, I found Sabrina anxiously waiting for me.

"So?" she grinned, raising her eyebrows at me, as if she knew something was up between Thomas and me. After all, she had seen us together here last night for her New Year's Eve dinner.

"So?" I repeated, frowning, as if I had no idea what she was referring to.

"Girlfriend, it's written all over your face. You can't hide the fact that you are in love, that you and Thomas finally got together. Right?" she whispered as she stepped closer, away from several other customers checking out some of the books on the shelf.

I could only nod, trying to suppress a grin.

"It's written all over your face, Angela. You're blushing, you know," she said in a teasing tone of voice. "All I can say is that it's about time!"

Way past time, I thought. We'd only been waiting to consummate this relationship for over a century. But I wasn't about to reveal that information to anyone, not even Sabrina. It sounded like total insanity.

"Sabrina," a female voice shouted from the adjacent big room, interrupting our conversation. "I need more coffee, Sabrina."

"My mother," Sabrina sighed, shaking her head. "She's having her morning coffee by the fireplace and needs my constant attention. Catch you later. Or, how about joining us? Actually, you may be interested in a new development here."

I followed her into the great room where Annette was seated in one of the overstuffed chairs before a blazing fire. Her slippered feet rested on an ottoman. A half-full cup of coffee sat on the tiny antique table beside her. She grinned almost impishly at Sabrina who was shaking her head.

"Mother, you still have well over half a cup of coffee left. Why don't you drink that first before I fill it up again?"

"Because it's getting cold."

"Fine, I'll warm it up for you." Sabrina began to pick up the cup of coffee when Annette shook her hand at her.

"No, I don't want it warmed up. I want a fresh cup!" she demanded.

"Anything else, Mother?" Sabrina tried to smile as she gathered the cup, dumped it in the kitchen sink and brought back a fresh cup of coffee.

After taking several sips in silence, Annette looked up. "Actually, I would like a lump of sugar. Just one."

I patiently waited, sitting quietly on one end of the sofa. Finally, Sabrina sat on the other end and introduced me to her mother—again. Apparently, Annette didn't remember having met me before, but she was friendly and told me she was happy to make my acquaintance. Quaint. Almost as quaint as the previous life I'd left behind in Virginia City, Montana.

"I do have some good news to share with you, Angela. My mother has been going through Justine's journal. She's deleted some parts that she doesn't want to share with anyone, not even me, but she's willing to share some of it with you. In fact, she tells me she actually found some references to your grandmother, Angelique. Justine knew her, too."

"What?" I had hoped and prayed that this would happen. Hopefully, some of the missing pieces of my mother's life would finally come together.

I leaned in closer to Annette. "I am grateful that you're willing to share some of this with me. I know you were little when you played with Emily at their cabin, but I understand that your grandmother Justine knew her and Emily's mother, Angelique?" I held my breath.

A confused look crossed Annette's face as she shook her head in frustration. "Who? Emily? Do I know someone named Emily?" She focused her gaze on Sabrina.

"Mother, you once had a playmate named Emily. You told me about her last week, about playing dolls together. Do you remember?"

Annette stared at the floor, twisting her hands in frustration.

"I know that was many years ago," I said, trying to soothe her. "Sometimes it's easy to forget. But if I can take a look at Justine's journal, maybe I can find out more?"

"What was her name again?" Annette whispered.

"Emily," I responded softly. "And her mother's name was Angelique."

A flicker of recognition sparkled in the older woman's eyes. "Ahh....Angelique. Yes, I think my grandmother knew her. Yes! I think she wrote about her in a little book that she kept."

Now we were getting someplace! Sabrina and I each breathed a sigh of relief. We shared a look of triumph before turning our attention back to Annette who was stirring her coffee with a puzzled expression upon her face.

"I don't like sugar in my coffee, Sabrina," she scolded her daughter. "Why in the world did you put a lump of sugar in my coffee?"

Sabrina shook her head sadly. I noticed a tear in the corner of her eye as she got up to dump her mother's coffee once again and start all over. Aging was not easy for anyone, but it was perhaps harder for an elderly person's loved ones to process. There were good days...and bad days.

I felt it was time for me to go. This wasn't a good time to pursue the journal I was dying to get my hands on. But Sabrina brought it up one more time when she returned with a cup of sugarless coffee for her mother.

"Mother?" She touched her shoulder gently. "About Justine's journal? Do you think we can let Angela take a look at it now?"

Annette bristled and bolted upright in her chair. "Justine's journal? What on earth are you talking about?"

So close and yet so far. I rose from the sofa, making an excuse that I had to go home.

Sabrina escorted me to the door. "I'm so sorry, Angela. It's not a good day. Hopefully she'll have a better day tomorrow. I'll find a way to get that journal to you. I know how much it means to you. I only hope there actually are entries about your mother and grandmother. Sometimes it's hard to know what's true and what isn't anymore."

"I understand." I gave her a hug goodbye. "You take care of yourself and let me know if I can do anything to help."

Yes, hopefully, Annette would have an easier day soon, or perhaps Sabrina would find a way to access that journal.

In the meantime, I had a backup plan to pursue.

CHAPTER TWENTY-ONE

*I*t wasn't easy but I finally convinced Mother to come up to my cabin with me. She was obviously afraid of old memories surfacing. I hoped they would surface so we could learn more about our past.

I was able to bribe her with lunch at Grand Marais' famous Angry Trout Restaurant on the shores of Lake Superior. Her favorite. Every summer when we'd make our annual North Shore trip, she always had to stop here to have a bowl of their fish chowder made New England Style with fresh-caught Lake Superior fish.

This year was no exception. I drove down and picked her up early one Monday morning. We then took a leisurely drive up the shore, arriving at the restaurant in time for lunch. I talked her into a glass of wine along with her chowder, hoping to loosen her up a bit before we drove to our cabin. While we usually sat outside on the deck overlooking the big lake, it was closed for the season. But we found a table by the windows with a view of the lake shrouded in a thin coat of ice that sparkled beneath the rays of the sun.

It was a beautiful relatively warm late winter day with very little snow to contend with. I carefully watched my mother for any reactions as we drove down my long driveway, the sun casting shadows through the trees. She stared straight ahead, her hands clenched in her lap.

She did not speak, nor did I, as we entered the cabin. She looked around carefully, then settled on the davenport by the fireplace as I lit a fire and offered her another glass of wine. She readily accepted. Still no reaction.

Did she not remember anything about the first three years of her life? About this cabin where she had most likely once lived? Or, had she buried old, possibly hurtful, memories so deeply that she could no longer access them?

I waited, checking my watch, knowing that Sabrina and her mother would be arriving soon. Just happening to drop in to visit. At least that's what I would tell my mother. Maybe seeing Annette would somehow stir up old memories. Although who knew what kind of a day Annette may be having? It was always a wild card, as my mother would say.

"Are you okay, Mother?" I asked.

She sipped her wine, staring into the fireplace, silently. Was she remembering anything? Anything at all?

"I'm all right." She sighed. "I just need time to try to think..."

I busied myself reading a book, or at least pretending that I was, while glancing her way to monitor her facial expressions. So far, no reactions.

Finally, there was a knock on the door. Mother startled, as if she'd suddenly returned to this world from another time and another place.

"Come in." I ushered Sabrina and Annette into the room. "What a pleasant surprise!" I lied, as I seated them by the fireplace and introduced them to my mother.

There was an awkward silence at first as Emily and Annette seemed to focus on each other. Sabrina and I waited.

"Is that you, Emily?" Annette finally broke the silence in a quivering voice. Thankfully, she seemed to be having a fairly good day today. A great relief!

"I used to come here to play with a little girl, one of my first friends," Annette reminisced. "Her name, if I remember right, was Emily..."

My mother's mouth dropped open, her eyes, wide. She just stared at Annette.

"We played dolls together. Sometimes your mother read us stories, and she always made us chocolate chip cookies. She was so nice..." Annette's voice trailed off.

While Mother continued to stare at Annette as if in shock, I asked Annette, "Do you remember Emily's mother's name?

"Oh yes. Angelique. She was just like an angel... and she had the most beautiful green eyes..." With that, she gazed into my mother's eyes. "Just like your eyes."

An angel? The mother who had deserted her own daughter? I could only imagine the thoughts running through my mother's head. She just shook her head slowly, back and forth. Back and forth.

"Tell me about your dolls," I said to break the silence, wondering if my mother would mention Susan, her favorite doll, who had disappeared when she did.

"Oh yes," Annette chimed in. "I had a baby doll that I fed with a bottle and changed her diaper. Her name was Mathilda."

My mother's voice croaked. "Mathilda? I think I do remember a doll like that...but it was so long ago. I thought it was a funny name. My doll was named Susan and she was so beautiful."

"Yes! I remember Susan!" Annette leaned toward Emily. "She has the most beautiful eyes that moved, and a pretty pink dress..."

The two aging women stared into each other's eyes as old memories resurfaced.

"Annette..." Mother wiped away a tear. "Annette. I think I do remember you now. You were my first friend. And I missed you so much when...when..."

I reached over to give my mother a hug. She clung to me.

"Why did you leave us, Emily? I never knew why. You just went away."

Sabrina and I both had tears in our eyes, as did our mothers, by then. Finally, Sabrina broke the tearful silence. "Maybe we can find that out in the pages of Justine's old journal?"

Annette nodded. "That's a good idea."

"Who is Justine?" my mother inquired.

"That would be my grandmother," Annette replied. "She knew your mother."

"She did?"

"Yes, and she wrote some things about her in her journal. Would you like to see it?"

Mother glanced at me, looking for help, unsure how to respond. Unsure if she did or did not want to know anything about the mother who had deserted her so many years ago.

"We would love to see it, Annette," I replied. "We will take good care of it and return it to you."

"Maybe...maybe...you can read it, Angela," Mother finally stammered. "I'm not sure how much I want to know."

"I can do that," I sighed, greatly relieved. We were finally getting somewhere!

Our mothers began to chat together, reliving their childhoods. As Annette shared some of her memories, it seemed to trigger more memories for my mother. Sabrina and I retreated to the kitchen, poured a glass of wine, and toasted each other on a successful reunion.

After a while, Annette grew tired and slipped back into the fog of early dementia. She wasn't sure who my mother was anymore. "Do I know you?" She frowned as she stared at her old friend.

My mother shifted in her chair uncomfortably, searching for me, not knowing how to respond. Sabrina immediately intervened, helping her mother up from her chair and escorting her to the door. "It's time for a nap, Mother," she said as she helped her into her coat. "I'm so sorry, Emily, but my mother forgets things sometimes. I know she'd love to visit with you more someday when...when she's feeling better?"

"That would be lovely," Mother replied, managing a smile.

Once they left, we settled in for the evening. While I tried to talk with her, she was quiet as she tried to process what had happened. I had to convince her to stay over, promising her that I'd take her back to Duluth first thing the next morning. She stared out the window of the car, anxious to get back to the world she knew. A safer place than having to deal with the mysteries that surrounded her up here in her childhood home.

I finally broke the silence surrounding us. "Are you okay, Mother?"

"How can I possibly be okay?" she snapped at me. "My mother...an angel? I'm not sure Annette knows what she's talking about. I mean, she even forgot who I was at the end..."

"But you do remember her? It sounded like you both remembered things about your early days together, right?"

"Yes, but...I just don't know. I feel like I'm in some kind of dream. Maybe a nightmare. I don't know what is real and what is not anymore. Maybe...am I getting like Annette? Forgetting things like she does?"

Her words tugged at my heart. Yes, I had observed Mother forgetting a few things sometimes. But didn't we all, especially as we got older? And my mother was certainly not at the same stage of life as Annette. In fact, she still led a very active life and played an important role on the various councils and committees she was involved with. I reassured her of that.

The next morning I drove Mother back home. "Do you want me to stay?" I felt compelled to ask after I'd seen her safely into the house where Beth was waiting, always there to help my mother.

"No, I just need to be alone, I think, to try to process what happened. It's so strange that you somehow ended up in the cabin where I once lived. How can that be?"

"Maybe it's meant to be, Mother." I hugged her goodbye. "Call and let me know how you're doing and if I can help."

While I was concerned about how she was handling this shocking glimpse into her past and how she might handle any additional information I was able to find out. I was also anxious to get back to my cabin. I couldn't wait to get to the lodge tomorrow morning and hopefully access Justine's journal.

CHAPTER TWENTY-TWO

$\mathcal{G}$t was dark when I pulled into my driveway and I was surprised to see lights on in the cabin. Had I forgotten to turn them off in all the excitement? Then I noticed Thomas's snowmobile parked by the door. The walk was shoveled, and I could smell the heavenly scent of a basil-laced Italian sauce simmering on the stove when I opened the door.

"You have no idea how happy I am to see you," I said as he turned from the stove and then folded me into his arms.

"You said you'd be home sometime this evening. I figured you could use some TLC and your favorite meal, my lovely. And I'm anxious to hear all about your day."

I told him everything over a plate of the most delicious spaghetti I'd ever eaten. He listened carefully. Afterwards, while he told he about his day, we cuddled together on the old sofa by the warmth of a fire in the stone fireplace. Just listening to the crackling of the fire, enjoying the warmth of each other, and the comfortable silence.

I fell asleep with my head on his shoulder, exhausted after a productive and exciting day. He kissed me goodnight and left for his place in Grand Marais, somehow knowing I needed time alone to process what had happened and to prepare for my adventures delving into Justine's journals, hopefully tomorrow.

As much as I was dying to get into those journals, I had a feeling that I may discover things that may not be easy to digest. Things that could perhaps have a major impact on my mother's life, if not my own. Secrets from the past that were important enough for Angelique to lead me to this place.

"There are no secrets that time does not reveal," a silent but comforting voice whispered into my subconscious as I slipped beneath the covers and shut off the bedside lamp. *"It is time,"* she reminded me once again.

...

Early the next morning I was awakened by the ringing of my phone. It wasn't light out yet and I was still lost in a dream about Thomas and me as David and Julia. He was proposing marriage, down on one knee, after securing my father's permission to take my hand in marriage.

I managed to grab my phone. "Hello?"

"Angela, I have Justine's diary!" an excited Sabrina whispered. "How soon can you come over?"

I bolted upright in bed, heart pounding. It was happening! "Really? Oh my God! It's...what...only six o'clock?"

"Yes, sorry, but I was so excited that I was able to retrieve it before my mother woke up, just in case she changes her mind again, you know."

"That's fine. I'll be there in fifteen minutes if that's not too early?"

"Great. Coffee is already on. See you soon."

"Perfect. Thanks so much, Sabrina!"

Why was my heart fluttering with both anticipation and dread? What was I going to discover in the pages of this book? It was probably a good thing that I could read it by myself and censor what I would or would not be sharing with Mother.

Throwing on yesterday's clothes, I ran a brush through my hair, brushed my teeth and headed out to my car in the dark. I gazed at a sliver of a moon hovering amongst the stars. A shimmer of light casting a beacon of hope in the midst of the darkness.

After brushing a light coat of fresh snow off my windshield, I climbed into my SUV and made my way to the lodge. There I found Sabrina waiting for me by the fireplace with two cups of coffee. A plain paper bag was on the sofa beside her. Justine's journal, I assumed.

She and I were the only ones up, I realized, as we settled by the fireplace. Sipping our coffee, we caught up on recent events before the lodge came to life. It was that peaceful time of day. Guests would soon arrive for breakfast, coffee, or to spend time reading or playing games. And who knew when Annette would decide to come strolling down for attention? I had to make my getaway before then, we decided.

"Here." Sabrina handed me the heavy paper bag as the stairs above us creaked and we caught a glimpse of Annette emerging at the top of the stairs. She would soon be needing Sabrina's attention, despite the fact that Sabrina had a lodge to run and staff to supervise.

I tucked the bag beneath my arm, grabbed my coat, and retreated out into the cold as the sun was beginning to rise through a bank of fog. It was time to head back to Angelique's cabin and try to discover what I could through the pages of the journal.

CHAPTER TWENTY-THREE

"*The tall dark pines, like figures in a black and white etching, stand draped in capes of snow. They flank the Gunflint Trail in elegant silence, their frosty caps tilted at stylish angles.*"

Justine's beautiful words emerged from the first page of her journal, perfectly capturing the scene outside my window. She was obviously a talented writer and a lover of nature. I reread her words several times as I sat at Angelique's antique desk.

I wondered how much time Angelique had spent sitting here in this old, wooden chair. Did she write, or perhaps sketch? Had she kept a journal? I'd have given anything to discover an old locked diary or any of her writings. I had searched this desk and the cabin from top to bottom. I'd found nothing so far.

Breathing deeply, closing my eyes, I invited her to join me here as I delved into Justine's journal. An intense swirl of energy suddenly engulfed me for a moment before disappearing. It seemed that her visits were shorter these days, as if her boundless energy was perhaps dwindling. Yet, there was an intensity about them.

I began carefully turning the pages of Justine's old leather-bound journal dating back to the 1950s. I was going back in time, seventy-five years into the past. I was drawn into Justine's beautiful and mesmerizing descriptions of her world around and her life. Maybe there wasn't anything about my grandmother after all.

I tried to pinpoint dates. Since Emily had been born in 1955, I should be searching for journal entries from 1955 to 1958. I knew she'd been adopted in 1958. I poured myself another cup of strong coffee to fortify myself against whatever I might discover as I paged through the journal.

Help me out here, Angelique, I whispered into the silence of the room. As I did so, I felt a gentle breeze sweep through the room emanating a sense of strength, hope, and confidence that I could indeed handle whatever I discover in these pages and in the future. Then she was gone once again.

With that, I began carefully turning pages, intrigued with Justine's artistic writing style, until the name "Angelique" almost jumped off the page at me.

June 15, 1958 – A lovely early summer day up here in God's Country! I took my little granddaughter Annette for a walk, stopping to admire the wildflowers peeking up through the lush forest floor. Delicate white woodland wildflowers. Brilliant yellow marsh marigolds. We decided to pay a visit to our neighbors Angelique and her adorable little daughter Emily. The girls had a wonderful time playing together with their dolls while I visited with Angelique. She's a lovely young woman and a doting mother, probably in her very early 20s. She treated us to homemade chocolate chip cookies. Her husband wasn't there since he's a mariner, away from home a lot while sailing on the Great Lakes. She seems perfectly content alone here with her daughter whom she obviously loves dearly. Lovely visit.

Very interesting. So perhaps Angelique had been a good mother after all? At least during Emily's early years. Intrigued, I paged through more entries, looking for clues. Finally, I found another entry that almost took my breath away.

July 2, 1958 – Well, some things may not be as they seem. I decided to stop in to visit Angelique and Emily after taking Annette for a short walk through the woods, stopping to admire the eagles swooping overhead and tiny chipmunks chattering in the treetops. I had heard that her husband was home for a spell the last few weeks but had left again. I hadn't wanted to intrude on their time together so I'd waited until he left. I knocked on the door several times. No answer. I knew she was there since I could hear Emily inside. I knocked louder.

"Angelique? It's Justine," I called out. Again, no answer. Was something wrong? I tried the door and found that it was unlocked, so I gently opened it. "Angelique?"

"Oh!" a startled Angelique carefully pulled herself up from the sofa, trying to hide her face from me. She was limping and appeared to be in pain as she moved slowly across the room.

"Are you all right? What happened to you?"

"I... I...had a fall," she stammered, unable to look me in the eye, trying

to shield her face from my gaze. She winced when I reached out to touch her arm. I walked around her to get a better look and discovered that she was trying to hide a black eye as well as bruises on her arms. Her ankle was also swollen. I managed to get her to sit down and tried to get her to tell me what had really happened to her.

Finally, she broke down in tears, admitting that she and her husband, Jonathan, had had a disagreement. A "disagreement?" Really?

He hadn't meant to hurt her, she tried to assure me, but he was stressed out about having to ship out again so soon. He'd probably had a few too many drinks when he was out with his buddies that night. And he'd accused her of cheating on him, which she assured me had never even crossed her mind. He also accused her of being a witch – because she seemed to have some psychic abilities to see and predict things, even to connect with deceased spirits.

"A witch! That's what you are!" He'd slapped her across the face, over and over again. "And you think I'm going to let you raise our daughter? She will be one hell of a lot better off without you. I will be back for her, as soon as I make arrangements, and there's not a damn thing you can do about it!"

With that, Jonathan had stuffed a few things into his duffle bag and left her in a heap on the floor, Emily wailing in the background.

I was shocked and terrified for her, Justine continued in her journal. *I finally convinced her to let me call the doctor who came out immediately. He checked her out, tended to her wounds, gave her pain medication and a brace for her ankle. She avoided answering his questions, just stared at the ground, shaking her head. After he left, I tried to talk to her about leaving her husband before he returns from his ship. That should be several months in the future. At least she has some time before she needs to make a decision. I plan to be there to encourage and support her anyway I can. The poor dear! How can something so horrible happen to such a lovely young lady?*

How can her husband be such a monster? I intend to find out more about this Jonathan!

Tears streamed down my face as I shook my head in disbelief. I could feel her pain. And I couldn't help flashing back to the last time I saw Jeff. I had also been lying on the floor of our bedroom, bloody and bruised, as he stormed out of the house and out of my life. I'd tried hard to block those memories from my conscious mind. Until now. Until this. Angelique and I apparently had more in common than I realized. But this was not the time to think about that or what happened to me. I had moved on, right? I had Thomas now and a wonderful life ahead of me. I needed to focus on my grandmother and what happened to her.

It was hard to understand how my hero of a grandfather, the brave sailor who went down with his ship, could have suddenly turned into an abusive monster. Or how the selfish woman who abandoned her own daughter was now being portrayed as a loving mother and abused wife.

How could this be true? But I had no reason to doubt Justine's words. She had no reason, no motive, to make up stories like this.

And how could this horrible truth have been hidden from my family for so long? Well, that answer was fairly obvious. My mother had refused to delve into her past history, afraid of what she may discover. I also knew that in those days, adoption records were closed, supposedly to protect the parties involved. And I really couldn't blame my mother. How would I feel if I'd been abandoned as a toddler? Would I want to dredge up hurtful memories of the past or simply try to put them behind me?

My head was spinning as I closed the journal, unable to read another word, afraid of what more I might discover. Still, I knew I needed to uncover the truth. Angelique needed me to solve the mystery of her disappearance soon. Time seemed to be of the essence. Was she running out of time – or were we?

First, I needed some fresh air. Throwing on my parka, warm hat, gloves and hiking boots, I made my way along the snow-covered trail down to the bench overlooking Gunflint Lake. I always felt a sense of peace here. Hopefully that would be the case today when I needed it most.

As I gazed out over the stillness of the ice-covered lake surrounded by forests of pine, I felt a comforting presence snuggle beside me. Nobody was there, except for Angelique's essence. I could feel her pain seeping gently into my soul, but it was much more than that. The initial pain seemed to swell upward into layers of acceptance, hope, and meaning that exceeded the evil lurking beneath it.

There's a silver lining in every cloud, Angela. The truth will set you, and my darling daughter Emily, free. I felt a gentle invisible hand stroke my cheek before she disappeared once again.

I wondered what my mother would think if she knew what I'd discovered in the pages of Justine's journal. Could she handle learning that her evil mother had actually loved her, and that her hero of a father was actually a monster? How much could or should I even tell her? For now, I needed to learn more before I made any rash decisions. Hopefully, the answers could be found in Justine's journal.

I don't know how long I sat there, deep in thought, trying to process what I'd just learned and figure out my next steps. I finally escaped from my reverie and realized that the sky was turning dark with heavy clouds hovering overhead. The wind began to howl as heavy snowflakes fell. It was time to go home.

I trudged through the snow back to the warmth of my cabin, Angelique's cabin. The place where she'd been abused by her husband. Had she taken Emily to escape from him, especially after his threatening words about not allowing her to raise their daughter? Maybe she decided to leave while he was away at sea, to find a place where she could raise her daughter in peace. If that was the case, how and why did she simply disappear and leave Emily behind? *What happened to you, Angelique?*

I lit a fire in the fireplace, got into my pajamas and made myself hot cocoa. Wrapped in a quilt that my mother had crocheted for me years ago, I stared into the flames, trying to make sense of all I'd learned. Trying to stay away from Justine's journal. As intrigued and anxious as I was to learn more, I wasn't sure how much more I could handle today. So, I tried to read one of the books I pulled from the library shelves surrounding the fireplace. But I couldn't concentrate.

I was just dozing off when my phone rang, startling me.

"Hello?" I whispered, not quite awake.

"Angela, are you all right? I've been trying to call you but you don't answer... I left you several messages." Thomas sounded worried.

"I'm sorry, Thomas. I was too distracted with Justine's journal to think about or check my messages."

"You don't sound okay, my dear. What happened?"

Where to begin? It was all too much, but I tried to briefly describe what I'd learned. Thomas listened, trying to comfort me, offering to come out and be with me. But with the storm growing in intensity and a forty-four-mile drive to get to my place, I declined his offer.

He tried to lighten my mood. "It sounds to me like our next step is to dig deeper into our research and find out where Angelique went and what happened to her. I can help you with that. How do you think I found you in this lifetime?"

"I'd love that, Thomas."

"Together, we can do anything. Always remember that."

"I will. You are the best thing that ever happened to me, you know."

"As are you to me. I love you, Angela, or Julia, or whatever your name is!" he joked.

"And I love you, my darling Thomas, aka David!"

Suddenly the lights went off. The storm outside was growing in intensity and we'd lost electricity. A common occurrence up here in the woods. It was time to light the kerosene lamps and make sure I kept the fire going until the electricity was restored. I'd spend the night sleeping on the davenport, keeping an eye on the fire and adding fire wood when needed.

"Are you sure you don't want me to come? Do you have enough firewood?"

"I'm fine. I don't want you out in this weather, Thomas. Besides, you've already filled my firebox to overflowing. I could last another month or more!" I teased him, feeling better after talking with him.

With that, we bid each other good night. I lit the kerosene lamps, the ones that Angelique had undoubtedly lit years ago, and threw more logs on the fire.

CHAPTER TWENTY-FOUR

I'm running barefoot through the woods – again – shivering in a thin nightgown, stumbling, trying to hide from an evil force that is following me, getting closer and closer. Ancient snow-laden pines swirl around me in distorted shapes. I hear the crashing waves of Lake Superior against the rocky cliffs far below me. I run harder, faster, trying to get away.

"Angelique!" That hauntingly familiar voice thunders through the forest as snowflakes fall and heavy footsteps close in on me.

"Help! Just leave me alone... please just leave me alone!"

Suddenly the lights in my cabin flickered back on, startling me, waking me from the nightmare that had haunted me for some time. Trembling, heart pounding, I got up, unable to sleep anymore. Peering through the frost-covered window, I saw massive drifts of snow. It had stopped snowing, however, and the glimmer of a rising sun lurked across the horizon.

I headed into the kitchen to make myself a badly needed cup of coffee. I couldn't help wondering if this nightmare had suddenly taken on a new meaning. Did Jonathan somehow find Angelique and try to hurt her—or worse? Is that why she disappeared? I would welcome Thomas's help in trying to find some answers to her mysterious disappearance.

It was time to confront Justine's journal again, I decided, as I turned on the desk lamp and settled on a pillow in Angelique's old chair. I could do this, I tried to assure myself.

July 21, 1958 – I've been so busy with our summer guests and leading fishing expeditions that I've neglected to update you, Dear Diary, on what I've learned about my neighbor Angelique's husband, Jonathan. It's not good, unfortunately. You see, I did a little sleuthing around the bars in our area, had a few beers with the regulars, and managed to get a conversation going about Jonathan. Did any of them know him? I was trying to find him, I told the guys sitting at the bar. I was a friend of his wife and daughter and had some important information to share with him.

You could have heard a pin drop as they all eyed me cautiously. Finally, one man decided to break the silence.

"Jonathan, the sailor guy?" An elderly man with a scraggly gray beard shook his head in surprise. "That crazy son-of-a-bitch? All I can say is stay out of his way when he's off the boat and drinking. Hell, last time I saw him here…maybe a month or so ago? Well, he was ranting and raving about his crazy wife. It wasn't good…"

I encouraged him to elaborate. "His crazy wife?"

Another older man wearing a red flannel shirt and suspenders chimed in. "Yeah…I heard about that wife of his. She's a witch, according to Jonathan. He said she talks to dead people and thinks trees are alive. What the hell?"

"Besides," the hefty, bearded bartender said from across the bar, "Jonathan said she was having an affair with someone. Didn't know who or have any details. He just knew she was up to no good when he was off sailing."

"Yeah." The scraggly bearded guy jumped in again. "He said she wasn't fit to raise their daughter and he intended to do something about that. He stormed out of here, all fired up. I have no idea if anything he said was true…because he says crazy things that make no sense. He usually makes threats and then forgets about it the next day."

"You bet ya. Besides, if his woman is really a witch, she should be able to take care of herself, right?" The man in the red flannel shirt smirked. "Yup, that guy is just a drunken sailor, that's what he is. I stay out of his way when he's back and stops in to get drunk. Never argue with him or question anything he says."

I'd heard enough. It was time to head home and process this before tending to our guests. And I needed to pay Angelique a visit as soon as possible. I'm not quite sure yet how to handle this situation and how much to reveal to her.

Poor Angelique! My heart aches for her and I am terrified thinking about what could happen if she doesn't leave and go into hiding. I simply have to convince her to take Emily and find a new place to live. At least we should have until December before he returns. That's about when the lakes freeze over and the shipping season ends.

Tears filled my eyes once again. Did Justine convince her to leave?

Oh Angelique, I pleaded silently. *Where did you go? What happened to you?*

No response.

I decided that shoveling the snow outside would be a welcome diversion. I tried to distract myself by focusing on the beauty surrounding me. The massive pines were blanketed in a fresh coat of snow that sparkled in the sunlight. The world was silent. I compulsively shoveled.

I stopped to watch several deer lurking at the edge of my driveway as if they were watching me. I'd forgotten to put corn out for my pals so I trudged through the snow to the shed where I retrieved a bucket of corn and spread it on the ground. They came running in, not the least bit afraid. One nudged my hand gently as I stood beside them.

"Good deer." I talked to them softly as I always did. They seemed to wag their tails at me, grateful for their daily snack. If deer could only talk. The wildlife surrounding me helped to ground me and connect me to nature. Maybe it wasn't so crazy after all if Angelique had talked to trees. Didn't the American Indians believe that trees had spirits within them? And hadn't I heard once, long ago, that Angelique had some Indian blood in her, along with French Canadian? Metis, I believed.

The silence was suddenly interrupted by a snowmobile roaring down my driveway. My heart fluttered when I recognized Thomas. He'd had that effect on me, totally unlike anything I ever felt for my ex-husband.

I greeted him with a hug. "What are you doing here?"

"I figured you needed some diversion, my lovely." He grinned down at me as he removed his helmet. "Look at the beauty around us. It's time for a photo shoot, don't you think? Come on," he led me back into the house. "Get yourself dressed and grab your camera. Please?"

"But...but what about Justine's diary?"

"That can wait. I'll help you later, but I think you need a break, Angela." He gazed into my eyes.

He was right. "Okay, but I'm starving. How about an omelet before we leave?"

"Exactly what I was hoping for." He laughed. "Why do you think I drove all the way out here?"

We fixed breakfast together, so comfortable, as if we'd always done this together. And we talked about our photography, our dreams to capture wildlife photos.

"It's going to be a long winter, you know, with awesome photo opportunities. And we should probably think about setting your work up in some of the galleries in town. There's more to life, you know, than your family history."

He was right. I had been, still was, consumed with the mysteries of the past. Maybe I needed to try to find some balance in my life. And Thomas was determined to help me do that.

We had a lovely day together, snowmobiling down snow-covered lanes, across frozen lakes, stopping to take pictures of the beauty surrounding us. We captured some fantastic photos of a moose quietly hiking along a trail. It was enough to almost make me forget Angelique's unfolding mysterious story. Almost.

After an early dinner at The Poplar Haus Restaurant, we returned to my cabin and settled in for the night. Thomas had the next day off and I was pleased that he could stay over. We cuddled by the fireplace for a while, talking about anything and everything—except Angelique. That could wait for tomorrow, he suggested. I agreed. Tonight was for us. Exhausted after a long day on the trails and the fresh air, we retired to my bed where we fell into each other's arms and made sweet, tender love until we fell asleep.

CHAPTER TWENTY-FIVE

*A*fter a quick breakfast the next morning, we were back to our research. I curled up on the sofa with Justine's journal and read.

September 1, 1958 – On my God! Listening to the news on the radio this morning, I learned that a Great Lakes ship, The Americana II, *has gone down on Lake Superior in a freak storm that came out of nowhere. It disappeared shortly after leaving Whitefish Point and was headed along the south shore of Lake Superior toward Grand Marais, Michigan. This is known as the "graveyard of the Great Lakes" due to the dangerous Herculean currents and horrific storms that have plagued this area. At least 200 ships have gone down along this treacherous 80-mile shoreline.*

Why am I so shocked over this? Because Jonathan, Angelique's husband, was sailing on this ship last I heard. They say there are no survivors and no possibility of retrieving the bodies of the crew who will spend eternity in this watery grave at the bottom of the lake.

I immediately rushed over to see Angelique. I found her sitting on her back porch, staring into space as she watched Emily playing with her doll beneath the old oak tree.

"Angelique? Have you heard the news? About the Americana *going down?"*

"I have," she whispered. "They say there are no survivors..."

"That's right. Isn't that the ship that Jonathan..."

"Yes."

"I'm so sorry. Are you all right? I mean, I know you had your problems and were thinking about leaving him. But...he was your husband and Emily's father. This has to be difficult for you." I pulled up a rocking chair beside her and waited for some kind of response. She seemed to be in a trance. Certainly understandable. But no visible tears. Barely any emotion. She must have been in shock, in denial.

"What can I do to help?" I reached out to touch her shoulder.

"Nothing. C'est la vie." She sighed.

I waited, giving her the space she probably needed.

Suddenly she rose, agitated, a fearful look clouding her eyes as she scanned the forest surrounding us. "Something's wrong here. Something doesn't feel right. I don't know. I can't explain it. He's not gone... I can feel it."

What? That made no sense to me. She was probably in denial, unable to accept her abusive husband's tragic death and the fact that he and his shipmates were now at the bottom of Lake Superior.

I tried to assure her that it would take time to process his death and that what she was experiencing was a normal reaction to something like this.

"Nothing's normal about this." She shook her head, now pacing back and forth on the porch, nervously glancing into the woods surrounding her. "I'm sorry, Justine, but I have to go. I have things to do. Thank you for being my friend and for caring about me."

I'd been dismissed and was utterly confused. I told her to let me know anything I could do to help and gave her a hug. She clung to me as if she didn't want to let go. Tears finally filled her eyes and she asked me to leave.

That was the end of Justine's entry.

My own eyes filled with tears, totally confused, heartbroken for my grandmother Angelique. Even for my grandfather, perhaps, who was now gone forever. It took me a few minutes of pacing around the cabin before I was able to speak.

"That's so strange, isn't it?" I finally asked Thomas who was sitting at our kitchen table researching Angelique on his laptop. I'd just read him Justine's journal entry and was trying to figure it out.

"It is, but you never know how people deal with grief, especially under these circumstances. A violent husband whom she was thinking about leaving. Now this...his death in a tragic shipwreck. Still...yes, a little strange."

Of course, we already knew about Jonathan's ship going down and the fact that there were no survivors. But it was Angelique's strange reaction that intrigued me. I poured us another cup of coffee and threw another log on the fire before summoning up the courage to return to Justine's journal.

September 8, 1958 – I am shocked and terrified and wasn't sure what to do. We were all worried about Angelique and little Emily, especially when she would not return our phone calls or answer her door. When I went to check on them, I found the door was locked, and the place looked deserted. Her husband's old truck was also missing.

The police responded to my plea for help and went out to do a welfare check. They had to break the lock on the door. They went in cautiously, after ordering me to stay outside until they determined it was safe. Just in case.

I was finally allowed to enter, my heart pounding as I almost tripped over Emily's beloved doll on the floor. Dirty dishes filled the sink. Clothing and other items were scattered throughout the cabin. Angelique and Emily were gone. It looked like they'd left in a hurry, taking only a few things with them.

I told the police everything I knew, including the abuse Angelique had endured from her now deceased husband. No, I had no idea they were leaving or where they might have gone. Yes, she was considering leaving him...but now that he was dead, why had she felt she had to leave? And why didn't she tell anyone?

Nothing makes any sense. I keep mulling it over and over again in my head. Did I miss any clues that could lead us to them? Or, did they not want to be found?

CHAPTER TWENTY-SIX

Where did they go? And how did my poor mother end up alone and placed for adoption? I could hardly imagine what it must have been like for her, a toddler, to lose her mother and never hear from her again. My head was reeling as I paced around the cabin. Somehow, we had to find out more about her adoption. Thankfully, my super sleuth partner, Thomas, was already searching through records on his laptop.

The ringing of my phone interrupted my thoughts.

"Angela?" Mother's worried voice brought me back to the present. "I've been trying to contact you. Is everything all right?"

"I'm fine, Mother," I lied. How could I possibly tell her what we'd just discovered? There seemed to be more questions than answers at this point in time. I didn't think she could handle this. Not yet. Not until I learned more and figured out how to tell her, and how much to tell her.

"And Justine's diary?" she finally asked quietly.

"I'm just getting into it, Mother, and I really don't have much to tell you yet."

"Hmm... I figured you'd have read the whole thing by now. You were so anxious to learn more."

"I am, but I'm taking it slowly, I guess. Trying to put the pieces together. I'm really struggling to make sense of some of this. All I know so far is that Justine and Annette enjoyed their visits to Angelique's. Justine liked her, Mother. I need to read more, and figure some things out. I promise I will let you know then."

"That's fine, I guess. To be honest, I'm not sure how much I want to know or need to know. This is not easy for me."

"I get that, Mother. But can I at least ask you if you have any information at all about your adoption? Your biological parents and their ancestors? Any papers around the house?" I held my breath, hoping I wasn't being too intrusive.

"Nothing. I actually looked yesterday. Just in case. Now that we're finally looking into our family history. But there's nothing. I don't know anything about my biological parents or who their parents were. Nothing."

We chatted a while before hanging up. I found Thomas still seated at the kitchen table with his laptop. He was absorbed in his research, making notes, lost in his own world, even talking to himself. "Hmm...I hadn't thought of that..."

"Thought of what?" I grinned as I walked over to give him a big hug.

"Something compelled me to check out a different database that I wasn't aware of. Great source for old news articles, in case there's anything about Angelique and Emily. You never know."

"Something compelled you? Perhaps the mysterious Angelique?"

"Could be... we need to find out what happened to her. She's the one with the answers we seek. She obviously has something important that she wants us to take care of."

"Unfinished business she has entrusted to us, Thomas." I grew serious as I sat down across the table from him. I would do whatever it took to resolve whatever it was that she still needed to do on this earth. And Thomas was obviously committed to helping me do that.

Restless, I decided to take a break and make us lunch. The morning had slipped away and it was already one o'clock. I warmed up the chili I'd made yesterday—perfect for a cold winter day—and threw together a salad.

Before long, I was buried again in the pages of Justine's journal. I made my way through her entries for the next several months. Her poetic descriptions of nature and wildlife were intriguing. But I was focused on finding out what happened to Angelique.

All I found were several brief paragraphs in which Justine expressed her worries and concerns about Angelique and Emily. Why had they disappeared so suddenly? Where had they gone? She prayed that they were all right, and hoped to hear from them soon. She couldn't understand why Angelique didn't say goodbye or tell her where they were going. Or had she simply decided to make a fresh start with her little girl, someplace where she wouldn't be haunted by memories of her late husband?

I was running out of hope as I neared the end of the journal. When

I flipped the last page, I was surprised to see that someone had obviously torn pages from the end of the journal. That was strange.

The last words Justine wrote in this journal were also strange and somewhat alarming.

At last! I am greatly relieved to hear from her – but very troubled about what is going on. I have been sworn to secrecy, of course, and will keep that promise. My lips are sealed and I will never reveal her whereabouts or any information that she has shared with

The end. The remaining pages had been ripped out.

"What the hell?" I exploded, startling Thomas.

I held up the journal for him to see. "Why would someone rip out the very pages that could shed some light on what happened? Who would do such a thing?"

"Maybe to try to protect them?"

"That's a stretch," I began to pace around the room again. "Who would want to hurt them? Jonathan's dead, don't forget. This makes no sense at all."

"Maybe there's another journal?"

With that, I bundled up and headed for the Gunflint Lodge to find Sabrina. It was worth a try. I placed the journal in a paper bag to conceal it, in case Annette was around. She still didn't know that Sabrina had loaned her grandmother's journal to me.

It was refreshing, almost calming, to hike along the snow-covered trail inhaling the fresh air. I left Thomas at his laptop, declining his offer to go with me. Maybe he'd find something, anything to help solve this mystery.

I found Sabrina organizing some of her handcrafted Northern Lights jewelry in the gift shop.

She grinned when she saw me. "Hey, stranger." She then stopped and frowned. "Something's wrong. Are you okay?"

"I...I don't know." I slumped down into a chair by the desk as I carefully retrieved the journal from the bag and handed it to her. "The pages at the end have been torn out, just at the point where Justine was starting to shed some light on this mystery." I read the last sentences to Sabrina.

"Oh no. Who would have done that? Justine? And why?"

"Do you think there could be another journal? Would Annette know anything about any more documents or letters or notes of some kind?"

"I doubt it, but I'll ask and let you know. I'm so sorry, Angela." She gave me a quick hug as customers drifted into the shop.

I made my way back home, kicking through the snow. I had been so close, but we'd hit a dead end. All I knew was that something was wrong. Justine was concerned. And she had known where Angelique was hiding out. Although, I reminded myself, she had not used Angelique's name in her last entry. I'd simply assumed it was Angelique that she was writing about. That made sense, based on her previous entries, right?

Later that evening, I was curled up on the davenport alone since Thomas had to go home to his place to prepare for a dog sledding excursion. While indulging in, perhaps, one too many glasses of wine to relieve my anxiety, I tried to connect with Angelique. I needed her help. How could we discover the truth if she didn't guide us? Why had she disappeared once again? Why now when I needed her more than ever?

"Angelique, please," I pleaded. Sometimes it felt like it was easiest to communicate with spirits telepathically instead of verbally. After all, they were unable to speak. At least that had been my experience.

Nothing. No response.

I tried again, over and over, until the ringing of my phone interrupted my efforts.

"Angela?" Sabrina didn't sound overjoyed. Not a good sign.

"Hi, Sabrina. Any news?"

"I'm sorry, but Annette has no more journals, papers, notes. Nothing. I double-checked to be sure. We can't find anything."

"I was afraid of that. Thanks for trying."

"I did ask her, again, if she remembered anything. If Justine had ever mentioned the disappearance of Angelique and Emily to her."

"And?" I held my breath, gripping the phone tightly.

Sabrina sighed deeply. "She asked who Angelique and Emily were...very confused. Not a good day, apparently. I'll try again on one of her better days. I'm really sorry. Is there anything I can do?"

"Not really...unless you want to stop over for a glass of wine? I'm drinking alone tonight..." I tried to laugh.

"I'll be right there, girlfriend."

We spent the evening chatting by the fireside about life in the Northwoods and the colorful people who inhabited it. Sabrina had fascinating stories to share about local history and happenings. Stories that had been handed down through the generations her family had owned and operated the Gunflint Lodge. Although there were no stories about my family, it was a perfect diversion for me.

...

Thomas and I soon settled into pursuing our photography and placing prints for sale at the Lake Superior Trading Post and several art galleries in Grand Marais. We tried to limit the time we spent researching my family's history. He made sure of that...and although that sometimes frustrated me, I was grateful for the balancing effect he had upon me. One more reason to love this guy I'd somehow always loved.

Finally, the snow began to melt and an early spring was upon us. As Justine had so eloquently described the season in the book she wrote years ago...

Spirits are returning to the trail, bringing with them drums that rumble under the lake ice with an ever-changing cadence. The treetops sway as if caressed by the spirits' gentle hands.

As I sat out on the bench overlooking the lake, basking in the warmth of the sunshine while reading my well-worn copy of her book, I gazed up at the billowy clouds drifting overhead.

Angelique, I whispered, *all I need now is for your spirit to guide me, to help me complete whatever tasks you need me to do.*

Suddenly I felt her comforting presence embracing me. Although I could not see her, or anyone else, I knew she was there. She was back, finally. I almost wanted to scold her, to ask what took her so long. But I knew that there was no such thing as "time" in the spirit world.

The truth shall make itself known very soon, my dear Angela. Her thoughts flooded into my mind. *Be open to the clues that are descending upon you. Timing is everything.*

CHAPTER TWENTY-SEVEN

"Angela! You aren't going to believe this!" Thomas's words echoed down the trail toward the lake where I was still perched on the bench. "Come quick!"

I met him half-way down the trail where he scooped me up into his arms and swung me around.

"What in the world?"

Grabbing my hand, he led me back to the cabin, to his laptop which was sitting in its usual place on my kitchen table.

"Look what I found! An old newspaper article that could very well be about your mother. The date and other data we've found seem to confirm this."

Heart pounding, I sat down at his laptop and was startled to see an old photo of a little girl. A little girl about three years old. Zooming in, I could clearly see a distinct resemblance to my mother. A slightly younger version of the childhood photos her adoptive parents had taken after they'd adopted her. I recognized those eyes, the slightly upturned nose.

The headlines screamed at me, "Help Needed to Locate Little Girl's Parents." The article was dated November 10, 1958.

Heart pounding, I began to read.

Authorities are seeking the public's help to identify this little girl and to find her missing parents. The little girl's name is Olivia, according to her unidentified young mother. She dropped the child off at the Maple Hill Church two months ago. She asked the pastor to take good care of her daughter. An urgent matter, a crisis of some kind, had supposedly called her away. She would be back as soon as possible to pick up her little girl. The mother seemed distraught, nervous, terrified of something that she refused to speak of, according to the pastor who could not calm her down or detain her. The mother hugged her daughter goodbye, holding on to her for dear life, sobbing, before she placed the child in the pastor's arms and ran away.

"Olivia?" I whispered, shaking my head in confusion as Thomas gathered me in his arms. I clung to him. "But I know this little girl is not Olivia. This is my mother, Emily! I've seen photos of her as a little girl..."

"It will be all right, my lovely." He stroked my hair, whispering into my ear. "We will find the answers we seek..."

My mind suddenly flashed back to another time, another place... *an elegant Victorian home in Virginia City, Montana. David (Thomas) and I (Julia) sat closely together on the veranda of my father's stately home. We were holding hands, unchaperoned at the moment, as a horse-drawn carriage passed. I had panicked, concerned about the two of us being seen together like that. It was not proper amongst the upper class of entrepreneurs who had migrated West to pursue their financial dreams. They still retained their traditional Victorian values.*

"It will be all right, my lovely," David whispered into my ear.

That was the evening he had asked my father for my hand in marriage. My father had approved out of his love for me, despite the fact that my beloved was not a proper wealthy businessman like himself. David had been a free-spirited cowboy at heart, managing his ranch and providing horses for the stagecoach lines passing through on their way to the gold fields.

Sadly, it was a marriage that obviously was never meant to be. At least not in that particular time and place.

"I know it didn't turn out all right back then..." Thomas said softly, bringing me back to the present, as if he was reading my mind. He had also flashed back in time to that magical day we had shared together in our past lifetime. "But this time, it truly will be all right. We are finally together and we will discover the truth so we can put all of this behind us and move on."

Early the next morning we were off, down the Gunflint Trail toward Grand Marais. Our destination was Spirit of the Wilderness Episcopal Church, built in 1902. It was formerly known as the Maple Hill Church.

Beams of early morning sunlight flickered through the forest lining the roadway. Birds chirped, welcoming an early spring to the northland as wild flowers began to poke their heads through the forest floor. Another beautiful day in God's country.

I tried to immerse myself in the beauty of the day instead of focusing on my lingering fears of what we might, or might not, discover. Thomas had arranged for the local pastor to meet us there at the church. Hopefully, he could shed some light on this mystery. However, it had been sixty-six years since a little girl, my mother, was left here with a pastor who was probably no longer alive.

We slowly bounced along the somewhat plowed back road winding past an old-fashioned cemetery. Just beyond that, a vintage white clapboard country church stood proudly amongst towering maple and pine trees. Its steeple loomed high into a brilliant blue sky, illuminated by sunbeams filtering through the trees.

We got out of the car and walked toward the church where a gentleman in a long black overcoat was waiting for us. He appeared to be in his mid-thirties. He obviously would have no personal knowledge of what may, or may not, have happened here so many years ago. Still, it was worth a try.

Could this really be the place where Angelique left my mother all those years ago?

"Pastor Jorgenson?" Thomas reached out to shake his hand, taking the lead. I was thankful for that since I was already feeling overwhelmed by all of this.

"Just call me Bruce." The pastor smiled, shaking our hands. "Please come in." He gestured to the church door.

We followed him into a small chapel filled with carved wooden pews, an antique pulpit, and old piano. A lovely stained glass image of Jesus holding a lamb in his arms cast reflections across the room. A part of me wanted to settle into one of the front pews and say a few prayers to help guide our search. Maybe later.

For now, we were seated together as Thomas began asking questions. He'd already told Bruce, on the phone, what we were looking for.

"I have no firsthand knowledge about your little Olivia," he began. "That was long before my time. But I did do a little research before you came."

My ears perked up. Thomas gripped my hand as Bruce pulled a manilla envelope from a briefcase.

"There was a Pastor Peterson serving this congregation, formerly the Maple Hill Church, back in 1958." The pastor handed the envelope to Thomas. "Fortunately for us, he kept extensive notes about anything and everything that happened here, including little Olivia's arrival and departure. She was placed for adoption after two months, when nobody could locate her parents."

Thomas toyed with the envelope as if he was deciding whether to open it now or later. He gazed into my eyes, looking for an answer.

"Feel free to take it with you and get it back to me later when you're done," the pastor said. "Do you have any questions that I can at least try to answer?"

"Her name was Olivia?" I couldn't resist asking. "Are you sure about that?"

"Actually..." Bruce frowned. "There are a few rather confusing entries regarding the little girl's name...can I show you?"

Thomas nodded and handed the envelope back to the pastor.

"Here...listen to this. These are Pastor Peterson's words." Bruce fumbled through several pages and began to read.

I remain somewhat mystified over the identity of this adorable little girl. I keep replaying the scene when her mother (also unidentified) left her here with me over a month ago. Our conversation went as follows:

"And what is your daughter's name, my dear? And yours? I need to be able to contact you, to stay in touch," I pleaded with her as she turned to flee into the woods, leaving the little girl behind with me.

The young mother stopped for a brief moment, appearing to be puzzled as if she was seeking an appropriate answer. Finally, she blurted out, "Her name...her name...is Olivia. I can't tell you anything more. Not yet."

Then she was gone.

The child did not speak much, probably traumatized after being abandoned by her own mother. She was understandably sad, cried easily – especially in the first few weeks – despite everything my wife and I did to care for her. I found it strange that she didn't respond to the name Olivia in the beginning.

So, it was possible, I thought to myself, that Angelique purposely provided a false name for Emily. To protect her? From what? I glanced into Thomas's eyes and was aware that he was thinking the same thing.

"Anything more about her name?" I asked cautiously.

"Yes," Bruce flipped through a few more pages and began to read once again. "This is one of his last entries about the little girl."

It's been over two months and we've been unable to locate this little girl's parents, despite assistance from the police. As much as we love her, my wife and I cannot keep her. My heart breaks to have to let her go, but the Cook County Social Services Department has made a decision to place this child for adoption.

We will greatly miss little Olivia...although I'm not convinced that is her real name. She still looks puzzled when we call her Olivia, a frown spreading across her little face. There have been times when she shakes her head, saying "No, no." Sometimes she mumbles something that sounds like "Emmy." I can't be sure, but I have my suspicions. Did her mother purposely give me a false name? Perhaps to protect her daughter from something or someone? Perhaps to prevent anyone from finding out her true identity? If so, I'm afraid she has succeeded. Only time will tell.

"Oh my God," I gasped before it hit me that this was probably not an appropriate phrase to use sitting in a church with a pastor. I nervously glanced his way, only to find a reassuring smile.

"It's okay, Angela. What is it?"

"Emmy...Emily. That's my mother's name. I think we've established her identity, that my mother was, in fact, this little lost girl called Olivia. But I've only ever known her as Emily. I've never hear of an Olivia."

My eyes filled with tears as Thomas hugged me close.

"Only time will tell," the pastor reiterated the late Pastor Peterson's words. "And that time has apparently come. I hope this discovery will bring you and your family—especially your mother, Emily—some peace. I wish you the very best in sorting out the rest of the pieces of this puzzle."

CHAPTER TWENTY-EIGHT

After bidding the kind pastor goodbye, Thomas and I settled into an easy silence, holding hands, as we began our drive back to my place. At least I thought that's where we were headed, until he turned the opposite way onto the Gunflint Trail.

"What? Are you lost?" I nudged him.

"No, but you appear to be, and we're going to do something about that, my lovely."

"Such as?"

"Such as...it's too beautiful a day to spend it researching. You've had enough excitement for one day, and I know how you love being on the water..."

"Yes, water does soothe my soul, I must admit. The sea, lakes, rivers, oceans, whatever... I guess we could spare enough time for a walk along Lake Superior?"

"Better than that." He grinned. "I just happen to have tickets for a sunset sail on the *Hjordis*. You were talking about it—"

"That's wonderful! They're open for the season already?"

"Yup, just for you!" He laughed. "Seriously, the North House Folk School decided to open tours a little early this year because of the early spring. We're in luck! An early dinner first at your choice of Grand Marais' restaurants."

"You are too good to me." My eyes filled with tears. The *Hjordis* was a rigged schooner or flagship, used for the education program at the Folk School.

"I'll find a way to have you pay me back," he teased, as we drove into Grand Marais, his eyes sparkling with a combination of mischief and desire.

"And I think I would like that very much." I cuddled up to him.

After a meal of fresh walleye for Thomas and coconut crusted shrimp for me, washed down with a mug of locally crafted beer at My Sister's Place, we found the sailboat. The sun was beginning to descend over the lake. Thomas just happened to have loaded warm jackets and our cameras into a duffle bag that he'd hidden in the back seat. Thank God for that!

We couldn't have asked for a lovelier evening on Lake Superior which was known for its wild and unpredictable weather. Gentle waves lapped against the shoreline overlooking the lighthouse. We boarded the ship, which was named after the mythical Norse goddess of war as a tribute to the Scandinavians who settled this region long ago.

"All aboard!" the captain called out as his crew hoisted the burgundy sails and we set out to sea, just us and another couple along with the captain and his mate.

Jake, the captain, entertained us with colorful stories about the lake's history as we sailed into the sunset. Stories about the Ojibwe Indians who lived here 3,000 years ago. Of Chippewa City, an Ojibwe settlement that thrived in the 1890s with more than one hundred Indian families living there. They'd built a church at this site in 1895 which still stood, nestled amidst tilting gravestones commemorating the lives of those who had passed on into their spirit world.

Thomas and I kept busy snapping photos as we listened. The setting sun, filtered through layers of dazzling light-rimmed clouds, cast reflections upon the waves. It was a magical evening, and I was sure we had some awesome photos that we'd be able to enlarge, frame and sell at one of the art galleries now handling our work.

"Can you tell us anything about Isle Royale?" the elderly gentleman named Bradley asked the captain. "My wife and I are planning to take the ferry over from Grand Portage in a few days, and we'd especially love to hear any stories about its past."

"Excellent question!" Excitement brewed in Jake's dark brown eyes. "Isle Royale's history is near and dear to my heart since my ancestors had cottages there for many years. Yes, that island has a most colorful history. There are over twenty-five shipwrecks lying on the bottom of Lake Superior along the dangerous reefs surrounding Isle Royale. Goes all the way back to the wooden sidewheeler *Cumberland* that sank there in a dangerous storm in 1877."

I was somewhat distracted, trying to capture the best shot of the sun sinking beneath the waves. Thomas nudged me back to the moment.

"And then there's the tragic legend of Angelique, an Ojibwe woman..." Jake lowered his voice. The others took a sip of the wine we'd purchased down below. Except for me... I was too stunned to respond or sip my wine.

Angelique? I froze as I gripped Thomas's hand. Surely this had nothing to do with my grandmother? Still...how many people were named Angelique? And we had discovered that she'd been part Ojibwe. I was already intrigued, listening intently as we rocked on the gentle waves, darkness descending upon the waters surrounding us.

"It was 1845," Jake began in a sober, dramatic voice.

I heaved a sigh of relief. My grandmother had not even been born in 1845. At least this legend had nothing to do with her. Thomas squeezed my hand, obviously thinking the same thing.

"Angelique and her voyageur husband, Charlie Mott, were dropped off on Isle Royale that spring by the schooner *Algonquin*. Charlie worked for this company and their mission was to find copper. It was Angelique who found a large mass of copper. She and her husband were left on the island to guard this valuable resource until Charlie's employer could send a barge to retrieve it sometime before winter set in."

Jake hesitated, building suspense amongst us all.

"But...what happened?" Bradley's wife asked, obviously immersed in this legend from the past.

"Well...that barge never came. They were stranded in an old unheated log cabin on Isle Royale until the next spring with very minimal provisions. All they had was half a barrel of flour, six pounds of butter, and some beans. They lost their canoe in a fall storm and their fishing nets were destroyed."

"How did they survive? Or did they?" Bradley chimed in when Jake took a break.

"Are you sure you want to hear the rest of the story? I mean, it's not easy to digest, to say the least."

"Yes!" We all urged him to go on.

"Okay. So, by January, Charlie went crazy from hunger and starvation. He took a knife and threatened to murder his wife...and eat her...so he at least could survive and fulfill his obligations to the company that employed him."

Bradley's wife had a horrified expression upon her face, but demanded that Jake continue.

"She managed to grab the knife from him, weak as he was, so he was unable to carry out his heinous plan. He died of starvation during that cruel winter. Angelique was unable to bury his body in the frozen ground so she moved out and let his body freeze in the cabin."

"What about her? Did she survive? Did someone finally come to rescue her?" I couldn't resist asking as the suspense grew amongst us.

"Well, she was smaller and didn't need as much food to survive. She built herself a crude hut nearby made of bark and leaves and whatever she could find. She ate roots that she was able to dig from the ground; trapped a few rabbits with snares that she fashioned from her own hair. And she made a crude fishing net as the spring thaw set in. They say she still visited her dead husband often and talked to him. At one point, she was almost dying of hunger and thought about making soup out of Charlie!"

"Really?" Thomas piped in. "Sounds like a legend to me, interesting as this is."

"Actually, she was rescued when a boat finally arrived after the ice went out that spring. The crew found a trembling, terrified, and starving widow. She lived to be interviewed about her ordeal later that year and the interview was recorded."

Bradley finally joined in. "What became of her?"

"She spent her remaining years in Ontario, Canada, where she died in 1874. They say she was never the same after all she went through. Probably PTSD, although, of course there was no name for such things back then."

A hush grew over the passengers on the *Hjordis* as we sailed back toward the welcoming lights of Grand Marais beneath a pitch-black sky.

It had been a long, eventful day. Thomas and I drove back to my place. While we were both basking in the beauty and serenity of our excursion, contrasting vividly with the horrific tale we'd just heard, we were also becoming intrigued with Isle Royale.

"Something is telling me that perhaps we need to plan a little trip out there, my lovely." Thomas's eyes met mine as the same thought surfaced in my mind. Of course. We seemed to be halves of a whole at times.

"It's more than that, Thomas…"

"I know. There's something for us to discover out there. Some clue. Somehow."

I knew that Thomas had commitments the next day and would not be able to stay with me, as much as I wished to spend the night in his arms.

"Are you okay?" He kissed me goodbye at my doorstep. "I can always cancel my excursion tomorrow and stay over if you need me to."

"I'm fine," I told him, though I wished he could stay. I was not about to interfere with his obligations. Besides, I probably needed some time alone, time to hopefully connect with Angelique. It wasn't long before I drifted into a deep sleep.

CHAPTER TWENTY-NINE

I'm settled into my tent for the evening, hidden away in the jackpines near a secluded lake on Isle Royale. I thought I was safe here, finally...until I hear the crashing in the brush. A bear? A moose? A wolf? Or one of the resident ghosts said to haunt the old Rock Harbor Lighthouse that I can see in the distance? Or, worst of all, Jonathan?? But Jonathan is dead...or is he?

I cautiously peek out through the flaps of my tent, praying to any gods that may still exist in this insane world. Thinking about my beloved daughter, Emily, and praying that I can somehow find my way back to her soon. But I could not let Jonathan get to her.

Heavy footsteps crunch through the brush, coming closer and closer. Heart pounding, I realize that it's now or never. I'm a sitting duck and I need to escape now, quietly, or it will be too late. I need to execute my backup plan that. Now.

I crawl out of my tent quietly, thankful for the distracting sound of the waves crashing against the rocky shoreline. I creep into the forest behind my tent in the opposite direction of the footsteps. There I slink down into the hideaway hole I'd dug into the ground, closing the hatch I'd made of twigs over me.

An evil voice echoes throughout the forest. "You can run...but you cannot hide..." Oh my God! It is Jonathan! Jonathan who is supposed to be dead and lying at the bottom of Lake Superior with his shipmates. He's alive! But somehow, I'd always known that, hadn't I? Maybe I'm not crazy after all. I wasn't simply in denial over his death when I'd decided to run for my life.

Jonathan's voice seems to explode, laughing hysterically, growing louder and louder as he closes in on my tent. It dawns on me that he's not just cruel and abusive. He's insane!

"Angelique!" he cries out in a low ominous voice that sends shivers up and down my spine. I hear him ripping open my tent. "What the hell? Where are you, you little witch?" He laughs hysterically. "You know, they *used to burn witches like you at the stake. But I have a better and much easier plan to rid the world of the likes of you..."*

I can hear him tearing apart my little refuge, throwing things around, kicking my camp stove, and hurling my few belongings into the forest.

"Yes, I know all about you and all the evil things you do every time I set sail. Don't think I don't. Where the hell are you?"

It is eerily quiet as I hide in my hole in the ground, terrified that he may hear the pounding of my heart. How long can I last here? When will he leave? And where can I go? Is there no place to find safety, no my way back to my daughter?

Finally, I hear him hike off, kicking sticks and stones along the path. He screams, "Wherever the hell you are, I will find you, bitch!"

The ringing of my alarm finally jolted me awake from another horrific nightmare. I was trembling, blanketed in layers of sweat, tears streaming down my face. Was this just a dream? Or had I somehow been flashing back in time to what might have been Angelique's last days? Did she survive? If she did, where did she go? And why didn't she find a way back to Emily?

"Oh, Angelique!" I cried out, aghast at what my grandmother must have endured...if, in fact, my nightmares were actually based on her true-life experiences.

I suddenly felt invisible arms holding me, comforting me. *It's all right, my dear,* her thoughts entered my mind. *I apologize for putting you through my trauma. But it's the only way for you to discover the truth. You and your mother deserve to know what happened, Angela, before it's too late...*

Then she was gone, disappearing as mysteriously as she always did. But leaving behind a shred of hope for me to cling to. I could do this...I could find out what happened to her, somehow, with Thomas's help.

Still, I was devastated. Maybe there was a reason she had abandoned my mother after all. A reason why she never returned.

Fortified with a few cups of strong coffee and a brisk walk down to the lake, I was ready to face the day. My first stop would be a visit to Sabrina at the lodge. I worried about her and all she was going through with her mother. And I was also anxious to find out if Annette had come up with any more information.

I found Sabrina and Annette sitting on the sofa by the stone fireplace in the lodge having a cup of coffee, their morning routine. As I plopped down in the chair beside them, I sensed that something was going on. Sabrina had a puzzled look upon her face. Annette seemed anxious, upset about something.

"Is this a good time?" I inquired quietly, wondering if they needed some time alone.

"Please stay. You need to hear this and help me make some sense of this nonsense..." Sabrina spoke quietly, shaking her head in frustration.

"You need to do something about this now!" Annette slammed her coffee cup down on the coffee table, her eyes burning with both fear and frustration. "She needs your help or something really bad is going to happen to her. Don't you understand?"

"Who are you talking about?" Sabrina patted her mother's hand, trying to calm her down.

"Angelique, of course!"

I almost dropped my coffee cup. Was she talking about my Angelique, my grandmother?

Sabrina and I exchanged looks. She was giving me the go-ahead to talk with her mother.

I touched her shoulder gently. "I understand, Annette. But do you know where she is so we can try to help her?"

"Finally." Annette breathed a sigh of relief as she searched my face. "She's out there in a tent someplace on a little lake in the middle of nowhere. Let me think..." She hesitated while we waited patiently.

"Yes, that's it. Lake Ojibway! Somewhere near a lighthouse. A Rock Harbor Lighthouse?"

Oh my God! Visions of last night's dream erupted in my head. Annette must be referring to Isle Royale, although I'd never heard of a Lake Ojibway out there. Could she be referring to the legend of the other Angelique who'd been stranded on Isle Royale many years ago and barely survived?

But she'd died long ago. Or, was this connected to my Angelique, and my dream?

Taking a deep breath, I finally calmed down and continued. "Why does she need our help?" I needed to learn as much as I could.

"You don't know?" Annette shook her head in bewilderment. "You didn't read her letter to Justine?"

You could have heard a pin drop as Sabrina and I exchanged glances. "What letter?" we responded in unison.

"Oh, oh," Annette wrung her hands, her eyes darting back and forth between us, hanging her head like a child who had been caught lying or doing something bad. "It was supposed to be a secret. That's why I had to get rid of it, you know."

So, she had perhaps found something more in Justine's papers after all. An old letter? One that she claimed to have destroyed?

I tried to stay calm. "You found a letter from Angelique to Justine? And you destroyed it?"

"I did. I had to be sure he doesn't find her. You can't tell anyone. You must promise me?"

We nodded in unison. "Who is *he*, Annette? And why does she need our help? What can we do to help her?"

"It's that horrible husband of hers. She's afraid he's looking for her. He's a very mean man. We need to help her!" She began to sob, drifting back in time as her voice quivered in a childlike manner. "Her little girl needs her. We play together all the time, but now she's gone. I don't know where she went, but I miss her."

Sabrina put her arms around her mother, rubbing her back. "It's okay, Angelique will be fine, and so will you."

"No, she's not going to be fine." Annette pouted. "We need to find her right away!" She straightened up in a fighting stance, then collapsed back against the cushion behind her, exhausted.

"We will," I tried to assure her. "What else can you tell us so we can find her? I'm a little confused. Maybe you can help me? You see, I thought her husband was dead...that he had drowned at sea."

"Dead?" Annette shook her head. "Then why is she afraid of him? Why did she tell my grandmother where she was and to be sure he never finds out? It was supposed to be a secret. But if he's not dead...what if he comes looking for her here?"

"We will figure all of this out, and we will help her," Sabrina said.

Annette shook her head, totally confused. "Help who?"

"Angelique. We will help Angelique," I replied wearily.

"Who is Angelique?" Her voice trailed off as her eyes closed in exhaustion.

Sabrina shook her head as she led her mother away for a nap.

CHAPTER THIRTY

$\mathcal{M}$y head was spinning as I made my way back to my cabin, barely noticing the colorful wildflowers poking their heads through the forest floor. A flock of migrating Canada geese flew overhead, coming home after spending their winter in the south. I was all the more determined that Thomas and I must make a trip out to Isle Royale as soon as we can get reservations on the ferry out of Grand Portage. And we needed to coordinate that with a reservation at the historic Rock Harbor Lodge there.

The pieces of the puzzle were perhaps starting to come together. We now had Annette's somewhat deranged claims about finding a letter—one that no longer existed—referring to a Lake Ojibway that was within viewing distance of a Rock Harbor Lighthouse. And my nightmare that could have taken place on any wilderness island. Also, the fact that the ghost of my grandmother had appeared to confirm that my dreams were actually a reenactment of what she had endured.

I couldn't help almost laughing out loud. The only clues we had were based on messages from a ghost, a relatively senile elderly woman whose mind transported her back and forth between the past and the present, and my strange nightmares.

Still, I felt like we finally had some direction to help us solve this mystery. Thomas agreed and started making arrangements for a trip out to the wilderness island of Isle Royale located twenty miles out into Lake Superior. I did some research and discovered that it was a large island, forty-five miles long and nine miles wide. It was mostly wilderness, home to wolves and moose. There were many small lakes and ponds nestled within the forests near campgrounds, cabins, and Rock Harbor Lodge.

Isle Royale was probably considerably wilder and more primitive, without modern conveniences, when and if Angelique had been there. Indigenous people, including the Ojibwe Indians, had inhabited this pristine island for over 4,500 years before the logging and copper mining days. It later became a commercial fishing settlement with Scandinavian immigrants settling along the coastline. And later, wealthy mainland families came to build cabins where they could escape from the hustle and bustle of life in the big cities. Today, it was a part of Isle Royale National Park.

Lake Superior's wild winds and waves could be ferocious as attested to by the many shipwrecks lying in its depths around the island.

So why would Angelique have decided to escape to such a harsh and remote place? Thomas and I were both puzzled as we bounced ideas around while sitting on our bench down by the lake one evening. We watched the sun sink into the lake as the soft wail of loons filled the air. After long months of winter, spring had finally arrived in the Northland.

"How could she expect to survive out there by herself, especially late in the fall? Once winter sets in, there would be no way to get off that island." Thomas took a sip of his beer.

"I understand she was very self-sufficient, a survivalist—maybe because of her Ojibwe background. She camped, hiked, picked berries, snared rabbits, fished. She chopped wood for fires to keep warm. She did have camping gear. That's what she did. At least that's how Justine described her in her journal."

"So maybe she thought Isle Royale was the most secluded and inaccessible place she could escape to? A place where Jonathan couldn't find her? A place to hide out until it was safe to return for Emily? Until Jonathan had given up and was no longer trying to find her—if he was, in fact, not actually dead?"

"Maybe..." A tear dribbled down my cheek as I tried to imagine how lonely and terrifying that could have been for her. Life-threatening. Thomas gently wiped my tear away as he put his arm around me, pulling me close.

"Listen, Angela...we need to remember that we may find absolutely nothing out there to solve this mystery. All of this happened so long ago. Or are you relying on messages from Angelique to help us out?" He grinned, trying to cheer me up.

"Maybe a little," I confessed. "Still, just being there, hiking around, finding that little lake and the Rock Harbor Lighthouse may help to open our eyes. We may find some clues, somehow, someway. If not...well, I've always wanted to visit Isle Royale." I smiled back at him.

Now if I could only convince myself that it would be fine, even if we discovered nothing and found no more clues. Something compelled me to believe that the answers we were seeking were waiting for us on Isle Royale. If only we looked hard enough. If only we opened our minds and hearts.

Later that evening, after Thomas returned to his place to prepare for his fishing charter early tomorrow morning, my mother called. Her voice quivered and she was very quiet. I could hardly hear her.

"Are you all right, Mother?"

"Just a little confused, Angela. I had a bad dream last night. It felt so real, like I was slipping back in time. Almost like a repressed memory of some kind was infiltrating my brain."

"Tell me more."

She took a deep breath. "Well, I was little and I was there...in the cabin where you're now living. My mother and my father were there. He was hitting and kicking her, calling her bad words, and threatening to kill her! I was hiding in the corner, crying, clutching my doll, Susan. Oh my God, it was awful!"

So, her memories were finally resurfacing after all these years. Memories she'd repressed because they were so hurtful.

"It's okay, Mother," I said as I tried to soothe her. "I know it's awful, but maybe it's just a bad dream."

"It's not a dream. It happened, Angela! I know that now. Oh, my goodness, my poor mother. Maybe that's why she left me? But why didn't she come back for me?"

"Maybe because she wasn't able to, Mother. I do believe she tried. She never would have left you behind. She loved you dearly."

"You don't know that," she reprimanded me.

I could not reveal all that I'd learned of course. Not until I knew more, until I knew what was true and what was not. All I could do was assure her that, based on what I'd read so far in Justine's journal, her mother had indeed loved her.

I hesitated a moment, trying to decide if this was a good time to ask her one of the questions that had been bothering me for some time, ever since Thomas and I met Pastor Jorgenson at the church. She was already regressing back into her early childhood memories, so I decided it may be a good time to broach the subject.

"Can I ask you a question?" I said.

"Why not? I'm already remembering things I don't like to remember…"

"Does the name Olivia mean anything to you? Do you remember anyone with that name?"

Dead silence on the other end of the phone. Then, she exploded. "I hate that name! Why did they keep calling me that? I kept telling them it was *not* my name!"

"Who called you that, Mother?"

"My new parents. I had to keep telling them that my name was Emily. They didn't understand me at first, I guess. I was little. Finally, they did…and I got my name back. Mommy always called me Emily…until she ran away…"

"Until she was forced to leave you, Mother. She always planned to come back for you."

"Maybe…" her voice trailed off into the distant past.

Some things were beginning to make sense to me, but it was time to change the subject before I stressed her out anymore. We chatted about her book club, the weather, anything except the past. And we made plans for a visit this coming weekend.

CHAPTER THIRTY-ONE

My dear Thomas insisted that it would do me good to spend the evening in Grand Marais with him. Besides, I needed to check on my photo prints at the art galleries to see how they were selling and if they needed more. So far, I was very pleased with my sales. My passion for photography was actually providing some extra income. And being out in nature taking photos was therapeutic. It gave me a break from obsessing over the details and lack of progress related to solving the mystery of my grandmother's disappearance.

I drove into town, stopping at several galleries including the Lake Superior Trading Post. That was one of my favorite places to shop for gifts, jewelry, books, and art work to spruce up my rustic cabin. I bought a little gift for my mother, a handmade ceramic mug engraved with a loon floating on Lake Superior. She loved loons and Lake Superior. Hopefully this would cheer her up a bit. Maybe I'd pick up her favorite hot chocolate mix to go with it. If she wanted to add a shot of Irish Cream to it, so be it!

When I arrived at Thomas's cabin overlooking Lake Superior just north of Grand Marais, his sled dogs, confined in a fenced area, announced my arrival. I made my way down the stone walkway towards the rustic cabin. Several rocking chairs were perched on the front porch beneath shuttered windows. I could smell something delicious cooking.

I could see why he loved this place, almost as much as I loved mine. He enjoyed water as much as I did. When we weren't relaxing on my bench overlooking Gunflint Lake, we sat in his gazebo perched on a cliff overlooking the big lake. That's exactly what I needed tonight after indulging in whatever he made for dinner.

Once again, I reminded myself how lucky I was to have found this man. I would be forever grateful to my dear grandmother Angelique for leading me back to him.

Thomas was also an excellent cook. Tonight, he'd made homemade beef pasties, a Scandinavian version complete with rutabagas. We enjoyed a glass of red wine and his famous Northwoods salad which included apple slices, walnuts, dried cranberries and feta cheese mixed with crisp lettuce and his own honey mustard dressing.

After dinner, we held hands as we hiked out to the gazebo. It was a lovely evening sitting together, basking in the breeze coming off the lake. The scent of spring filled the air as seagulls swooped overhead and several sailboats glided past. Now and then a large ore carrier passed in the distance on its way to or from the Duluth harbor.

A blanket of fog eventually rolled in, obscuring any view of the sunset. Still, we felt relaxed and peaceful. Lake Superior had that effect on us. We returned to his cabin, took an invigorating shower together and soon fell into his bed, wrapped in each other's arms. It was a night to remember...

I awoke early the next morning, before sunrise, to the smell of coffee brewing and Thomas trying to quietly get dressed in his fishing clothes in the dark. He had another excursion first thing this morning and he swore that early morning was the best time to catch the big ones.

"Are you awake, my lovely?" he whispered as he set a cup of coffee and a warm blueberry scone on the bedside table beside me. "As much as I'd love to stay here with you longer," he said, his hand gently caressing my outstretched leg, "I do have passengers waiting."

"I know." I reached out to caress his face as he leaned in to kiss me goodbye. "I could get used to this, so used to this..."

"Someday we will need to do something about that, you know...I mean someday when you're ready."

"Who said I'm not ready?" I teased as I slipped my hand beneath his shirt and down his chest.

"Wow, if you don't stop that now, I'm going to be too late." He laughed as he reluctantly slipped his boots on and headed out the door.

"Until tonight? My place?"

"You got that right. I love you."

"I love you more." I threw him a kiss before burrowing myself beneath the covers, warm with memories we'd made together last night.

CHAPTER THIRTY-TWO

"This simply makes no sense." I paced back and forth in front of my fireplace while Thomas lounged on the davenport reading a book about Isle Royale National Park and its history.

"Umm hmm..." he mumbled, absorbed in whatever he was reading.

"Does it make any sense to you? Why would Angelique simply head all the way out to Isle Royale? How could she have even gotten there?"

No response. So, I continued, my frustration rising every moment. "And why is Angelique so damn secretive? Why can't she tell us what happened instead of leaving little clues around and driving me crazy trying to figure this out?"

He sighed, finally slamming his book shut. "Listen, Angela. We don't even know that she went to Isle Royale. You need to quit pacing back and forth and obsessing about all of this. Just stop, please?"

I stopped dead in my tracks. "What did you say?"

"You heard me. Enough is enough. It does no good to beat yourself up like this. What if this? What if that? Just stop it." He shook his head, obviously annoyed with me.

"Don't tell me what to do, Thomas. You have no idea what I'm going through, do you?"

I stormed out of the cabin and down to the lake. I needed a break. Maybe I was being obsessive. Still...he'd never gotten this angry or frustrated with me before. As I hiked down the trail, taking deep breaths, trying to calm myself, I finally decided he may have a point. Maybe he deserved an apology.

By the time I returned, he was waiting on the porch. "Look, I'm sorry if I lost my temper with you. It's just that this is getting to be a lot, you know. I worry about you. Can't you just chill a little until we find more answers?"

"I came back to tell you that I'm sorry, Thomas. You were right, and I will try harder to control myself and quit obsessing over this."

With that, we fell into each other's arms and enjoyed the rest of our evening before he had to leave once again.

After he left, I finally fell into a restless sleep. But it felt like someone or something was hovering in the little alcove adjacent to my bedroom. I'd hear noises that sounded like a chair being moved, papers rusting around. Turning on the bedside lamp, I peered across the room into the alcove. Nothing was there. The sounds ceased and I eventually fell asleep again.

First thing the next morning, I decided to check out the alcove more carefully. Of course I'd searched it thoroughly in the past, just in case there was any information about Angelique. There was nothing. But this morning I noticed that the old chair and rug beneath it had been moved just slightly.

Bewildered, I trudged down the stairs into the kitchen to make a cup of coffee when I saw something in the middle of the kitchen table. It appeared to be an old photo album—a string-tied leather album that I'd never seen before.

I sat down at the table and carefully opened the album. The handwritten message scrawled on the inside front cover jumped out at me: *Angelique's Photo Album.*

Heart pounding, I began to carefully turn the brittle black pages that held square black and white glossy photographs attached with white adhesive corners. An inscription was written beneath each photo, identifying the individuals in the photos.

There were photos of Angelique as a child with her mother and father. Just the three of them picking blueberries by a little lake. Standing together beside an old church. One of Angelique proudly holding a little birch bark basket that she had made. She had long dark hair, big eyes, and a cautious smile. Another of her dancing at a pow wow in a jingle dress, concentrating on her dance steps.

"My mother making her delicious fry bread," one caption read. Her mother wore moccasins and beaded jewelry. She appeared to be of Indian descent.

As I turned the pages, I found several of them all in a birch bark canoe on Lake Superior. One of a large moose grazing near a fog-covered swamp. Another of them camping in the wilderness near a little lake that she labeled "Our campsite on Minong." Minong...wasn't that what the natives originally called Isle Royale?

Intrigued, I could not put the album down. Finally, I came upon a photo of her parents together with the caption "1953 – The last photo of my dear parents before they drowned while catching fish near Minong. May they rest in peace."

Tears welled in my eyes. So, Angelique had been left alone after the death of her parents. Just like her daughter would be someday. Who were her parents? What were their names? I had to find out more. I was not disappointed as I flipped the page to find an obituary for Awenita (1915-1953) and Andre Gauthier (1912-1953).

I learned that Awenita ("Fawn" in Ojibwe) grew up in Chippewa City. She married Andre in 1935. He was French Canadian and had settled in the area after working as a fur trader, later becoming a fisherman. They had drowned off the coast of their beloved Isle Royale (also known as Minong) where they spent time fishing, trapping, hunting, maple sugaring, gathering greenstones and engaging in the spiritual practices of the Anishinaabe (Ojibwe) culture. They left behind their beloved seventeen-year-old daughter, Angelique. They would be buried in the little cemetery beside the Chippewa Church in the now abandoned Chippewa City.

At the bottom of the page, Angelique had written, "I believe their lives were claimed by Mishipeshu, a dangerous manitou or spirit known to lurk like an underwater lynx beneath the waters surrounding Minong. The many shipwrecks scattered in the depths around this island attest to his deadly presence. But why did that evil spirit choose my parents, two wonderful people who did so much for others? Why did he take my loving parents from me?"

I needed a caffeine boost as I tried to process all of this. Still in my pajamas, I went out onto the deck to take some deep breaths and try to lose myself in the wind and waves surrounding my place.

I was beginning to understand Angelique's connection to Isle Royale. Had she gone back there, after fleeing from Jonathan, to try to reconnect with the spirits of her parents? To revisit the memories they'd made together at this special place? Maybe to lose herself in nature and seek guidance from the spirits that be? Did she encounter, instead, the horrific events that were portrayed in my nightmares?

When I returned to the album, I found a wedding photo of Angelique and her husband Jonathan. Was he really as evil as we now thought he was? They actually looked happy together in those days. She had been only nineteen when she'd married him, two years after the death of her parents.

Before long the album was filled with photos of little Emily with detailed descriptions. "The love of my life..." one read. Yes, Angelique had loved her daughter. I could hardly wait to show my mother this album.

I'd spent most of the day pouring over the photos, too absorbed to think much about how and why it had mysteriously shown up on my kitchen table. I checked with Thomas and with Sabrina, just in case they knew anything about it. They were also stunned.

Finally, I got dressed. It was already two o'clock in the afternoon. As I passed the alcove by my bedroom, I felt compelled to check it out a little more. The corner of the rug beneath the chair was now flipped over, exposing the floor boards beneath it. Getting down on my knees, I pulled the rug off to the side. There, beneath the rug, I found a trap door that I pried open after inserting an old metal letter opener that someone had left behind.

There, hidden away in a cubby hole just large enough for that album and other important papers, I found an envelope addressed "To Whom It May Concern." I sat down on my bed, turned on my bedside lamp, carefully opened the letter, and began to read:

I hope with all my heart that someone will find this letter someday. My name is Angelique. I have an adorable little daughter, Emily, whom I love with all my heart. I am very sad that I am going to have to leave her at a nearby church until I can come back to pick her up. That is IF my husband does not find me first and kill me as he said he would.

They say that Jonathan went down with his ship, the Americana II. *All hands drowned. No survivors. Yet something is telling me that he was not on that ship. That he is still alive and will be hunting me down. Somehow, I know this to be true. I have always had special abilities, and Jonathan has accused me of being a witch.*

143

I am hiding this photo album here with the hope that it can go to Emily someday. I am leaving today for Minong, out in the middle of Lake Superior. A place where I used to go with my parents. Maybe I can find their spirits there. Maybe they can help me figure out what to do next.

I pray to God that I will be back someday soon to pick up my daughter – and this photo album. Just in case that is not meant to be, I am leaving this letter behind.

I must go. Now.

Angelique

But she never returned. What happened to her? Did Jonathan find her, like he did in my dreams?

Clutching her letter to my chest, I slumped down on the bed. My poor grandmother! It was hard to imagine what she had suffered through. I was all the more determined now to discover the truth about her life and her disappearance.

CHAPTER THIRTY-THREE

The sun was rising over Lake Superior when Thomas and I arrived at the abandoned Chippewa City. There wasn't much left of what was once a thriving Ojibwe community. We pulled off Highway 61 by the restored St. Francis Xavier Church which had been built in 1895 of hand-hewed timber in the French style, according to the research that Thomas had done online. Listed on the National Register of Historic Places, it was now owned and cared for by the Cook County Historical Society.

From what we could figure out, my great-grandmother, Awenita, had probably lived there with her family until she married Andre. They would have attended the historic church standing before us. Angelique would have been born the year the church closed its doors in 1936. I wondered if she'd perhaps been baptized there. Did she, as a baby, attend that last Christmas mass with her family? If only those walls could talk...

We stood in silence, lost in thought, as a gust of wind swept around the steeple and the bell rang out. Was that a sign of some kind? Was Angelique here with us? Or was that just my wishful thinking?

Thomas took my hand. "Should we stroll over that way to the old cemetery?"

I nodded.

It was sad to see how the years had taken their toll, although there appeared to have been efforts in recent years to clear the brush and downed trees and make it more accessible. A red cardinal called out to us from a birch tree as we hiked deeper into the remains of the old cemetery.

Old gravestones tilted into the forest floor, some crumbling into the earth. Some were impossible to read. Other graves seemed to be marked with large rocks or tilted wooden crosses. A number of aging spirit houses stood guard over other graves. An Ojibwe spirit house was a miniature wooden plank cabin erected beside graves of the dead.

I had been intrigued with the concept of spirit houses and done a little research in the past. They were designed to keep good spirits in and bad ones out. They also provided a home for the deceased's spirit before they traveled the Path of Souls into the afterlife. There was a small doorway in one end of the spirit house to allow the spirit to escape, and a shelf to hold offerings for his or her journey to the spirit world. Those offerings included food, incense, candles and wild flowers.

Somehow, I knew, beyond a doubt, that my great-grandparents would have had a spirit house. Angelique would have seen to that. So, I focused on the remaining spirit houses. Unfortunately, many had crumbled into the earth and it was difficult to read any inscriptions. Still, I searched, as Thomas waited patiently, wandering through the old graveyard.

I was about to give up when that red cardinal flew over my head and landed on what was left of an old spirit house. I followed quietly. A chill swept through me as I got closer. The cardinal did not move.

Simply made of hand-hewn wood, moss-covered and battered by time, the spirit house upon which the cardinal still perched slumped into the earth, almost hidden by weeds and a few wildflowers. As I stood before it, I felt Angelique's invisible presence folding her arms around me.

*My beloved parents. Your great-grandparents...*her unspoken words infiltrated my mind. Then she was gone, as usual.

Tears in my eyes, I got down on my knees in the tall grass, said a prayer, and paid my respects to my long-lost and newly discovered ancestors. Thomas soon joined me and wrapped his arms around me. We sat together in silence until he led me back to the car.

CHAPTER THIRTY-FOUR

My dear Thomas managed to snag us a reservation for a week at the historic Kettle Falls Hotel on Isle Royale, as well as transportation over and back on the *Voyageur II* out of Grand Portage. He'd been prowling online for any cancellations since people usually booked reservations a year in advance. The spirits seemed to be lining things up for us!

I was pleased that he seemed to be more enthusiastic and optimistic about this trip, especially after seeing Angelique's letter and photo album. He was no longer reminding me, at least not as often, that we may—or may not—discover anything out there to solve this mystery.

"At least you will see the places that your grandmother and her family loved." He grinned at me. "And who knows what more we may discover? Especially if Angelique decides to help us out."

"I love you, Thomas." I curled up in his arms that night to the sound of waves gently lapping along the shores of Gunflint Lake and the cries of loons echoing through the fog.

Early the next morning we were off for Grand Portage with our oversized backpacks and a few snacks to eat on the long journey across Lake Superior. It would take us seven hours to arrive at Rock Harbor after making a few stops around the island to let passengers on and off the boat.

The forty-six foot silver boat was gleaming in the morning sunlight when we arrived at the docking area. Built in 1937, it was named the *Copper Queen* initially and used for commercial fishing until 1955 when it began transporting visitors to what became Isle Royale National Park.

The captain and deckhand welcomed us and helped us board and stow our backpacks. We kept what we needed for the trip over—snacks, water, a book to read. Since it was a calm and beautiful day, so far, Thomas and I settled into seats on the front upper deck. Hopefully, the waters would remain calm. That wasn't always the case on Lake Superior.

Before long, we were headed out, rocking on gentle waves. A sense of peace washed over us as we basked in the sunshine. We saw little but open water for the first several hours as we crossed eighteen miles of increasingly choppy water. But as we neared Isle Royale and the first stop at Windigo, we began to see rocky islands surrounding us. It was magical, as if we'd entered another world, a primitive wilderness.

And then, perched on a tiny rock outcropping in the middle of Lake Superior, the historic Rock of Ages Lighthouse towered above us.

"The lighthouse was built in 1855," the deckhand announced. "Initially it served as a beacon for copper miners coming out to the island, warning them of the underwater reefs that had claimed a number of ships passing through these waters."

He continued to entertain us with stories about the Lake Superior Indians who came over from the mainland in their birch bark canoes years ago to hunt, fish and trap during the summers. Families like my ancestors. Lumbermen, then the commercial fishing families who later settled on the big island before the tourists came and built cottages around the Tobin Harbor area.

As we got closer, we were amazed at its vast size. There were a number of lakes within this heavily forested island, rustic hiking trails, campgrounds. Although it was primarily a primitive world, the historic Rock Harbor Lodge had all the comforts of home. What more could we possibly want...except to, somehow, discover more about my grandmother and the time she spent here.

We learned that Isle Royale was created 1.2 billion years ago when lava seeped up through the cracks of the Superior Basin and formed basalt, the bedrock on the area. Glaciers added the final touch as four major ice sheets pushed down from Canada. After the last glacier melted about 11,000 years ago, Isle Royale appeared. It was over 5,000 years ago, they say, that early inhabitants began extracting copper on the island.

By mid-afternoon, we arrived at the last stop, Rock Harbor. Our boat docked at an impressive marina that housed some large, fancy boats, much different than it would have looked in 1958 when my grandmother was hiding out here. Still, it was beautiful, tucked away in a wilderness setting with grand views of Lake Superior. It housed a number of old wood buildings including a visitor center, office, and a restaurant with a nice deck overlooking the marina.

After checking in at the office, we made our way down the Stoll Trail to our lodge which was coincidentally named the Ojibway Lodge. Perched along the shoreline of Lake Superior, it offered amazing views of the lake and surrounding islands.

Refreshed, but exhausted after our long day afloat, we went down to the Greenstone Grill for a Greenstone Burger and glass of wine which we enjoyed out on the deck as the sun sank into the lake, casting reflections upon the lake and boats bobbing on the waves in the harbor.

We retired to our room and settled into the wooden Adirondack chairs by the large window overlooking the lake. With Isle Royale maps and information spread out on the little table between us, we began planning our stay. Of course, Lake Ojibway was our number one priority.

It wasn't long before we climbed into bed and drifted off to sleep to the sounds of waves crashing against the shoreline below our window. My last thought was a silent plea to Angelique to please help us discover the truth about whatever happened to her on this island so many years ago.

CHAPTER THIRTY-FIVE

We were ready to go as soon as the morning fog lifted off the lake. Backpacks were filled with water, snacks, rain gear, sunscreen and mosquito repellent. Summer seemed to be arriving early this year and that could mean an early mosquito hatching season. The weather was always unpredictable here or anywhere around Lake Superior. Dressed in layers, wearing hiking boots and carrying our hiking poles, we walked along the Rock Harbor Trail overlooking the harbor. Our initial destination was Daisy Farm campground where we'd branch off along the Mount Ojibway Trail toward Lake Ojibway.

It was going to be a long day, many miles on these secluded trails, but we were ready and anxious to be on our way. Once we left the busy Rock Harbor area, we were alone, just the two of us, hiking through a primitive forest. Rays of early morning sunlight filtered through the trees. I could only imagine Angelique walking along these trails, perhaps running in fear, carefully watching for any movement in the brush. Watching for Jonathan to suddenly appear as he did in my nightmares.

The silence and serenity of the old growth forest was suddenly shattered as we neared the Daisy Farm Campground, the largest campground on Isle Royale with individual and group tent sites as well as a number of shelters. The world was waking up. We began to encounter other hikers on the trail. Quite different from the isolation that my grandmother would have experienced when she was here with her parents as a young child.

We found a secluded spot near Lake Superior to rest and eat the lunch we'd picked up at the Greenstone Grill before leaving Rock Harbor. Across the bay we had an awesome view of the Rock Harbor Lighthouse that Annette had mentioned as she'd rambled about the letter she found in Justine's papers. The lighthouse that Angelique had supposedly seen from her hideaway by Lake Ojibway. We were getting close...just not close enough.

We began the gradual climb up the rocky Mount Ojibway Trail

leading to the old fire tower that loomed above the trees. It had been built by the National Park Service in 1939 after the devastating Greenstone Ridge Fire that I'd read about. That was at least twenty years before my grandmother hid out here in her tent on nearby Lake Ojibway.

We were surrounded by forest on all sides. No campgrounds here. No people. Just red squirrels scampering around, bluejays singing. Now and then a crashing sound in the brush.

"A moose?" I whispered as we stopped along the path, scanning the woods surrounding us. Waiting. Listening. Hearts pounding with anticipation.

Thomas nodded, quietly retrieving his miniature camera from his pocket. Just in case.

It wasn't long before a big bull moose crossed the path in front of us and slowly meandered towards Lake Ojibway where he began to feast on whatever lurked beneath the waters of a shallow bay. As Thomas snapped photos, I quietly retrieved my camera from my backpack and got a few of my own.

We were blessed to have encountered a moose here. It was no longer a regular occurrence on Isle Royale. Or, was this perhaps some kind of message from beyond? A message of hope? Maybe. Maybe not. But I was free to find whatever meaning I chose, right?

After a while the moose retreated into the forest and we began hiking along the lakeshore, looking for something. Anything. Any signs of something that may have happened here in 1958. What were the chances after all those years of finding anything beneath the new forest growth?

Still, we searched until we were tired enough to take a break on a large boulder along the shoreline. Even if we couldn't find anything here, we could bask in the knowledge that my grandmother and her family spent time here many years ago.

Closing my eyes, I snuggled against Thomas and tried to envision what life had been like for Angelique and her family. What memories they had made. Had she been able to connect with her deceased parents while hiding out from Jonathan? Had she received the spiritual guidance she was seeking?

What about the awful nightmare I'd had of him stalking her in a place like this? I wondered if that had actually happened, and if it could have happened right here.

"Are you ready?" Thomas gently stroked my hand. "We do have a long hike back along the Greenstone Ridge, you know."

I sighed, reluctant to leave this place that I'd hoped would help solve the mystery that had haunted me for so long.

"We can come back again, you know, if you need more time to process all of this," he offered.

"It's okay. Nothing seems to be speaking to me here, not now. Maybe we need to explore other areas. Maybe I just need to sit on a rock tonight and try to connect with Angelique."

"We can do that, my lovely." He grinned that magical grin of his, gave me a kiss and helped me to my feet. We had just enough time, we figured, to check out the fire tower before the long hike back to Rock Harbor.

Exhausted after returning to the lodge just before dark, we grabbed a quick dinner and decided to sit out on the rock formations by the lake near our room, alone beneath a star-studded sky. I tried hard to be "open" to whatever messages the universe may be sending me, to the spirits that were said to hover over this island, to any messages from Angelique. There was nothing.

The next day Thomas rented kayaks for us. He had planned an excursion through nearby Tobin Harbor. Just for a change of pace, he said, and to rest our tired feet. I dragged myself out of bed, tired, but anxious to check out other places on the island where we may find some clues to solve this mystery.

It was a lovely day on the harbor paddling past old cabins where commercial fishermen once lived. Wealthy people from the cities later moved up and built some nice retreats to get away from their stressful lives. I could only imagine living in a world like this back then. As we paddled, we searched the shoreline. For something, anything that could shed some light on Angelique's plight.

Several days passed as we asked questions of local park rangers and personnel, and visited the tourist center searching for historical information that may help us in our search. We also hiked the trails, paddled, and took excursions to historic lighthouses. Sometimes we enjoyed simply sitting by Lake Superior at various secluded sites. Just listening to the sounds of the waves and the wind while watching surreal sunrises and sunsets together. Still, my heart ached for what we had not yet discovered on this remote island. I wanted so badly to find out what had happened to my grandmother. Whatever it was, wherever she now was, I needed to know. My aging mother also needed closure before her time on earth was over.

Then one night, after a strenuous but incredibly scenic hike along the Tobin Harbor Trail, I fell into a deep sleep, flashing back into an unknown time and place.

CHAPTER THIRTY-SIX

*T*ears are streaming down my face as I drive north along the highway to Grand Portage, passing the now abandoned Chippewa City where I grew up, where my beloved parents are now buried beneath the spirit house I had built for them. All that is keeping me going is my hope to find their spirits out on the island of Minong where we'd spent so many memorable times together. I am running for my life...and I need their help to guide me in the right direction. I have no place else to run. No one to turn to without jeopardizing their lives. Not even Justine, who has become like a grandmother to me.

Tears for what I am leaving behind. My adorable little daughter, Emily, whom I love with all my heart and soul. At least she is safe with the nice pastor. She would not be safe with me, not with Jonathan trying to kill me.

Lost in thought and tears, I swerve left, recovering just in time as an oncoming car approaches. Clutching the steering wheel, I take a deep breath, hoping this rusty old truck can make it all the way to the fishing marina at Grand Portage. From there, I hope to catch a boat out to Rock Harbor – the nearest access point to Lake Ojibway where my family has roots.

I crawl down the road, pushing this worn-out piece of trash to its limits. It's Jonathan's old truck and it hasn't been driven in years. I have not had a vehicle to drive since we moved to our cabin in the woods a few years ago. But this was my only way to escape.

I finally make it to Grand Portage, heaving a sigh of relief. I manage to find a secluded wooded area within walking distance of the marina where I abandon the old truck after removing the expired license plates and tossing them out into the woods. I slip my heavy backpack over my shoulders, cautiously slip back out onto the road and hike to the marina. I hope I have everything I need to survive. A small lightweight tent, rain gear, sleeping bag, a few changes of clothing. Bug spray. Warm jacket. Flashlight. Matches. Fishing hooks. A tiny framed photo of Emily...

As I approach the harbor, I try to come up with a logical reason for requesting a lift to the island. First, I will need a new name...how about Emily? Yes, that should work just fine, a name I'd never forget. And why am I going to Rock Harbor with a backpack full of camping gear? Well, I have friends over there. I plan to do some camping. Maybe I'll think about getting a job at the Rock Harbor Lodge if I like it there.

A number of boats are bobbing around at the harbor docks when I arrive. I muster up the courage to approach a middle-aged man who looks respectable. He's standing beside a large classic wooden Chris-Craft boat that certainly looks seaworthy. The boat's motor is running. A younger man is loading items onto the boat, while a middle-aged woman is seated inside.

"Sir?" I manage a smile as I approach the man. "I'm looking for a ride out to Rock Harbor. Is there any way you'd have room for me and my backpack?"

He extends his hand to shake mine although a slight frown creases his busy eyebrows. "And may I ask your name and your business out there?"

"Emily..." I begin nervously pitching my story, aware that the woman in the boat is listening carefully. He hesitates as if uncertain about what to do when the woman calls out, "Honey, we have room. I think it would be nice to give...Emily?... a lift out to Rock Harbor. "That's close to our place, and we're not in any big rush."

It is settled. We are soon off across Lake Superior. Thankfully, the noise of the motor drowns out the possibility of much conversation. They offer me water and snacks which I gladly accept.

The lady, who introduces herself as Alice, and her husband as Steven, is very welcoming. As we pass Tobin Harbor and slow down, she points out their lovely cottage perched on a cliff overlooking the harbor, and begins to make conversation. She invites me to visit them, or to let them know if I need anything. I sense she is picking up on the fact that I may be running or hiding from someone or something. I make a mental note of where they live before we are off again to nearby Rock Harbor where I disembark, thanking them for the ride.

"We hope to see you again soon," Alice calls out. "It's just a short hike down the Tobin Harbor Trail to our place. Not far from Scoville Point."

Now where do I go? How do I get to Lake Ojibway from here again?

I see before me the rustic Rock Harbor Guesthouse perched on the rocky shoreline overlooking the lake. A little restaurant. An office and supply store. An old post office box that fosters a sense of hope in me as far as connecting with the rest of the world someday. A few guests and campers are milling around.

Starving, I decide to grab a bite to eat at the restaurant before I figure out my next moves. I have enough cash (that I'd dug up from our underground safe before I left) to cover some food and other essential expenses. Enough to cover lunch anyway. At least I feel safe here, out on this remote island in the middle of Lake Superior.

The food is good and the service friendly. The waitress asks too many questions, however. Who am I? What am I doing here? Where do I plan to camp out? And...am I at all interested in a part-time job at the lodge and restaurant? They are short-staffed, she tells me. I am relieved to learn that should I need a job to earn some money, there may be one here. But for now, I have no idea how long I will be here or where I'm going. For now, I am anxious to be off to set up camp at Lake Ojibway. The waitress, Martha, points me in the right direction.

...

Before long, I am settled into my tent tucked in the woods beside Lake Ojibway just a stone's throw from the lake. I am alone with nature, the birds and squirrels, an occasional moose. I catch fish in the lake, pick berries, and occasionally hike to Rock Harbor for supplies and basic groceries.

I'm getting to know Martha although I'd never divulge the nature of my visit or my background to her or anyone else. And I've spent some time with Alice and Steven at their lovely cottage overlooking Tobin Harbor. They invited me for dinner and are so welcoming. I sense, however, that Olivia in particular is concerned about me living alone out in the woods. I'm afraid she knows I am hiding from something or someone. She keeps repeating her offer to come and stay in their guest bedroom. It's good to know I have a backup plan. Just in case. They will be leaving for the winter, back to their primary residence in Illinois. But they have shown me where they hide the spare key to their cottage...in case I ever need a warm place to stay while they are away.

But how long do I have to hide out here? When will it be safe to go home to my little girl and find a place for us to start a new life together? I spend long nights sitting silently, alone, on the rocky shoreline of Lake Ojibway beneath a brilliant canopy of stars with the moon casting reflections upon the lake. Trying to connect with the spirits of my mother and father. Praying to Gitche Manitou for guidance. Seeking any kinds of signs or messages from the universe or the heavens above. Every night, before I crawl into my sleeping bag, I retrieve my little framed photo of Emily and kiss her good night.

...

Then one evening, when I'm settled in for the night in my tent, hidden in the jackpines, I hear something crashing through the brush. A bear? Moose? Wolf? Or...worst of all, Jonathan?

I cautiously peek out through the flaps of my tent. I see nothing...but I hear heavy footsteps crunching through the brush, coming closer and closer. Heart pounding, I realize I need to escape now. I quietly crawl out of the tent and make my way to the little dugout hole I'd prepared at the edge of the woods for an occasion like this. I lower myself into the dark hole and pull the makeshift roof of twigs and bark over me.

"You can run but you cannot hide," an evil voice echoes throughout the forest. Oh my God! It is Jonathan! Jonathan who is supposed to be at the bottom of Lake Superior with his shipmates. Somehow, I'd always known he was alive, that he wasn't on that ship, that he was going to try to find and kill me. But how had he found me?

"Angelique!" he shrieks as he closes in on my tent. I hear him rip it open. "What the hell? Where are you, bitch? You know, they used to burn witches like you at the stake. But I have a better plan to rid the world of the likes of you."

I hear him tearing apart the tent, throwing things around and hurling my few belongings into the forest. Finally, I hear him hike off, kicking stones and sticks along the path. "Wherever the hell you are, I will find you, bitch!" were his parting words.

I'm shivering in my hole in the ground, terrified to leave but with no place to go. I wait until I can no longer hear anything – nothing but the howling of a wolf somewhere out there. I tiptoe back to my campsite, retrieve my sleeping bag, a bottle of water, and Emily's picture before retreating back into the woods. There I find a little patch of weeds hidden beneath towering pines where I can hide until dawn. Then what can I do? Where do I go?

I decide that I need to get back to Rock Harbor, maybe to Alice and Steven's place on Tobin Harbor. I need help. I begin my hike just before sunrise, anxious to get there as soon as possible. Heart pounding, I startle anytime I hear a noise of any kind.

Finally, I trudge into Rock Harbor and slip into the restaurant, nervously glancing all around me to make sure Jonathan isn't there.

"Oh my God, Emily! What has happened to you?" a shocked Martha greets me. I know I'm a mess – disheveled, dirty, obviously terrorized. I can't even respond as she quickly leads me into the kitchen, slamming the door behind her.

"Look, whatever has happened to you, we will help. For now, I'm taking you over to the guesthouse and checking you into a room so you can clean up and be safe, okay?"

I can only nod in agreement and follow her to the guesthouse, too exhausted to object or to think. She settles me down onto a comfortable bed and pulls up a chair, a puzzled look on her face as she studies me closely.

"What?" I manage to mumble.

She hesitates before finally staring into my eyes. "Emily...do you know of a young woman named Angelique by any chance?"

"What did you say?" I gasp.

"I don't want to upset you anymore than you already are, but you look exactly like a photo that I just saw the other day of a young woman named Angelique..."

"Where did you see a photo like that?" I can only gasp as my hands grip the bed for support.

"Well, a young gentleman showed up here a few days ago with this photo that he showed us. He was looking for his good friend, Angelique, whom he was supposed to meet out here to do some hiking together. Sounded like they were more than good friends and he wanted to surprise her. He even carried a red rose with him, telling us that Angelique loved red roses."

"Oh my God! What did he look like?"

"Probably about twenty-five? Dark hair. Brown eyes. A long scar on his left cheek."

I slump down onto the bed, feeling faint, tears welling in my eyes. Of course, I knew it was Jonathan tearing my tent apart last night, intent on killing me. But this confirmed it.

"That's my husband!" I finally manage to speak. "How could he have known I was here? How did he find me? He tried to kill me last night. Dear God, where is he now?"

Horrified, Martha gets up quickly to lock and bolt the door. She returns to the bedside and quietly strokes my back. "I'll call the park ranger. But you need to know that this guy was in early this morning for breakfast. He said he was taking a boat back to Grand Portage this morning, but he planned to return soon."

"Can you find out if a Jonathan Edwards has a reservation on the Voyageur II*?" my brain finally engages once again.*

"Jonathan Edwards?" A puzzled look crosses Martha's face. He said his name was Robert Andersen...and that he was a dear friend of yours."

Robert Andersen indeed. That was the name he'd used on his boat reservation, we soon discover. And he had actually boarded the Voyageur II *heading back to the mainland this morning.*

After a hot shower and changing into a set of clothes that Martha kindly donated to me, I find a pen and paper to scrawl a quick letter to Justine, my only reliable contact in this world. Someone has to know that Jonathan has found me out here and is going under the assumed name of Robert Andersen. I give the letter to Martha when she returns to check up on me. She promises to put it in the mailbox immediately. The mail will go out tomorrow on the next boat, she assures me.

With that, I push a heavy chair against the door, close the curtains, and pass out on the comfortable bed after making sure the door of my room in the guesthouse is securely locked.

...

A knock on the door of my room startles me early the next morning.

"Emily?" Martha announces herself. "It's just me with some breakfast for you."

Janet Kay

I stumble to the door to let her in, thanking her profusely for the tray she'd delivered. Scrambled eggs. Sausage. Toast. A glass or orange juice and large mug of coffee.

She opens the curtains to expose a lovely sunrise over the lake and settles herself on the chair by my bed. "So, what am I supposed to call you anyway? Emily? Angelique?"

"Let's stick with Emily...my little daughter's name." I sigh, missing Emily's early morning hugs badly.

"We need to come up with a plan." She grows serious.

So, it's "we" now. I have a partner in crime, which is probably a good thing as fried as my brain is.

She continues. "The park ranger has checked the boat schedules and there's no Robert Andersen scheduled to return today at least. But... you know you're not safe here. He could come by private boat, just like you did. We need to find another safe location here, someplace warm enough... just in case you are still here after it gets cold this fall. You know, you could even stay with me for a while in Grand Portage if you like, after we close up for the season. We could pick up your little girl."

Tears of gratitude fill my eyes as I reach out to give her a hug.

"But for now..." She glances nervously around the room. "I have to get back to the dining room, and you need to figure out where to go. I'll be back later."

I devour my breakfast at the little table overlooking the lake. Trying to find some sense of comfort and hope within the beauty of the sunrise reflecting across the waters of Lake Superior. Wondering how such evil things can happen in such a beautiful world. Sipping my coffee as I try to figure out where to go next – and when.

Once my brain fog lifts enough to think straight, the answer is obvious. Alice and Steven's place on Tobin Harbor, of course. I'm not sure they will still be here since they were planning to head back to Illinois soon. But I know where the house key is and that I am welcome there.

I pack up my few belongings, knowing that I have a long hike ahead and that time is precious. I think about stopping to see Martha, to tell her where I'm going. But that could also jeopardize her life if Jonathan comes back looking for me. Instead, I find a napkin and pencil and scribble her a note.

160

Thanks so much, Martha, for all your help. I hope to see you again in Grand Portage. For now, I need to be on my way. I have a safe place. It is best not to let you know where I'm going – just in case my ex shows up and pressures you in any way. Take care.

I do not sign the note. I just leave it on the pillow before quietly sneaking out and finding my way to the trail.

As I hike along the trail, I can't help startling at every noise in the brush. Thankfully, I have the trail to myself today. Now and then a canoe or kayak passes by. I hide behind a tree until they are out of sight.

Fall is already in the air. A stiff breeze off the harbor sends a chill through me. I keep thinking about a nice warm fire in the fireplace at Alice's cottage. As much as I'm looking forward to hiding out there, I do worry about endangering their lives if Jonathan somehow tracks me there. Or am I just being paranoid? Maybe it's best if they have left for the winter.

Finally, I arrive at their cottage. No signs of anyone. I knock on the door. No response, so I recover the key in its hiding place and let myself in. They are gone.

As I toss my backpack onto the floor, I notice a note on the kitchen table.

Emily, just in case you need a place to stay, you know you are welcome here for as long as you like. We have stocked plenty of food in the pantry, firewood in the shed. Please take care. God bless.

Alice and Steven

How could I possibly have found more kind and helpful people out here on this island in the middle of Lake Superior? But would it be enough to save my life?

After settling in, I build a fire and make some macaroni and cheese for dinner. I find a pile of clothing – almost my size – that Olivia left on top of the bed in the guestroom.

I feel safe here, as safe as anyone can feel after what I've just been through. It's warm and comfortable, but how long do I need to hide out here? When will it be safe for me to go home to my little girl, to find us a new place to live? Besides, it looks like an early winter is already setting in. Before long, the boats going back and forth to the mainland will quit running. I see fewer passing by every day. I could end up here, alone, during what could be a harsh and brutal winter.

Days pass slowly, turning into weeks. I want to go home to my daughter. I'm getting restless, feeling like I have to get outside into the natural world. I can't just hole up in this cottage forever. I long to hike the trails again, to go foraging, to lose myself in the wonders of nature. There's still time before the snow falls to pick some honey mushrooms, blueberries, thimbleberries. Who knows what more I will discover along the trails? I used to forage out here with my mother and father. I know what is safe to eat and what is not.

They say that the trail out to the scenic Scoville Point has edible plants. I may need them over the winter...just in case.

It's been over two weeks since Jonathan's visit. Shouldn't I be safe by now...at least safe enough to take a hike? I mark an X on the calendar every day to keep track of time. My plan is to wait until the night before Rock Harbor Lodge closes for the season, until the last ferry leaves for the mainland. Then I will show up and go back with Martha.

For now, I grab one of Alice's warm jackets and a bucket and set off along the Stoll Trail toward Scoville Point. It feels so good to breathe in the fresh air, to get some exercise, to take in the amazing views along the winding trail that goes back and forth from the forest to the craggy bluffs and rocky cliffs overlooking Lake Superior.

The big lake is churning today as I get closer, wild waves crashing against the cliffs below. The wind is picking up, but I don't care. I stop to gather mushrooms and berries, filling my bucket.

Peering through the canopy of trees hovering above me, I can see the massive stone cliffs of Scovill Point ahead at the end of the trail. How I'd love to perch out there on one of the rocks and bask in the sun and the wind. But for now...it's getting late and the sun is going down. A full moon is rising in the distance. That's okay. I can find my way home in the dark. In fact, that may be safer.

Suddenly I hear a crashing in the brush behind me. A moose? Something tells me to run, run faster. Something is not right. The wind begins to howl and turns bitterly cold, twisting the trees into contorted shapes.

I run faster, deeper into the forest, trying to catch my breath as I stumble over rotted tree limbs strewn along the trail. I hear the pounding waves of Lake Superior crashing against the rocky shoreline below. I run harder, faster, trying to escape from an evil force that is now crashing through the brush behind me. Angry trees swirl around me in distorted shapes as if they are reaching out to grab me.

"Help me! Leave me alone!" I scream silently as heavy footsteps seem to be closing in on me.

"Angelique!" Jonathan's voice thunders throughout the woods as snowflakes begin to fall, dancing around me, obscuring my vision. Oh my God, he has found me – again!

Heart pounding wildly, I try to hide behind the massive trees, to head deeper into the woods. But those footsteps are closing in on me as darkness descends over the island.

"Angelique," he roars in an ominous voice. "You have no place to go, no place to hide."

"Why? Why are you doing this to me?" I whimper as I trip over a protruding limb and fall to the ground. Trembling in fear, I curl up in a ball beneath a tree, trying to hide, trying to protect myself from his fury. I can no longer feel my limbs. I can no longer think.

Suddenly the forest grows eerily still. I can no longer hear his footsteps. I cautiously open my eyes, listening for signs of danger.

Finally, I dare to move, to cautiously rise, trying to figure out where I am in the pitch black of night and where I need to go – until a gunshot shatters the stillness of the forest and my world goes black.

CHAPTER THIRTY-SEVEN

" *A*ngela, wake up, Angela!"

"He killed me! Oh my God, He killed me!" I shouted as I thrashed about, trying to escape from arms holding me tight. I had to get away. Was I dead? Or was I alive? Who was I? Where was I?

"Angela, you are all right. It's just a nightmare. Take a deep breath. You are all right," a familiar voice spoke softly as someone stoked my forehead gently. I began to settle down, exhausted but totally confused.

I finally recognized Thomas's voice, not my mother's this time, trying to wake me from the same nightmare that still haunted me. Only this time, it was not a nightmare. It was not just a dream. It was real.

And I knew beyond a doubt that I had flashed back into my grandmother's life, into her last days out here on Isle Royale. She had finally shown me the way and left more clues for us to pursue.

I began to sob as I clung to Thomas. "He killed her!" I was finally able to blurt out in between my heaving breaths. "My grandmother...Robert Andersen...Scoville Point."

Thomas continued to rock me gently as if I were a baby in his arms. I began to relax when I felt a second set of invisible arms enfold me, that familiar comforting presence of my dear departed grandmother. Her unspoken words filtered into my mind.

Now you know. Hopefully you can understand why I waited to convey this horrific information to you until I knew you were safe with your dear soulmate Thomas. He will take care of you, Angela. You will be all right. And now you can help your dear mother, my beloved daughter, to find the closure she needs.

"But wait." I spoke out loud this time. "Don't go! We need your help to find this...this Jonathan monster...or Robert Andersen, or whatever he calls himself. We need justice for you."

Thomas startled, his eyes searching the room, on high alert. "What's going on? Is she here? Angelique?"

His eyes suddenly closed as he took a deep breath and relaxed.

"She's here, isn't she? I can feel her presence..."

Angelique's final unspoken words infiltrated my mind as she once again disappeared. *Together we will find him and seek justice.*

Jonathan should be close to ninety, I figured, based on the birth certificate Thomas had found for him on one of his research sites. Hopefully, he was still alive. But how many Robert Andersens were there in this world?

I stumbled out of bed, grabbed a notebook and began making notes, trying to capture every detail of my dream. My vision. My flashback into my grandmother's life. I wasn't quite sure what it was. I only knew it was important to record the details.

Thomas waited patiently until I finished, then suggested a walk to clear our heads and work up an appetite before breakfast.

We enjoyed a hearty breakfast on the deck of the Greenstone Grill, quietly watching the marina come to life as fishing boats headed out for the day. The crew of several dive boats were loading their boats with gear and suiting their passengers up to dive some of the shipwrecks scattered around the island. A gentle breeze caressed us as we basked in the early morning sunlight sipping our coffee.

After a short hike along the Tobin Harbor Trail, we found a secluded cove and settled on a rock overlooking the harbor. I finally divulged all the details of my flashback into Angelique's life. He shed a tear or two and held me close once I finished.

"He could easily be dead, you know," Thomas cautioned me. "But I, for one, would like to get that bastard and make him pay—if he's still alive. I need to get back to my laptop and my research now that we have more information. What do you think?"

"I'm in, totally in."

We got back to our room as the wind began to pick up. Looked like a storm could be moving in. Hopefully not, since our plan was to head out to Scoville Point tomorrow morning, to the scene of the crime I'd envisioned. We had two more days left here on Isle Royale. We had work to do.

I took a badly needed nap while Thomas settled down with his laptop at the little table by the windows overlooking the lake. As I drifted

165

off to sleep, I could hear his frustration as he tried repeatedly to connect to the sporadic internet service from out here in the middle of nowhere. He finally slammed his laptop shut and joined me in bed.

...

In the middle of the night, we were awakened by crashing sounds and ferocious winds howling. Rain and hail pelted the windows so fiercely that we couldn't see anything outside. It sounded like a tree or two crashing onto the rocky cliffs below as huge waves roared into the harbor. Then the electricity went out.

From our bed, we could see a frightening display of lightning flashing through the sky as bolts of thunder shook the building. Of course, there was no internet or television or radio for us to try to figure out what was happening and what we needed to do. So, we hunkered down, stayed away from the windows, and said a little prayer as the storm raged on throughout the night.

By morning, the electricity flickered back on to the sounds of a generator. The rain and wind had ceased, leaving behind some flooded areas, washed out trails, and trees down. Chain saws buzzed. We put on our hiking boots and navigated the muddy, limb-strewn trail down to the grill where staff were busily trying to clean up the mess.

Signs hung on the doors of the office and restaurant advising that all trails were closed until further notice and ferries running to the mainland hoped to resume service by late afternoon.

So much for our hike to Scoville Point! When we asked one of the park rangers how soon we could get out on the trail, he advised that it was too dangerous until they'd had a chance to scope out the trails. And of course, the internet was down.

Seriously frustrated and disappointed, especially since we finally had a lead to follow and only one more day to do it, we resolved to drown our sorrows in coffee and a good book on one of the benches by the restaurant. But Angelique's oft repeated words haunted me: *Time is of the essence.* A chilling sense of urgency swept through me. Now was the time.

As we tried to focus on our books, we also watched the activity surrounding us as staff did their best to clean up the mess that the storm had left behind. I could see several of them gathered outside the old guesthouse by the office where an antique mailbox was located.

That old mailbox was now lying on the ground, apparently taken down by a fallen tree that another ranger was cutting up with a chainsaw. I couldn't help wondering if anyone used the box anymore or it was just an artifact from days gone by.

"Look at this!" one ranger exclaimed.

I watched him retrieve what looked like an old envelope from the broken mailbox.

"What the hell? An old letter? That mailbox hasn't been used in years. Can you read the address?" Another ranger moved in.

I felt compelled to move in closer so I could hear better.

"Damn, this looks old. Hmmm...looks like it's addressed to a...Justine Kerfoo?"

My heart almost stopped as I recalled my flashback. Angelique had, in my nightmare, mailed a letter to Justine before she left the guesthouse. Was it possible that this was the letter, stuck in that old box for the past sixty-six years? A letter that Justine never received?

I approached cautiously, Thomas following.

"Excuse me, but can I see that letter? You see, Justine Kerfoot was a friend of my grandmother who spent time out here on Isle Royale way back in 1958. Please. It would mean a lot to me."

The ranger holding the letter frowned slightly, as if trying to decide if he should release the letter, or if he needed permission to do so. Finally, he smiled sympathetically, and handed me the letter.

"Thank you, I will give it back as soon as I read it. Okay if I read it over there on that bench by the office?"

"That's fine, ma'am. In fact, I see no reason why we need an old letter like that back. You can keep it. Have a good day."

Thomas put his arm around me as we settled on the bench, giving me courage to open the faded envelope and carefully extract the frail paper.

Dear Justine, the letter read, *As you know from my previous letter, I have escaped to Isle Royale. I did not dare take my little Emily with me since I feared Jonathan would find us. I had to leave her with a kind pastor at the Maple Hill Church for now. Jonathan is alive and has now found me here at my campsite on Lake Ojibway, the one place I thought I would be safe. He is trying to kill me! I will be hiding out somewhere around Tobin Harbor, staying with a kind couple, until I can safely take a boat back to the mainland, back to my little Emily. First, I need to figure out a few things and make arrangements for us to start a new life together someplace safe. For now, someone needs to know that Jonathan is going under an assumed name of Robert Andersen.*

Just in case he finds me again and something bad happens so I can't return, please find my dear Emily and take care of her for me. Let her know how much I love her and always will. Thank you for everything you've done for me. I'm sorry I didn't get to tell you goodbye. I had to leave fast and did not want to jeopardize you or your family.

Love, Angelique

So, since Justine never received this letter, she'd have had no way of knowing that Angelique had left Emily behind. No way of connecting the news of an abandoned little girl called Olivia with the disappearance of Angelique and Emily. She probably assumed that Angelique and Emily were together, hiding out somewhere. At least that part of the mystery was beginning to make sense.

Most importantly, I now had written proof to show my mother that her mother had, in fact, loved her and always would. But how and when could I share the rest of the grizzly contents of this letter with her? Would it totally shatter her to know that her hero of a father was, in fact, an evil man who had killed her mother? Maybe that part would have to wait until we discovered more details.

CHAPTER THIRTY-EIGHT

The pressure was on. Our time on Isle Royale was running out. We kept checking with the Park Service to find out how soon we could navigate the trail to Scoville Point. Finally, they informed us that the trail crew had checked out and cleared the trails enough that we were allowed to take our hike along the peninsula to Scoville Point. We weren't sure, of course, exactly what we were looking for. Anything. Any signs from above or from Angelique. Even another terrifying flashback if it would help us to discover the truth about what had happened to my grandmother so many years ago.

Had she actually been murdered someplace along this trail as portrayed in my dreams? If so, where? After all these years, could there be any visible signs, any evidence that a horrific crime had been committed here on this island?

We hiked silently, lost in our thought. While I longed to discover the truth and find closure for us all, a part of me was afraid of what we may, or may not, find.

Instead of enjoying the warmth of the sun bouncing across the gentle waves and casting reflections through the canopy of trees surrounding us, our eyes swept every detail along the rocky trails. We cautiously climbed boulders for a better view, then retreated back into the forest.

As we got closer to the cliffs of Scoville Point, we began to see more storm damage including several major washouts that the trail crew had marked with red flags to prevent hikers from tumbling down towards the lake.

"Wow, look at that!" Thomas pointed downhill at a huge landslide. Trees, large boulders and massive amounts of dirt had washed down the cliff and into the lake. Grabbing his binoculars, he focused on something protruding from the dirt, something glistening in the sunshine.

As he did so, I felt strange images seeping into my mind once again. I sat on a large rock, taking deep breaths, trying to control the feelings now surging through my body. There was something about this place...

"We need to go down, Thomas, now!" I finally jumped up, determined. "This is it. I know it. This is where it happened!"

I began to bolt past the red warning flags as Thomas gripped my hands and held me back. "No, it's not safe. Stop!"

"Let me go! She's down there. Let me go!" I melted into a puddle of tears as he restrained me in his arms, trying to comfort me.

"Look, we'll get the park rangers out here to check it out. They'll know what to do, what's safe and what's not."

I finally consented. I wasn't sure what they would find. All I knew beyond a doubt was that this was the place where my grandmother had been murdered at the hands of my grandfather.

Thomas zoomed in with his camera to get a few photos to show to the park rangers, anything to convince them that there could, in fact, be something down there that they needed to check out. He did capture a blurry image of something that I at least thought could be human remains. Or was that just my overactive imagination perhaps?

I reluctantly allowed Thomas to guide me back to the ranger station where we met with William, the head park ranger. I let Thomas handle the conversation with him. He was at first wary of our request to check out a strange object that had apparently been exposed as a result of the massive landslide.

"I know this sounds bizarre, but to me it almost looked like skeletal remains. Here." Thomas showed him a photo he'd taken. "It's blurry from that distance and with the glare of the sun, but someone needs to check this out."

With that, William consented and radioed for several of his rangers to join him in the search, emphasizing that it was also important to make sure the area was safe and secure. He didn't want anyone getting hurt.

William agreed to let us tag along so we could pinpoint the exact location. Once again, we traipsed down the trail, this time following the rangers who were equipped with shovels, sensors, a camera, ropes, bags and other equipment.

A chill swept through the air as we arrived. I wasn't the only one who noticed it, I realized as several rangers shivered and zipped up their jackets. But I was the only one who could identify that chill as

Angelique's presence. She was there with Thomas and me, standing on top of the cliff while the rangers carefully made their way down using ropes attached to the rocky formations with large hooks.

A shocked voice from down below called out, "Whoa! Whoa! Look at that!"

"What the hell?" William exclaimed. "Oh my God! Stand back. Do not touch or go anywhere near it. We need to get law enforcement out here ASAP. This could be a crime scene, or the remnants of one that was exposed by the storm."

Although we got as close as we could to the edge, we could not see exactly what they were looking at. We could, however, see them taking photos from various angles.

Before long, the crew, led by William, carefully climbed back up the side of the cliff, lugging their equipment. They were silent, somber, respectful.

"Keith, I'll need you to stay here guarding the skeleton until law enforcement arrives," William quietly ordered. "No one is to go near the scene, got it? I'll send someone out with the gear and provisions you'll need overnight."

As the others trudged back down the trail, William walked over to thank us for the heads-up and cautioned us to stay at the lodge until law enforcement interviewed us. I felt him watching me closely with a puzzled look upon his face.

"Ma'am, I know it's disturbing to see something like this...but..." He chose his words carefully. "Is there anything I should know, anything you want to tell me?"

I shook my head, staring down at the ground, as my eyes began to fill with tears. He waited until I finally looked up.

"It's just that...well, my grandmother was here on Isle Royale years ago. She disappeared and nobody ever knew where she went or what happened to her."

With that, his ears perked up and he sat down on a rock near us. "I'm sorry. Any idea about when she would have been here?"

"Nineteen fifty-eight," I blurted out, surprising him with my rapid response.

Janet Kay

"Of course, this could be totally unrelated," he tried to assure me, obviously aware of my emotional state of being. "Or maybe not. I need to get back to call law enforcement. They will want to speak with you and ask you a few more questions when they arrive. They can do an analysis and DNA testing to hopefully determine any possible connections."

"Any idea when someone will interview us? We're supposed to head back on the *Voyageur II* early tomorrow," Thomas announced.

"Hmmm...unlikely the investigator will be here until tomorrow afternoon, unless he can catch a seaplane over earlier. Where you staying?"

"The Ojibway Lodge at Rock Harbor."

"We will extend your stay, no charge. So, stay put until I let you know, okay?"

"Thanks," Thomas mumbled.

"Sorry, but I need to get back to make my calls. Take care." He tipped his hat as he hurried back down the trail.

Once he was gone, I began to sob as I lingered on the rock beside Thomas. "Oh Angelique," I whispered as I felt her invisible tears mingling with mine.

Closure, at last...almost, she whispered into my ear.

"Not yet. Not until we find that monster and you get the justice you deserve," I replied.

Thomas cocked his head, bewildered at first. "Of course, Angelique is here, right?" He sighed as he pulled me close. We sat huddled together staring out over my grandmother's remains as the sun set over the island.

While I was reluctant to leave, we decided it was time to hike back to our lodge beneath the light of a full moon.

CHAPTER THIRTY-NINE

We were awakened early the next morning, after a night of very little sleep, by a loud knocking on the door. Chief Ranger William apologized, but he wanted us to know that Detective Korpela's seaplane had landed at the Mott Island Park Service Headquarters on Isle Royale. He'd assembled his team and they were on their way in one of the park service's boats and scheduled to arrive within an hour. He was anxious to meet with us before he and his team headed out to recover the skeletal remains.

We hurriedly dressed and grabbed a quick breakfast at the grill before hiking to the office where we were ushered into a small room and seated in front of a large wood desk. The detective should arrive shortly, we were advised after the friendly staff person offered us each a cup of coffee.

Maybe that would help settle my nerves. My biggest concern was saying too much. I wasn't about to divulge anything about the ghost of my grandmother leading me here and making her presence known. I didn't want to sound like a crazy person. I only wanted to establish a good relationship with this detective so we could stay in touch and learn what happened.

A pleasantly plump, large man entered the office. "Good morning, I'm Detective Korpela." He shook hands with both of us before settling in the leather chair behind the desk.

He didn't waste any time making small talk. He scribbled notes on a yellow legal pad as we answered the questions that he fired at us about discovering the remains.

Then he settled back in his chair and began asking about my grandmother and her mysterious disappearance.

I told him all I knew and also produced the letter to Justine that had been found in that old mailbox. He read it over several times, obviously intrigued.

"We may have something here. We will have our forensic

anthropologist do a skeletal analysis to determine cause and estimated time of death as well as identity of the victim. We will need to do a DNA analysis… I would like to obtain a DNA sample from you, Angela, just in case this is in fact your grandmother. It wouldn't hurt to get one from your mother also if that's possible?"

"I'm more than happy to provide my sample. What do you need from my mother? I don't want to upset her any more than she already is…"

"I'd like a cheek swab from you. As for your mother, we could probably go with a piece of clothing or an imprint from a coffee cup for now."

"I can do that.

"So, we will proceed with our analysis. If the DNA determines that this is actually your grandmother, and if it appears that foul play was involved, we may decide to use your letter as evidence to try to find this Jonathan Edward—or Robert Andersen person. If he's still alive."

"That would be wonderful. Thank you so much."

"I'll have the clerk make me a copy of that letter. You may have the original back for now. Oh…one more question before I head out to recover the remains…what are the two of you doing out here on Isle Royale anyway? Does this have anything to do with your grandmother and her mysterious disappearance?"

I tensed up a bit, trying to decide how to answer his question. Thomas obviously sensed my discomfort and answered for me. "Angela knew her grandmother had loved Isle Royale and spent time here with her family of origin. That this was supposedly the last place she was seen. We decided to take a little trip, do some hiking, enjoy Lake Superior. Maybe this was a way for her to connect with the grandmother she never had the opportunity to know."

Detective Korpela nodded as he pulled his large frame up from his chair, shook our hands, and walked out the door. "Leave your home contact information with Ranger William. We'll be in touch."

We still had time to board the *Voyageur II* and head back to the mainland. Thomas was anxious to get back to reliable internet service so he could begin searching for this Robert Andersen. And I needed time to process our discovery. Spending hours crossing Lake Superior and losing myself in the wind and waves was exactly what I needed.

We found our favorite place on the front deck of the boat and settled in, just staring out at the lake. Several hours into the trip, one of the deckhands found us. "Are you Angela? And Thomas?"

"Why, yes," Thomas replied. "Why?" Something seemed a little off to both of us, based on the concerned expression upon the guy's face.

"The captain would like to meet you, privately. Please follow me."

With that, we were ushered through the boat and up into the cockpit where the captain was waiting for us. He turned to us, a sympathetic look on his face, as he cleared his throat and took a deep breath.

"We just got an important call for you from Chief Ranger William," he began hesitantly as he handed the phone to me. "He's on the line."

"Hello?" my voice squeaked as I clutched the phone.

"Hello, Angela. We have recovered the skeletal remains, and sadly..." he hesitated. "Is Thomas there with you?"

"Yes," I whispered as Thomas put his arm around me.

"There was a bullet hole in the skull. They have classified the cause of death as homicide. I'm sorry, but I thought you needed to know."

I crumbled into Thomas's arms, feeling like I was about to pass out. Of course I'd known this would be the outcome. But now it was official.

"We still need to find out for sure that this is your grandmother, Angela," Thomas reminded me. "And if it is, we will find that bastard...assuming he's not already dead."

CHAPTER FORTY

Once we'd returned from Isle Royale, it was time to pay my mother a visit. Time to let her know what we had discovered. While I dreaded being the bearer of such horrific news, news that would change her world and shatter her beliefs about her family, I knew it was time. I arranged a weekend visit to Duluth.

"Let's sit down in the gazebo," Mother suggested shortly after I'd arrived. Although she was obviously glad to see me, I could see the anxiety flickering in her eyes as she fidgeted.

I was also nervous, knowing I had to relay some important news to her while being careful not to say too much. Not to upset her too much. I'd decided to photocopy and share segments of Angelique's letters and Justine's journal entries; the parts that should reassure her that her mother had not abandoned her for no good reason, that she was loved.

I took her arm and we strolled out through the gardens and down to the Victorian gazebo overlooking the lake. It was a beautiful, early summer day. Birds chirping. Flowers beginning to bloom. Gentle waves caressing the shoreline below.

"Beth has already set up some hors d'oeuvres and wine for us. I thought we could use a little this afternoon..."

I poured us each a glass of wine and we settled into the wicker rocking chairs.

She finally spoke. "So how was your trip to Isle Royale?"

"Very interesting. We did discover some important information out there. Between our visit and Justine's journals—and a few of Angelique's own letters that we found..."

"What?" She leaned forward in her chair. "Tell me."

"Are you sure you're ready? I don't want to upset you, but the truth is not what we've always thought it was. There are some things you need to know..."

"Go on." She refilled her wine glass.

I retrieved my doctored photocopies. "The most important thing you need to know is that your mother loved you dearly. She did not abandon you. Something happened, something that prevented her from coming back for you."

Mother gripped the arms of her chair as I began to read.

"My name is Angelique. I have an adorable little daughter, Emily, whom I love with all my heart. It is with extreme sadness that I am going to have to leave her with a nearby church until I can return to claim her. That is IF my husband does not find me first..."

I paused to gauge her reaction.

"But...but my father was dead. He died when his ship went down! That makes no sense!"

"We have good reason to believe that he was not on that ship, Mother, that he jumped ship at the last port before his ship went down. The authorities are checking it out. Your mother goes on to say that she is leaving for Isle Royle, a place where she can hopefully hide out and reconnect with the spirits of her deceased parents. They had all spent time together on that island. And, as you know, her parents had drowned out there when she was only seventeen."

"Oh no! Dear God, how can that be? All these years...all these years I've hated my mother for leaving me. I thought my father was some kind of hero because he went down with his ship. Now you're telling me that is not true?"

"It doesn't appear to be true. Do you want me to read more, or is this enough for now? I don't want to stress you out."

"Go on. I cannot hide from the truth any longer, not at my age."

"I have escaped to Isle Royale where I am hiding from Jonathan. He is alive and has found me here at my campsite on Lake Ojibway. I will be hiding out somewhere around Tobin Harbor, staying with a kind couple, until I can return for little Emily and start a new life together someplace safe. Someone needs to know that he is going under an assumed name of Robert Andersen. Just in case I'm not able to return, please let Emily know how much I love her and always will. I did not dare take her with me out here but left her with a kind pastor near Grand Marais."

Mother began to sob. I held her in my arms, stroking her back, trying to comfort her. Finally, she sat upright and asked the question that I was

Janet Kay

not able or willing to answer. Not yet.

"What happened to my mother?" She could barely get the words out.

I stretched the truth, to say the least. "We don't know yet, but the authorities are trying to figure that out." That was true. There was no official identity of the skeletal remains yet.

"And what about this Robert Andrews?"

"Andersen. They're also trying to find him, if he is still alive. We just don't know yet, Mother. But I wanted you to know that you were loved, and that your father was not the man we thought he was."

"I needed to know that," she whispered. "Knowing she did love me and had a reason for leaving me behind...you have no idea how much that means to me, Angela. Thank you."

"I was totally shocked myself. I can only imagine what you are going through. Is there anything I can do to help?"

"Just sit with me. I need to hear the waves and feel the healing power of Lake Superior."

"I do have one good thing to share with you, something I found in my cabin, something Angelique wanted you to have." I pulled the photo album from the bag beside me and gently placed it in her hands.

"What is this?" She gasped as she opened the album and began carefully turning the pages.

"Something your mother wanted you to have. She hid it before she left, with a note to make sure that it went to you if she did not return."

More tears, from both of us, as we paged through that album together. My mother was finally discovering her roots and learning how much her mother had loved her.

I led her back to the house, beneath a canopy of stars glittering across the sky. Trying to convince myself and find comfort in the fact that we, and our problems, were just a tiny part of a giant universe.

I made sure that she carried her own wine glass back to the house and set it on the table. I did not want to touch it. After I gave her a big hug and she retreated to her bedroom, I took a pair of rubber gloves from my purse and carefully placed her wine glass in a little box. I would get that to the forensic anthropologist for DNA analysis. I'd already done my cheek swab and had sent it to their Michigan office.

Overall, I felt as good as I could about how the evening had gone. Mother seemed grateful to finally know the truth, and I felt that I had spared her most of the grizzly details for now. I climbed into my old canopy bed later that night and called Thomas.

He picked up his phone immediately. "How did it go?"

"As good, maybe better than expected." I filled him in on the details.

"That's a relief. Good job, my lovely. And you even confiscated a wine glass with her DNA on it?"

"That I did. How about you, Thomas? How are you doing?" God, I missed that man. I'd have given anything to curl up with him in my canopy bed.

"Aside from missing you..." He must have read my mind. "My fishing excursions went well. We're catching some big lake trout, walleye too. Happy clients. But I'm frustrated with my research into this Robert Andersen."

"No luck?"

"Too much luck. Do you have any idea how many Robert Andersens there are? How many guys about his age with that name? He picked a good one all right."

"I assume you've checked obituaries?"

"Yup. No luck so far. You know, law enforcement is also going to be trying to find him once they establish the skeleton's identity."

"But how long is that going to take? I wonder if they don't prioritize more recent murders?"

"Probably. I guess we could wait to see what they come up with once we know it really is Angelique?"

"No!" I gasped. "I need the satisfaction of finding out, of maybe even trying to see him if he's still alive. Does that sound crazy?"

"Why? So we can kill him like he killed her?"

"No, although I'd love to do that," I admitted. "I'd like to dig up enough dirt to frame him so he goes to prison for the rest of his life, even if he may not have many years left. That would make me...well, almost make me happy. Justice for Angelique and for my mother."

"I'm in," Thomas agreed. "I'm also checking into criminal records. If he killed his own wife, who knows what other crimes he may have committed?"

"And I'm going to help Sabrina scour every inch of their place to see if we can find any more information from Justine's days. Maybe we could even check out that bar where he hung out? Maybe some of the old-timers would remember something, or there might be stories handed down about him if he was as crazy as Justine's journal implied."

"Great idea. You're becoming a super sleuth." He yawned. "Early morning charter tomorrow. If you're sure you're okay, maybe we should call it a night. Try to enjoy your time there with your mother and I'll see you in a few days."

"I love you and miss you."

"Not as much as I love you, my lovely. Sweet dreams."

CHAPTER FORTY-ONE

"Robert Andersen?" The bearded bartender shook his head. "Nope, never heard of a dude around here with that name. How long ago would he have been here?"

"Way back—like the 1950s?" Thomas replied as he took a swig of his beer.

The bartender laughed out loud. "What? Hell, he's probably dead or in a nursing home. Anyone who might have known him is probably also long gone."

"We know that," I pitched in, trying to conceal my frustration. "But have you ever heard any stories about a weird guy with that name who got drunk here often?"

"Never." He turned away to wait on another customer.

"How about a guy named Jonathan?" Thomas called after him. "Look, this is important. We need to find this dude if he's still alive. His daughter is looking for him. Kind of a medical emergency."

The bartender heaved a sigh before returning and leaning his heavily tattooed arms on the bar. Several older men seated at the bar also quit talking and began to listen as Thomas continued.

"All we know is that this Robert, or Jonathan, was a sailor on Lake Superior. He had a wife and baby girl who lived here with him, not too far up the Trail. When Jonathan was home, he hung out here, got drunk, sometimes beat his wife. He thought she was a witch!"

"Oh!" One elderly man with a scraggly gray beard, wearing a red plaid flannel shirt and suspenders, joined in. "Yeah...I do remember a bastard called Jonathan. He was one mean SOB when he was drunk, picked a lot of fights around here. But that witch bullshit...yeah, he thought she was a witch because she knew things she shouldn't know."

"Any idea what happened to him?" I asked.

The old man shook his head, took another gulp of his beer. "Well, they say he went down with his ship. But before he left, he said he was planning to get rid of the bitch and take his little girl." He laughed. "She might have been a witch but he sure as hell wasn't fit to raise no kid."

Thomas and I took deep breaths and waited.

"Funny thing." The old man shook his head. "The wife and kid both disappeared about the time his ship went down."

"Do you remember anything else about him? About his plans to take his little girl?" I asked.

"Nope, just that he had a mean streak and we stayed the hell out of his way when he was drunk. Can't say we felt bad when his ship went down. Except for the other guys on that ship, you know."

"And his daughter?" I had to try once more.

"If I remember right..." He took a deep breath. "He said something about some island in a big lake somewhere where they would live happily ever after. Yeah, right. That poor kid would have had one hell of a life if that bastard had lived."

"Anything else?" Thomas asked.

"Nope, that's about it. Hey, I could use another beer here." He slammed his mug on the bar.

"I've got it." Thomas tossed a ten-dollar bill on the bar. "It's on me. Thanks for the info."

Thomas and I walked out of the old shack of a bar that had probably not changed since Jonathan was here all those years ago. We began to walk back to my place.

"Well, that seems to confirm Justine's observations," I said.

"And more...interesting that he talked about raising your mother on an island in a big lake somewhere. Not much to go on, but something to keep in mind, right?"

"Right. I hope to God he's not dead," I lamented. "It's not fair if he died a peaceful death instead of in prison where he belongs. It's not fair if he got away with what he did to my grandmother. You know that Sabrina and I have scoured every inch of their place. Nothing. No more clues. We can't find any leads online. What now?"

"Look." Thomas stopped and pulled me into his arms, his eyes boring into mine. "I know how you feel. I'm also frustrated as hell, but I don't know what more we can do unless and until we stumble across something else. Maybe timing is everything, like Angelique has told you several times. Once we get the investigator's report and DNA analysis, we should have more to go on."

"But when will that be? How long can it possibly take?"

He shrugged his shoulders. "You and I are going to sit out by the lake and try to relax," he announced. "If I didn't have a trip scheduled for early tomorrow morning, I'd stay here with you. Will you be okay?"

"I'll be fine." I sighed.

So, we settled on our log bench overlooking Gunflint Lake and drowned our frustrations in the gentle lapping of the waves against the shoreline.

Thomas kissed me goodbye later that evening. "I hate having to leave you. I hate not spending every night with you. We belong together, don't you think? Like for the rest of our lives? One house, one life..."

He eyed me cautiously, waiting for my response. He'd been careful not to push me too fast. And I'd been too preoccupied with my grandmother to give too much thought to my own future. But tonight, as I gazed into his eyes, I knew the answer.

"Yes, Thomas, that's exactly what I want also. As soon as we can get through this and have time to figure things out...that's exactly what I want and need. I need you and I always will. And I want to be here for you always."

We held each other closely, feeling that unbreakable bond between us, knowing that we were now committed to a future together.

...

I finally drifted off to sleep that night after tossing and turning, trying to quit thinking about our search for my elusive wicked grandfather. If only the investigation results were released. If only we could find some clues.

If only Angelique would guide us. Where was she? Shouldn't she know where Jonathan was or if he was alive? Didn't spirits on the other side of life know about things like that?

Angelique, I pleaded silently, *we need your help. Please! Where are you?"*

I was awakened abruptly by something settling at the foot of my bed. Startled, I bolted upright in bed, straining to see what or who was perched on my bed.

A transparent image glowed dimly. I relaxed as I sensed Angelique's presence. Finally! But something was different. She wasn't as bright as usual, not as visible, not as easy to feel her essence.

"Oh Angelique. I'm so happy to see you. We need your help. We need to find this Robert Andersen person or figure out what happened to him."

She did not respond at first. I strained to grasp whatever messages she was trying to commute telepathically like she always did.

Finally, something came through faintly.

It's time. Almost time. Running out of my earthly energy. Jonathan... Find Jonathan.

She emphasized the name. Should we be looking for Jonathan instead of Robert Andersen?

Where? Where can we find him? Please! We need justice for you. We need closure. Please, Angelique!

Kettle...Kettle...

Her light was getting dimmer, flickering like a candle about to go out.

"Kettle? What about a kettle? Don't go. Please," I pleaded with her, now talking out loud instead of sending silent messages the way we usually communicated. The louder the better.

Falls... Her faint voice managed to filter its way into my mind. Then she was gone, leaving behind a fading thread of hope and what felt like a weak hug. Tears welled in my eyes. Was that the last I'd ever see of my grandmother? Was there any way that a spirit could recharge their batteries, so to speak, and come back to visit again? Or was she gone forever?

Still, perhaps she had left us a few clues to pursue. But what did "Kettle" and "Falls" mean? I was quite sure that those were the words she had whispered into my mind, although they made no sense to me.

Did a kettle fall? But what did that have to do with finding Jonathan? Or was she trying to tell me about something Jonathan had once done to her, something about a kettle?

My mind was too tired to figure it out right now. Maybe the answers would come to me in my dreams.

Unable to sleep, I got up and settled into the rocking chair on my deck where I could watch the sun rise over the lake.

My reverie was interrupted by the ringing of my phone. I rushed in to grab it, thinking that it was probably Thomas checking up on me before he headed out on today's fishing trip.

"Angela?" a vaguely familiar male voice inquired once I answered.

"Yes?"

"This is Chief Ranger William O'Brien at Isle Royale..."

I gripped the phone tightly and sat back down. "Hello... do you have any news for us yet?"

"I do. We have a DNA match based on your and your mother's DNA samples and the skeletal remains. The remains belong to a woman, probably at least half Ojibwe, about early to-mid-twenties when she died by gunshot. Estimated time of death is around mid-nineteen-fifties. Does that seem to fit?"

"Oh my God." I grasped the arms of my chair. I'd always known it was Angelique, but now it was confirmed. That small shred of hope that I'd clung to had been severed. Images of the horror she must have experienced at the hands of her evil husband filtered through my mind. It had to be him, right? Who else would have killed her?

I could almost feel my heart breaking. Taking a few deep breaths, I forced myself back to the present. We had work to do. We needed to find justice for my dear grandmother soon. She was running out of time on this earth.

"Yes, that is my grandmother, Angelique Edwards. The profile fits perfectly. Thank you so much. Now...what happens next? How do we find her killer? This Jonathan Edwards. Or his alias, Robert Andersen."

He was quiet for a moment. "The investigator has secured a few DNA samples on the few remaining remnants of clothing, dried blood stains, etcetera, and will run that against our databases. They can't assume that her husband or any particular person killed her, not unless and until they get a match. To be honest, chances are good that the perpetrator is dead by now. And as long ago as this crime was committed, it's probable that there wouldn't be much DNA evidence for them to find. But they will do what they can do. There is no statute of limitations for murder. We will keep you posted if they discover anything. Someone will call when the remains are released."

It didn't sound encouraging. At least we knew that it was Angelique. It was time for Thomas and I to intensify our search. At least we had a few hints from Angelique to follow up—Jonathan... Kettle... and Falls. Whatever that meant.

CHAPTER FORTY-TWO

After dinner the next evening, Thomas and I talked. He was as baffled as I was as we discussed Angelique's visit. Before long, he was back at his laptop, lost in his research, shaking his head, mumbling a few swear words. "So, a kettle falls...what the hell does that mean?"

"Why don't you take a break, honey." I came up behind him, massaging his shoulders. "Let's go sit by the lake to clear our minds. Maybe something will come to us, something we're missing here."

He agreed and we hiked down the well-worn path to our bench. An eerie layer of fog was drifting over the lake, fitting for the mood we were in. It was all so mysterious, just like the universe that surrounded us. Sometimes that universe, and our little lives here on Planet Earth, were shrouded in fog so dense that it prevented us from seeing or knowing the truth. Sometimes rays of sunlight, of truth, filtered through. At times, some of us were able to capture those truths, to see beyond this little world.

And sometimes deceased spirits like Angelique found a way to come back and make themselves known to those who were open enough to communicate with them. Like me, perhaps. And Thomas. And obviously Angelique who had been accused of witchcraft because of her ability to tap into things that others could not. And that's why her evil husband killed her?

As we sat in silence, holding hands, these thoughts filtered through my mind. I took a few deep breaths, trying to clear my mind, trying to be open to any messages from beyond. If I could just let go of my anger and my sorrow, maybe I could focus.

Suddenly it hit me. "Kettle Falls! Maybe we need to put the words together. Maybe there's a waterfall called Kettle, or a place called Kettle Falls?"

We rushed back to the cabin, back to our laptops. It wasn't long before we identified several possible locations. There was a Kettle Falls Trail down in Arkansas. And a City of Kettle Falls in Washington. And a

Kettle Falls Hotel in Voyageur's National Park in northern Minnesota.

If Jonathan had escaped and gone into hiding someplace, he'd probably pick a remote place off the beaten path. Certainly not a far-away city in Washington. And a trail in Arkansas didn't make much sense either—unless that's where his body was buried?

The Kettle Falls in Voyageurs National Park seemed like the most logical option, although it could be a wild goose chase. It was located on Rainy Lake along the international border between the United States and Canada. About a 250-mile drive from our cabin, followed by a boat ride out to the island. A logical choice if Jonathan was trying to escape into Canada or hide out on the wilderness islands that surrounded Kettle Falls.

"An island in a big lake!" Thomas exclaimed.

"Yes, just like the guy in the bar said."

The more we read, the more intrigued we became with the historic Kettle Falls Hotel and the wilderness surrounding it. The Ojibwe fished there many hundreds of years ago. French Canadian voyageurs portaged their canoes around the waterfalls. In later years, lumberjacks drove tons of logs through the dam that had been constructed. Commercial fishermen auctioned off their catch in 100-pound wooden crates at the Kettle Falls docks. And during Prohibition, bootleggers distilled and sold their liquor here. They also smuggled Canadian liquor across the international border for mobsters as far away as Chicago.

Kettle Falls was accessible, we learned, only by boat or floatplane. Or snowmobile or snowshoes in the winter. A perfect place for a criminal to hide out.

"That's it! I can feel it, Thomas. There is definitely some connection to Jonathan out there. We need to visit soon."

He was quiet for a moment. "Look, we need to think this through a little more. What do we hope to accomplish out there, exactly?"

"We need to find any trace of that horrible human being. Was he there? What was he like? Is he dead or alive?"

"If he's dead, maybe we could find a local obituary or some evidence, even a grave. That's true. But what if he's still alive? Then what? Do we gather any information we can and turn that over to law enforcement so they can investigate and hopefully put him away for the rest of his pathetic life?"

"If he's alive...and I hope to God he is...we need to do more than that."

"Such as?" A puzzled look crossed his brow, although he obviously knew I had plans to pursue. He knew me only too well.

"I need to try to meet him, Thomas. And I want you to come with me. We need to get information out of him that will help nail him. We can do that. He's too old to hurt us. And you can bring your pistol. Just in case."

"Hold on, my lovely." Thomas drew back. "How can we meet and talk with him when we want nothing more than to kill him ourselves? How can we possibly act normal, even friendly, after what he did to your grandmother?"

"Where there's a will, there's a way." My mother's words somehow escaped from my lips. "If we want information badly enough, we can manage to control ourselves and put on an act. We can block our feelings and our need for revenge, if that's what it takes to discover the truth. To finally get justice for Angelique."

"I hear you," he said, "but are you sure you are up to this? It could be traumatic, heartbreaking. Or we may find nothing at all."

"I know, honey. I can do this, and I feel strongly that we at least need to try."

With that, he was back to his laptop, ready to book a hotel reservation at Kettle Falls Hotel. First, he had to find one of his fellow boat captains to cover the fishing expeditions he'd already booked.

A hotel shuttle boat would pick us up at the Ash River Visitor Center and transport us across the lake to the hotel on the eastern end of the Kabetogama Peninsula where the Kettle Falls Hotel was located.

CHAPTER FORTY-THREE

The boat ride to Kettle Falls was an adventure in itself. We were immersed in the beauty of pristine blue lakes sparkling in the sunshine. No wonder they called it "the land of sky-blue waters." We were surrounded by numerous rocky islands that dotted this wilderness landscape. Our boat driver occasionally pointed out an eagle perched in a tree or a flock of white pelicans gathered on a rocky outcrop. Aside from a few fishing and tourist boats, it felt like we had entered another world, a wilderness untamed by man.

We learned that the Kettle Falls Hotel where we would be staying was built in 1910-1913 by a timber baron, reputedly financed by the infamous Madame Nellie Bly. After years of wear and tear resulting in sloping floors from an unstable foundation, the National Park Service purchased it in 1977 and began a major renovation. The hotel was listed on the National Register of Historic Places and the renovation preserved its historical integrity. They even repaired and preserved the sloping floor in the bar room.

The boat docked at the landing and we disembarked with our luggage. A friendly staff member picked us up in a golf cart and transported us through the woods and along a dirt road leading to a sight that took my breath away.

"It truly is the jewel of the forest," I gushed, "just like it says on their website." At the end of the road, surrounded by forest, the historic white clapboard hotel stood before us in all her splendor. Old-fashioned red awnings provided shade over the windows and the screened veranda.

We had obviously stepped back in time. You could feel it in the air, in the breeze that wafted through the towering pines. This was another world filled with stories from the past. Perhaps a ghost or two? Maybe even the ghost of Jonathan?

We checked into our room upstairs in the lodge and freshened up in the shared bathroom before heading out to explore. A black bear rug hung on one wall of the sitting room. Old white wicker chairs lined the veranda where guests could sit and enjoy a drink from the nearby bar before enjoying a dinner of fresh caught walleye in the dining room. Photos of old-timers who had owned or frequented the hotel were displayed on the rustic knotty pine walls.

While we were tempted to check out the bar and enjoy a cold beer, we decided to save that for later. We were anxious to hike around the premises and take in the magical Kettle Falls that bridged Canada and the United States. We climbed up onto the observation deck overlooking the falls that were roaring today due to recent rainfall. Cascades of water flowed over the dam, swirling through what looked like underwater kettles boiling beneath the surface of the lake. Plaques on the deck told the story of the French-Canadian voyageurs who once portaged around these falls.

After a fresh walleye dinner, we ventured into the bar and across the sloping floor beside the pool table. An antique victrola was displayed in one corner, and an old wooden bar dominated the room. Historic photos were mounted on the walls and behind the bar.

"Good evening," a friendly middle-aged man with a mustache greeted us from behind the bar. He was wiping down the bar before pouring a glass of wine for a guest at the far end.

"Good evening," we responded as we seated ourselves at the bar, busily taking in the history that surrounded us.

"What a fascinating place!" I said. "What must it have been like to have lived here, or stayed here, years ago?"

The bartender chuckled as he moved closer. "I could tell you all about that if you'd like. But first, my name is Mike." He extended his hand to each of us. A firm, warm handshake.

"Thomas and Angela." Thomas nodded. "Our first time here, and we're very much interested in the history of this place, the people who stayed here."

"Just so happens..." Mike leaned in. "That it was my grandfather, Robert Williams, who bought this place in 1918 for a thousand dollars and four barrels of whiskey. I pretty much grew up here summers and served as dam keeper and caretaker year-round for some years. My daughters were born here, in that little caretaker's cabin down by the lake."

"Amazing!" I chimed in. "Tell us more."

"First, can I get you something to drink?"

"Cabernet for me."

"Make that two."

Mike poured our wine and began to share stories about stills in the woods during bootlegging days. Gangsters smuggling booze in from Canada during prohibition. Some of the "ladies of the night" who frequented the place when the lumberjacks visited.

"With a history like that," I commented, "one would think there could perhaps be a ghost or two hanging around?"

"As a matter of fact, we have heard footsteps roaming the halls when we were the only ones in the building. One time, just before we were ready to close for the season, my mother was unable to sleep because of the racket going on downstairs in the bar. There were no guests and the bar had been closed up for the evening. She finally tiptoed down the stairs, through the veranda, and opened the door into the bar. Well, guess what she found?"

"What?" Thomas and I were both totally intrigued.

"Nothing. Nobody there. The music from the old victrola suddenly quit. She could smell cigar smoke, and several empty whiskey glasses cluttered the bar."

"Wow, that is spooky," I chimed in.

"So does anyone live out here, or on any of these islands, year-round?" Thomas asked.

"We close for the season these days, but there still are a few folks who live year-round on their little islands. We've gotten to know a number of these locals. They like to stop in now and then for a beer and to catch up on what's happening in the world."

"Interesting." I mustered up my courage to ask a few questions although I wasn't sure I really wanted the answers. "A friend of mine told me that he once knew an old man...well, he'd probably be close to ninety by now if he's still alive. She thought he'd had some connection to Kettle Falls and this area."

"Really? Do you know his name?"

"I believe it was Robert. Robert Andersen?" My heart began to pound in my chest.

"Hmm... a common name." He hesitated a few moments, frowning as if trying to remember something. "But there was a guy over on Rabbit Island by that name. At least that's what he used to call himself—until the last few years when the old codger decided to start calling himself Jonathan instead."

I almost dropped my glass. Thomas placed a steady hand on my leg, trying to calm me.

"Maybe that's him." Thomas took over. "What's he look like? What's he like?"

"Old guy, hunched over. Long scraggly gray beard. Big scar on his left cheek. He uses a cane these days, but still drives his old boat over every Friday night to have a few drinks at the bar, usually more than a few." Mike laughed, shaking his head.

"He barely spoke for years. Very secretive. Never told us anything about his life or who he was," Mike continued. "He seemed like an angry, sad man who was running from something. But now, ever since he changed his name to Jonathan, he's been talking. Telling crazy stories. Probably senile."

I managed to get the words out of my mouth. "What kind of stories?" I had to learn to put my emotions behind me and play this game.

Mike refilled our glasses, poured one for himself, and pulled a stool up on his side of the bar. "Mostly about witches, would you believe? He hates them and thinks they should all be burned at the stake. Stories about going down with a ship. Crazy stuff. Seems to be losing his mind. Nothing he says makes any sense." He shook his head as he took a sip of his wine.

"And he lives alone?" Thomas asked.

"Far as we know. But we really know very little about him. He must have ended up on Rabbit Island sometime around 1960? He settled into an old abandoned cabin there, still in pretty good shape at that time. We've never been there, or course. Don't think anyone else has either. But we have boated past and it looks like it's in really bad shape now. The old boat shed is falling down. Sections of the dock missing. Can't imagine what that old cabin looks like these days."

Janet Kay

"How does he survive the winters?" Thomas wanted to know.

"Beats me. They say he used to grow a garden. Probably shoots deer and rabbits for meat. Used to hear a chainsaw buzzing over there, like he was cutting up firewood. But as far as I know, nobody but him has set foot on that island for years. Doesn't seem like he has a friend in the world, but he seems to like it that way. He's a true hermit."

"Still..." Thomas was obviously intrigued. "An old guy like that could just freeze or starve to death out here with nobody around to check up on him."

That would be one kind of justice, I couldn't help thinking. I wasn't sure where Thomas was going with this.

"You're right about that," Mike replied. "Social Services in International Falls is aware of his situation and has tried to contact him to offer him senior housing or services over the winter. He tells them to go to hell. He tells them he has no relatives and to mind their own damn business."

"He owns this place on Rabbit Island?" Thomas asked.

"Guess so. The Park Service was suspicious of his claim to the island when they took over, so they checked it out. He did have a deed to the property. That's all I know."

"Do you think he'd be willing to talk with us?" I finally regained my ability to speak and interact. "I am fascinated with what it must be like to live on an island out here, alone. In fact, I'm thinking about including a character like this in a novel I'm working on."

Good move, I congratulated myself. This story had suddenly slipped into my mind and was certainly a good excuse to talk to this guy whom I was convinced had to be my wicked grandfather. A good excuse to try to get some evidence that could be used to destroy the rest of his pathetic life.

Besides, I was actually planning to write a novel someday... someday after the mysterious disappearance of my grandmother had been solved and justice served.

Thomas patted my leg, proud of me and my comeback.

"Interesting," Mike said. "I bet anything he'd love to talk your ear off. However, be prepared to hear lots of crazy stories. He should show up here tomorrow evening, in fact. Usually at six o'clock sharp."

194

Other guests began to arrive, taking seats at the bar. Some were playing pool. Others were playing tunes on an old jukebox. Mike excused himself to wait on his customers. It was time for Thomas and me to take our drinks out to a quieter place on the veranda.

"We did it, my lovely." He pulled me close as we settled together on a wicker settee. A cool breeze filtered in through the vine-covered screens. We had a big, and very important, day ahead of us tomorrow. We could do this—and we would!

Thank you, Angelique, I whispered silently as I curled up in Thomas's arms that night, a gentle breeze filtering through the lacy curtains. *Thank you for leading us to Jonathan.*

No response. I strained hard to open my mind, to let her in.

Are you there?

Still no response. My eyes began to fill with tears. Was she gone forever? Had she depleted all her earthly energy? How can I get her back?

"It's going to be all right, my lovely." Thomas pulled me close, tuning into my silent tears. "She'll be back. She knows what's happening. Remember how she always tells you that timing is everything? Spirits have a different concept of time."

How I loved this man, my soulmate. My other half.

CHAPTER FORTY-FOUR

"We can do this," I reminded myself once again as we strolled into the bar the next evening shortly before six o'clock. We ordered a drink and began chatting with Mike. Minutes passed. No Jonathan. I was getting nervous.

"He should be here shortly," Mike assured me, aware that I kept glancing at the clock on the wall over the bar.

"If he doesn't show up on a Friday, would anyone know or care or check on him?" I couldn't help asking. Even if my grandfather was a monster who deserved to die, it was hard to imagine anyone slipping away into death, into hell in his case, without anyone knowing or caring.

"Hmm...well, I guess we'd probably contact Social Services or the Sheriff's Department to do a welfare check. That is, if they dared to venture onto his property without getting shot. The old man has confronted others with his gun when they got too close to his property. Scares the hell out of tourists who are curious about what looks like an abandoned shack on a remote island that they'd like to explore."

Still no Jonathan. It was half past six.

Finally, we heard a golf cart pulling up outside the hotel. Thomas and I had settled into a booth, making room for other guests at the bar. We held our breath, our eyes focused on the entrance to the bar. Waiting.

An elderly couple entered and seated themselves in another booth. Where was Jonathan? We waited impatiently. Finally, another figure hobbled into the room. An elderly man, bent over, using a cane. A scraggly gray beard, just as Mike had described. A faded, dirty jean jacket with holes at the elbows. As he slowly limped past us on his way to the bar, the scar on his left cheek was visible.

It was hard to wrap my head around the fact that this fragile, elderly man was undoubtedly my evil grandfather, the man who had murdered my grandmother. My head began to spin as I tried to control my conflicted emotions. Hatred. Anger. Remorse. Pity. I felt sick to my stomach.

"Are you okay?" Thomas whispered. "We don't have to do this, you know. We can leave right now."

I took a few deep breaths. It was now or never. We'd come so far. I simply had to regain control of myself. Suddenly a chilling but comforting presence swept through me, conveying a sense of strength and peace. Angelique! Then she disappeared...but I was back on track.

"Jonathan!" Mike called out as the old codger pulled himself up onto a bar stool. "The usual?"

"Yup, Jack Daniels, triple," a shaky voice replied.

"Here, or out at your usual spot?" Mike asked.

"Out there. Too damn much noise in here." He plunked a handful of change down on the bar.

Where was out there? What was he talking about?

"We can bring it out to you if you want to go have a seat. Veranda or outside at the picnic table?"

"Picnic table. Too damn many people in here."

We watched Mike talk quietly to him, but couldn't hear what he was saying. Mike pointed at us and Jonathan turned to gaze our way. Chills ran up and down my spine. I could clearly see a resemblance to my mother—the shape of his nose, a dimple on his chin. He finally looked back at Mike and nodded in agreement. Had he just consented to visiting with us, to answering a few questions to help me write my novel?

Then the old man carefully climbed down off his bar stool, steadied himself with his cane and slowly walked around the sloping floor, past the pool table, down the veranda and out the door.

Mike gave us a thumbs up and a friendly grin, gesturing for Thomas to come over to the bar where he handed over a big glass of Jack Daniels for us to deliver to Jonathan who was waiting for us outside.

We refilled our wine glasses, in need of all the reinforcement we could muster up before meeting my grandfather. My grandfather? I had to remove that thought from my mind fast. I could not think of him as my grandfather or as the devil who had murdered my grandmother. I had to block these images from my mind or I'd ruin everything.

I donned a pair of dark sunglasses that would hopefully help to hide any tears or any expressions that I did not want anyone to see. We

197

plastered friendly smiles upon our faces and walked to the picnic table where Jonathan was seated, nervously glancing around.

"Jonathan?" Thomas set the tall glass of whiskey on the picnic table before the old man, and then extended his hand to shake.

"Yup." He grunted as he picked up the glass with a trembling hand and took a few big gulps.

"I'm Thomas and this is my wife, Angela." He sat down across from Jonathan and nodded at me to join him.

His wife? I loved that. Not sure why he'd introduced me that way but it didn't matter. Maybe it would lead Jonathan to thinking about his own wife.

"My wife here is writing a novel about an older man who lives on an island out here on Rainy Lake and Mike thought you might be able to tell us what it's like, how you ended up choosing a place like this to live."

Jonathan's pale cloudy eyes seemed to twitch as he tried to focus on the two of us. As if he was trying to decide if he should talk to us or not.

"Don't worry." I forced myself to smile. "It's fiction. I won't use your name. But I am curious why people, you or others, decide to live out here on an island so far away from civilization?"

After a few more swigs of his whiskey, the old man seemed to loosen up. He chuckled. "Maybe because I don't like people, ya know. I mean, people are bad enough. But witches? Did you know that this world is full of witches?"

"No, I didn't."

His eyes gleamed as he grinned a toothless smile. He'd probably never been to a dentist in his life.

"Oh, the stories I can tell you!" He chuckled. "But first, I think I need another Jack Daniels." He handed his empty glass across the table to Thomas who quickly grabbed it and headed for the bar, after a questioning glance at me to be sure I was okay alone with this guy. I nodded.

"Actually, I am fascinated with witches, although a little scared of them? How do you know if someone is a witch? Have you ever known a real witch?"

"Witches know things they sure as hell shouldn't know before they even happen. They talk to trees and spirits that aren't there. They are evil. They hurt people, and they cast spells on others to drive them crazy. Crazy enough to do bad things sometimes..."

He shook his head as if unable or unwilling to continue. I waited. We were sitting in silence when Thomas returned, a frown and questioning look upon his face. I nodded to assure him that everything was all right.

We waited patiently while Jonathan took a few gulps of his second drink. He had a faraway look in his eyes as he fidgeted with his wrinkled hands. Maybe he was struggling with flashbacks from his life, trying to decide whether or not he should reveal more information. Maybe I needed to try to reassure him.

"I'm hoping to find someone who has actually had some experiences with a witch. I'd like to know what it was like, if it hurt them in any way..."

Jonathan finally came back to the present. "Look no further." He slammed his glass down on the table, a fierce look spreading across his face. "My fuckin' mother was a witch! Look what she did to me!" He pointed at the long scar on his left cheek. "She cut me. She whipped me. She threw me out of the shack we lived in when I was only thirteen years old."

Stunned, I managed to say, "Oh, I'm so sorry. And your father?"

"What father? I never knew my father. The fuckin' witch had guy after guy in and out of the place. Guys that did bad things to me when I was little. She was evil."

Thomas tried to change the subject, to focus on anything but my grandfather's horrendous past. "But at least you're safe now, right?"

I was horrified, wondering if what Jonathan said was true. Or was it just a figment of his imagination? A sign of dementia?

"Oh yeah...safe as hell." Jonathan relaxed a bit, staring into the distance as he took another gulp of his whiskey.

I simply had to follow up. "Can I ask what you did after you were kicked out of your home as a young boy?"

"Hit the streets like a homeless bum for a while. Got a few jobs. Moved into Grand Marais and made the biggest mistake of my life." He shook his head.

"And what was that?"

"I married a gal I fell in love with. We even had a baby together." He wiped a tear from his eye before continuing. "Yup, my little Emily. God, I miss her. Anyway, my wife turned out to be a witch, just like my mother. You see, my mother kept coming back from the grave, haunting my wife, turning her into an evil witch just like her. Making her do bad things. My wife even stole my little girl before I had time to snatch her away and save her from the evil spirits of my mother and my wife. Little Emily is gone. I never could find her."

He wiped another tear from his eye as he took another big gulp of his whiskey, staring into the starry night, almost as if he'd forgotten we were there at the table with him.

"You see, there's nothing ya can do to save a witch like her. Sometimes ya just gotta do what ya gotta do, even if you still love her. And I did, still do, love my witch of a wife. It's been a while since I've seen her though."

"Anyway..." He suddenly refocused on us as if he remembered he had company. "Do you know what you're supposed to do with witches like them?"

"What?" I managed to squeak out a response.

"Burn them at the stake like they did in the old days. That's what they deserve. Wicked witch women are all alike. Ya gotta get rid of them before they multiply and spread evil throughout the world."

I shook my head, unable to respond, glancing at Thomas for some help.

"I get that," Thomas finally replied, nodding in agreement. "How about that evil wife of yours? Do you need any help taking care of her?"

I almost fainted but managed to hold it together. What in the world was Thomas doing? What was he thinking?

Jonathan began to laugh hysterically, his eyes on fire. "I already took care of that bitch, my friends. Long ago. She's gone, gone to hell or wherever evil witches spend eternity. But thanks for offering."

He drained his glass of whiskey as we sat in silence, stunned. Finally, he leaned in towards us with an odd gleam in his eyes. "Yeah, she thought she was so smart. Ran away, thinkin' I couldn't find her. But I did. I got the last laugh." He chuckled.

"How did you find her?" Thomas dared to ask.

"She stole my truck and ditched it in the woods near the ferry landing. Took the license plate off and threw it into the woods. Well, I got a call one day from the town. They were clearing land there to widen the road or something. Found my license plate and tracked me down. Wanted me to move the old truck."

"But how did you find your wife then?" Thomas asked.

Jonathan straightened up as if he was proud of himself. "I ain't no fool. The truck was not far from the marina so I took a photo of my wife over there and asked around. Lots of fishermen there. They all know each other and everyone's business. Well, one guy recognized her. Told me that she'd been there a few weeks or so ago looking for a ride out to Isle Royale, somewhere around Rock Harbor. His friend, Steven, who had a place nearby on Tobin Harbor gave her a lift."

Timing was everything all right. For good—or for bad. If only the town hadn't been working on that road. If only they hadn't found that license plate and contacted him. If only that fisherman had not recognized her photo. If only...

It was all Thomas and I could do to hold it together at that point. We had a confession. We'd accomplished our mission. But still...we were horrified. Devastated.

"Cheers and good riddance to all the witches in our lives!" Jonathan raised his empty glass of whiskey to toast us. His eyes were glassy. He was obviously drunk. "Well, it's getting dark out there. Guess it's time for me to head home." He tried to get up.

"Just one more question?" I had to ask.

He slumped back down on the bench. "Sure."

"How did you end up out here on Rabbit Island?"

"Long story," he mumbled. "Ya see, I was lookin' for a place for me and Emily to live, once I got rid of her mother. Just happened that an old guy on my ship owned Rabbit Island and wanted to get rid of it. Guess he felt sorry for me once he knew all about my wife. So, he deeded it to me. I was supposed to pay him back later. But...he went down with our ship. He and all of the others. Except me. You see," he leaned in, an evil gleam in his eyes. "I jumped ship the day before it went down. Yup, that's what I did!"

He tried to stand but fell to the ground. "What the hell?" he sputtered. "Call for the damned golf cart so they can get me to my boat!"

The old buzzard was in no condition to drive his boat across the lake to his island. That was for sure. The wind was picking up, waves crashing against the shoreline as a sliver of a moon tried to peek through the clouds.

While Thomas proceeded to pick him up off the ground and settle him back on the bench, I went into the bar to find Mike and ask him what to do. Maybe we should have helped him into his boat so he could get out there on the wild waves, crash his boat into one of the rocky outcroppings and drown. Maybe that's what he deserved. Still...a tiny part of me had a sliver of empathy for the grandfather who had survived such a brutal upbringing. If that was even true.

"Drunk again?" Mike frowned as he followed me out to the picnic table in front of the hotel. I removed my sunglasses to wipe away a few tears and gathered a hand full of napkins off the bar before I left.

"All right, Jonathan," Mike announced firmly. "You're not going anyplace tonight, once again. I'll put you up in the room by the fish house until morning."

"Bullshit." The old man started to argue before his eyes began to close and he slumped back down on the picnic table. Mike summoned a few of his staff members and a golf cart to transport Jonathan to a place where he could sleep it off for the night.

As they loaded him into the golf cart, Jonathan looked back at me, a shocked expression upon his face. "Those eyes...your eyes..." He shook his head. It can't be! Angelique, is that you? You came back to me?"

Once again, I could barely speak. Standing on the lawn beneath the light emanating from the hotel, without my sunglasses, my unusual green eyes had been visible to my grandfather. He had recognized the similarity. He still remembered Angelique's eyes after all those years.

Then they were gone.

I retrieved his whiskey glass and placed it in the napkins, being careful not to touch the glass myself. More DNA evidence to turn over to the authorities investigating Angelique's mysterious death. Hopefully this would establish the identity of the murderer.

I should have been thrilled that we'd pretty much solved this case, but conflicting emotions surged through me.

My grandfather was certainly not the person I thought he was. He wasn't the hero who went down with his ship. He was a murderer! He was insane!

But he was also, perhaps, a victim of a horrific childhood.

CHAPTER FORTY-FIVE

After a sleepless night trying to digest what had happened, Thomas and I stumbled into the dining room for breakfast early the next morning. We had a few more questions for Jonathan and were hoping to catch him before he left.

The sun was just creeping over the horizon as we arrived at the fish house where we'd been told Jonathan should be sleeping it off. Thomas knocked on the door of a room adjacent to the fish house. No response.

"Jonathan?" he called out. Again, no response.

He tried the door. It was unlocked so he slowly opened it. "It's Thomas. Just checking up on you," he announced himself.

Still no response. Flipping a light switch, we entered. It was a tiny room dominated by a cot with a few rumpled blankets. That was all. No sign of Jonathan. We hurried down towards the lake where his boat had been tied at the dock.

"Good morning," an approaching figure called out. It was Mike who had already been down to the dock. He stopped to chat with us a moment. I could tell he had some questions for us. "If you're looking for Jonathan, he's gone."

Hie eyes searched mine. "Something tells me that you know more about this guy than you're letting on. Whatever it is, I need to know. It may help us understand what the hell is going on."

Thomas and I exchanged glances. He nodded. It was time to tell the rest of the story.

"We do," I finally responded. "Yes, I'm writing a novel and want to learn more about life out here on these islands. But...well, I was hesitant to say too much right off. It's just that... if I was wrong in my suspicions, it would all sound so stupid."

"Nothing's stupid." Mike smiled gently. "You wouldn't believe the stories I've been told."

I instinctively knew we could trust this man. "After talking with Jonathan last night, my suspicions were confirmed. Jonathan is my grandfather, for good or bad. He went missing sixty-six years ago, and nobody had a clue if he was dead or alive. Or where he could be hiding out. Something, some strange force, led us here to Kettle Falls as if we were meant to find him while he was still alive."

"Wow," Mike exclaimed. "Congratulations on a job well done. I hope this brings you some kind of closure or relief or...I don't know. I can only imagine."

"I'm still in shock," I confessed. "I'm not sure what this means. There's a lot of bad blood running through my family so my emotions are conflicted. I don't know what the future brings, if anything. Not yet."

"I get it," Mike agreed. "Maybe we all have some skeletons in our closet."

Skeletons? He had no idea how closely he had hit home. My home, my life. But I wasn't about to go that far. Not yet. Not until the official investigation had confirmed all of this.

Thomas jumped in again. He had a knack for doing so anytime I was too stressed to proceed with a conversation. "We'd actually like to drive by this Rabbit Island if you have a boat for rent and directions to get there."

"I have a boat available tomorrow if that works for you? And I'll give you a map to get there. It's not that far or that hard to find. But be careful not to get too close. He tends to fire at anyone within shooting range. Are you familiar with boats?"

Thomas grinned. "Oh yeah, I happen to be a licensed charter boat captain and fishing guide on Lake Superior, out of Grand Marais."

"That's awesome. I'd love to get out there someday. Maybe we can stay in touch."

"Absolutely."

With that, Mike headed back to the hotel. Thomas and I decided to hike around the trails and enjoy a leisurely day. Maybe fit in a badly needed nap.

After dinner at a little table on the veranda, we hiked down to the observation deck and settled on a bench overlooking the falls. The swirling motion of the root beer-colored kettles was mesmerizing and comforting. It was a beautiful evening—until we heard what sounded like a loud blast from a gun echoing across the lake.

"What the hell?" Thomas grabbed me, pulling us both down upon the bench. After a few minutes, he cautiously sat upright. Whatever it was, the danger seemed to have passed. No more gunfire. Just one shot.

We trekked back to the hotel where other guests were also buzzing about having heard a loud gunshot nearby. Some had been out on the lake fishing and immediately headed back to the hotel. As we all gathered on the veranda, people speculated about the gunfire. Was someone hunting out of season? Was there a problem?

Mike was there within minutes, assuring guests that there was no imminent danger. He had already contacted the Sheriff's Department and they would begin an investigation. In the meantime, he suggested we all remain on the premises and off the lake.

We settled back on the veranda with the other guests. As we climbed up the stairs to our room later, ready to get a good night's sleep before our boat trip tomorrow, we overheard Mike on the phone in the office.

"No, Sheriff, we have no idea what happened. Sure, that sounds good. Tomorrow morning?"

"Something's up. Something's not right." Thomas gripped my hand tightly. A sense of dread seeped through my bones.

"Yes," Mike continued. "I'm on my way over there to see if I can help identify the body."

"Oh my God." I stumbled on the stairs. "A body?" I mumbled. "It can't be him...can it?"

CHAPTER FORTY-SIX

A loud knock on the door woke us early the next morning. Thomas climbed out of bed to answer. "Who is it?"

"It's Mike," a weary voice answered. Thomas opened the door to let him in as I huddled beneath the coverlet.

"Sorry to wake you, but we have a problem." Mike shook his head sadly. He was disheveled and looked as if he'd been up all night.

I knew instantly what had happened. I could feel it. Jonathan was dead! Dead from the gunshot we'd heard last night. "Oh my God," I cried out. "Jonathan?"

Mike was too exhausted to show any surprise at my reaction. "I'm afraid so. A fisherman found a boat floating not far from Rabbit Island. Didn't think there was anyone in the boat—until he got closer and found a body, blood all over, and a bullet wound to the head."

"Oh my God" was all I could utter as Thomas sat down beside me on the bed and pulled me into his arms.

"You're sure it's Jonathan?" Thomas asked.

"I am. I saw him..." he looked down at the floor. Saw his boat. The sheriff asked me to come out and identify the body. He knew that Jonathan was one of our regulars."

"What happened?"

"The sheriff thinks it was suicide based on the evidence in the boat. He's on his way over and wants to talk with you and anyone else who may have any knowledge at all about Jonathan. Can you come down shortly?"

Mike excused himself, expressing his condolences. "I'm really sorry. It's like you finally found him...and now he's gone."

And now he's gone." I shuddered.

Of course, Mike didn't know the whole story. As Thomas and I got dressed, brushed our teeth, and I ran a comb through my hair, I struggled with how much we should tell the sheriff. Maybe it no longer mattered. Jonathan was dead.

Why, dear God? Why now? My head was reeling, alternating between waves of grief, shock, anger, sadness, and yet, a sense of justice. Did that make any sense?

How would Angelique feel? Does she know? And how will my mother react to this? I shuttered, just thinking about sharing this news with her.

Sheriff Dawson, a big and imposing middle-aged man with a bushy head of gray hair, sat on the sofa beneath the bearskin hanging on the wall. He got up as we descended the stairs and extended his hand to each of us.

"Sheriff Dawson," he introduced himself. "Just a few questions for you folks." He got right down to business. "Let's find a private place to talk." He led us to the empty bar which was not yet open for the day and settled his large frame in one of the booths. Thomas and I sat across from him.

"I understand you know this man, this Jonathan Edwards? That he is actually your long-lost grandfather?" He directed his questions at me, looking me directly in the eyes. "Seems no one here knows much about him. Where he came from. Nothing. Can you fill me in?"

I took a deep breath and decided it made no sense to withhold anything, except any references to ghosts or Angelique's spirit guiding us here. That could hurt my credibility. But it was time to let him know that there was an investigation going on back in Michigan related to the skeletal remains of Jonathan's wife who had been murdered long ago.

The sheriff's eyes widened with shock and excitement. There was a crime here to solve, something big that he was now a part of. Then he erased all emotions from his face and began firing questions at us. Why had we come out to Kettle Falls? What happened last night when we met Jonathan? What did we talk about? What was our impression of him? Did we think he could have murdered his wife, my grandmother? We tried to answer his questions to the best of our abilities.

Thomas had a few questions for him also. Was he sure it was suicide? Pretty sure, the sheriff replied, although an autopsy would be done to confirm this.

"What happens to the body now?" I asked.

"Well..." He hesitated a moment. "After the autopsy is done, it goes to the next of kin for burial or whatever. That would be your mother, I believe, his daughter. Or you?"

"I...I don't know. Perhaps," I mumbled. That was crazy if it was my job to bury the man who had killed my grandmother! But I could not lay this responsibility on my poor mother. I didn't even know how or when I should tell her about this. I had yet to claim my grandmother's remains.

Sheriff Dawson thanked us, wrote down our contact information and excused himself. He would be in touch.

"You did well, my lovely," Thomas put his arm around me. "But I think we could use some fresh air. We have a boat waiting, you know. Let's go for a cruise."

"Yes." I grabbed his hand as we headed down the trail to the boat landing where our rental was waiting for us. "I think we need to get out there on the lake to try to clear our heads and make some sense of this."

"We do. Are you all right?" He gazed intently into my eyes, our eyes merging. A connection that only soulmates can truly understand. He knew I wasn't really all right.

"I will be, with you by my side, Thomas. I don't know how I ever would have gotten through this without you. I love you so much." My tears began to fall as he pulled me close and rocked me gently.

A red cardinal flew overhead and landed in a nearby pine tree. A sign from the other side? From Jonathan? Or from Angelique? Red cardinals were known to appear when departed loved ones were trying to communicate with us, trying to help us overcome grief. I wanted to believe that.

I remembered the ceramic statue of a red cardinal that I'd found in my cabin when I first arrived. It had been sitting on the antique dresser in my bedroom where it remained to this day. I liked to believe that it had once belonged to Angelique, that it was a sign that she was there with me.

"I'm ready. Let's go." I dried my tears and attempted a smile. "We need to head out to Rabbit Island first. It's important."

"What?" Thomas stopped along the trail, a puzzled expression upon his face. "I thought you needed a break..."

"Something just came to me, telling me we have to go there. Now."

"Well, okay. Mike did give me directions yesterday before, well, before all of this."

"Before my grandfather committed suicide. We can say it. We can deal with it, no matter what we may find. Right?"

"Right." He grinned that irresistible grin. "Together, we can do anything."

It felt so refreshing to get out there on Rainy Lake, taking in the pristine beauty of the wilderness as the wind whipped our hair and sunlight danced upon the waves. Just being in and connecting with nature was always therapeutic for me. My problems seemed to drift away on the crest of the waves, or at least become more manageable.

Thomas skillfully navigated around the buoys, the falls and rocky islands at a good rate of speed before he slowed down and motored toward a small island. As we got closer, I saw a dilapidated old wooden dock, some sections loose and floating or scattered along the shoreline.

"Rabbit Island," Thomas announced as he found a safe place to tie up. We carefully climbed over the halfway stable sections of the dock and onto a rocky shoreline. Several old moss-covered structures came into view, partially collapsed, still housing an assortment of old rusted gas cans and ancient boat motors.

The place looked abandoned. Fallen tree limbs and debris littered a trail leading to a small log cabin nearby. It was almost hidden within a forest of massive pine trees that threatened to take over the place.

As we hiked to the cabin, we wondered how an old man like Jonathan had been able to walk these trails with his cane much less drive his old boat. Or how he'd been able to live out here alone, surviving the harsh winters and isolation. But that no longer mattered. He would not be doing that anymore.

An old stone fireplace covered one side of the tilting cabin. Tree limbs hung over a faded tarp covering the roof and several windows were boarded up. Pieces of glass were scattered in the brush and debris surrounding the cabin. Weeds and vines crept up over a few rotting stairs leading to a heavy door that stood partially ajar.

We looked around carefully to be sure we didn't have any company. Thomas had his pistol, just in case we encountered any problems from anyone who had known Jonathan or were nosing around on his property. But all was silent, no trace of anyone around. Thomas carefully opened the door and entered, giving me an "all clear" sign to follow.

The one-room cabin consisted of a tiny kitchen with a table and two wobbly chairs, an ancient stove and mini-refrigerator. A lumpy unmade bed was on the opposite wall, and a well-worn sagging sofa sat before an old stone fireplace. Piles of books and magazines were strewn around the room along with dirty clothes. It looked like the place had not been cleaned or the rotting floor boards swept in years. A few dead mice in various stages of decay were scattered about and I heard a squirrel or some kind of critter running around above the ceiling.

"How could anyone live like this?" It was beyond disgusting.

Thomas quietly called me over to the table which was covered with an assortment of items—an ammunition box, hammer, miscellaneous papers, a dirty plate with leftover food (Jonathan's last meal?), and an empty bottle of Jack Daniels. "Look at this."

Thomas was held something in his hand which he handed to me solemnly. An old picture in an antique frame. A young couple with a baby. The man, with a warm smile on his face, had his arm around the woman who was gazing up at him lovingly. He held the baby in his arms while the woman held her tiny hand. They looked like they had once been a happy family. What had happened?

Feeling faint, I slunk down onto a rickety chair. Angelique, Jonathan, and Emily. There was no doubt in my mind. "And he saved this photo?"

"It was on the table in front of his dinner plate, as if he was sharing his last meal with them."

Thomas searched through the pile of papers on the table while I stared at the photo, rubbing my finger across the glass as if trying to connect with what once was. How can one's life change so drastically? How can a loving family end up like this? What happened?

It was Thomas's turn to drop into the chair opposite mine, a shocked expression upon his face. In his hand he held a sealed envelope, addressed in shaky handwriting, to Angelique! He gave it to me.

I summoned the courage to open it as Thomas came to stand behind me, his hand on my shoulder. I began to read out loud.

My dearest Angelique,

So, you found me. You came back to me from beyond the grave. I always knew you would. And I knew it was you when I saw those eyes of yours last night at Kettle Falls. While I was delighted to see you after all these years, I can't trust a witch like you. I know what you're going to do. I know you're going to turn me in. But you know what? I will have the last laugh because I won't be here when they come knocking on my door.

Do you know where I'll be? I will be in another world – probably in hell – maybe with you once again. But that's okay if that's what it takes to be with you. You see, I never stopped loving you, even if you are a witch. And I need you to know that I'm sorry for what happened. But you really can't blame me. It wasn't me who killed you, Angelique. It was those voices in my head – especially my mother's. You see, she made me do it. It's all her fault. She was a witch – just like you. But she was the mother of all witches – the devil herself.

If you get this letter someday, in this world or another, I ask two things of you. Forgive me, please. Still, I will never forgive you for taking my little Emily away from me. Tell her that I will always love her, wherever she is.

Time to go. Time to trade my hell on earth for the other one out there somewhere. Guess that's where I belong even if all of this really wasn't my fault. Time to pull the trigger and end my life the same way yours ended. I don't want no funeral. Nothing. Just throw my ashes into Lake Superior where I probably should have gone down with my ship years ago.

Forever yours, Jonathan

Neither of us could speak when we finished reading his letter. His suicide note included a confession of murdering Angelique, just what we needed for the investigation into her death. But did it matter anymore? There would be no justice now that he was gone.

Yet he had also proclaimed his undying love for her and Emily. It made no sense.

Thomas finally broke the silence. "Those voices in his head?"

"I know. Sounds like he was schizophrenic! But even if he was, that's still no excuse for murdering your own wife!"

Once again, my tears began to fall as another harsh reality invaded my consciousness. "It's all my fault, Thomas. It was my eyes that pushed him over the edge. Just because I have her green eyes."

"Beautiful eyes." He pulled me up off my chair and into his arms. "Maybe it was your eyes that resulted in justice for Angelique. Think about that. Maybe it was your eyes that will soon close the investigation and give your mother the closure she needs."

"Thank you," I whispered as my lips met his.

We were suddenly startled from our embrace when we heard sounds approaching through the woods. We knew we really shouldn't be here. Maybe it was the someone from the Sheriff's Department. They could be checking out the place where a suicide victim had lived. Or was it someone else lurking in the shadows?

Thomas drew his pistol, told me to get down beneath the table, and cautiously skirted along the wall toward the door. He slowly opened the door and nosed his way out, trying to hide in the brush along the trail. As he did so, I flashed back to our past life together in Virginia City, Montana when he was my gun-slinging cowboy—until he was murdered.

"False alarm!" Thomas whooped loudly. "Come on out, Angela. Let's go. It's only a moose crashing through the brush!"

I tucked Jonathan's letter into my backpack and headed out to join Thomas. He stood there mesmerized as a large bull moose stood nearby, watching us. The black pupils of the moose's bulging eyes were highlighted with golden irises that glowed eerily. The moose stared at us, showing no fear, acting as if he belonged here. Maybe he had been my grandfather's only friend.

A chill swept through me. Had my grandfather returned to his island, his home, manifesting himself as a moose? Was he here to bid Rabbit Island goodbye...and was he also trying to reach out to me? Or perhaps still searching for Angelique and Emily?

We made our way back to the boat, leaving the island to the moose...and Jonathan's ghost.

...

An autopsy confirmed that Jonathan died by suicide. We provided the information we had about his birth date, birth place, and the names of his deceased wife and daughter.

What do to with the remains of his body? We did not wish to see my grandfather's body, but finally agreed to take responsibility for having him cremated at the closest funeral home in International Falls. We'd stop there to pick up the urn of his ashes after we left Kettle Falls.

We decided to honor Jonathan's wishes to have his ashes cast into the depths of Lake Superior later, maybe in a few weeks when we were ready to do so. After I broke the news to my mother. We could take Thomas's boat out onto the big lake at sunset, we decided, probably just the two of us, unless my mother decided to come along once she'd had time to digest all of this.

As we left Kettle Falls, Mike found us and asked about any burial plans. He said he felt like he was one of the few people who had any connection at all with Jonathan. He'd seen him coming and going at the hotel since he was a young boy. He told us that he'd be honored to be included in the burial of his ashes in Lake Superior. Of course, he didn't know the whole story. But did that matter anymore?

CHAPTER FORTY-SEVEN

Ꮝ called my mother to arrange a visit several days after we returned from our Kettle Falls trip, after the forensic analyst in Michigan contacted us to let us know that the mystery was solved. The DNA analysis revealed a match between DNA from Jonathan's body and incriminating evidence found on clothing remnants and remains of Angelique's skeleton. Jonathan had murdered Angelique. Case closed. It would now become an official record.

I dreaded telling my mother, but she needed to know. She needed closure. Hopefully she would finally find that once she'd had time to recover and digest this horrific information.

After I arrived, I suggested we settle in the library with a cup of coffee and some of Beth's delicious homemade blueberry scones.

Mother loved this room, the place where her adopted father spent many hours working at his massive mahogany desk. She'd told me often that he had always made time for his little girl to climb up on his lap. He'd taught her to love reading books from his vast collection housed on shelves lining the walls of the library. I knew she visited this room when she was seeking comfort. That's why I'd suggested we sit here while I updated her on what I'd learned.

I did my best to be gentle, not to upset her. But there was no good way to tell your mother that her father had killed her mother, hid out on a wilderness island for over sixty years, and then committed suicide right after we found him and got his confession.

"He killed my mother?" she shrieked, shaking her head from side to side, her eyes wide open as she frantically gazed around the library where we were seated together on the antique loveseat before a cozy fire in the fireplace.

She collapsed against the cushions of the sofa and began to sob as I held her in my arms, stroking her back. My tears also began to fall.

Mother finally collected herself and erupted in a fury. "How could he? Mentally ill or not, he killed my mother! And he has the nerve to kill himself so he never gets the punishment he deserves? You know what he deserves? He deserves to go to hell! And my poor mother...she never got the justice she deserves. How could he?"

"It's going to be okay," I tried to assure her. "You needed to know the truth. We found the truth, for Angelique's sake, and for yours. Time will help us to heal, Mother. At least we know he's going to hell, right? Maybe that's the justice we seek..."

She got up and began to pace back and forth. I called Beth, who was standing by in another room in case I needed her help. "Beth, would you please bring us a bottle of cabernet?"

Beth came in with a silver platter on which she balanced two wine glasses, a bottle of wine, and a plate of cheese and crackers. She had tears in her own eyes. We could never have asked for a better and more compassionate companion—one who had become a dear friend to my mother over the years.

"I'm so sorry, Emily." Beth gave her a big hug. "I'm here for you. Anything I can do, let me know."

"Thanks, Beth," she attempted a weak smile before taking a sip of the glass of wine I'd just poured for her.

"Let's try to relax, if that's possible," I told her gently. "Angelique loved you dearly and would not want you stressed out. She wanted you to know how much she loved you, that she would have done anything to come back for you, if she was alive."

"That means the world to me. But I'm still heartbroken. And my father?" She shook her head. "Is it wrong to hate the father I'm supposed to love? But he must have hated us both to do what he did. How could he? And why would he do such a thing?"

With that, I thought it was time to produce Jonathan's suicide letter. I hesitantly took it out of my purse.

"What's that?" She tensed up.

"I have a suicide note from your father. It's up to you if you want to read it. It may help you to understand a few things about him and his frame of mind. His obvious insanity."

She took a deep breath, and asked me to read it. She sat in silence as if trying to sort through her conflicting emotions.

"He still loved my mother, despite the fact that he killed her? And he wanted me to know that he would always love me? And…and he was planning to take me out to that island to live with him? That makes no sense. I don't understand."

"Of course it makes no sense to us. We need to understand that he was insane, probably schizophrenic. He was hearing voices, including that of his mother whom he told us horrific stories about." I went on to tell her more details about the one and only conversation I'd ever have with the complicated man who was my grandfather.

It was an exhausting evening and Mother was ready for bed. I tucked her in for the night in her bedroom just beyond the library.

Then I retreated to the library, re-stoked the fire, shut off the lights and settled back onto the loveseat. After staring at the dancing flames in the fireplace for a while, I decided to spend the night here instead of going to my bedroom upstairs. Just in case Mother awoke or had nightmares and wanted me. I went up to grab my pillow and a blanket and then came back down to the library for the night.

"Mommy!" I heard my mother's voice call out sometime in the middle of the night. "Oh, Mommy, it's you! You've come back to me!"

She sounded thrilled, not at all fearful. Her dream appeared to be comforting her instead of terrifying her. I listened carefully in case I needed to intervene. But there was nothing more. I fell back asleep.

...

I awoke the next morning to the smell of coffee brewing and bacon frying. Trying not to wake Mother, I tiptoed upstairs to change clothes and clean up a little before going to the kitchen where Beth was making our breakfast.

Surprisingly, I found my mother already sitting at the table sipping her tea and looking so much better than she had last night. She even had a smile on her face.

"Well, good morning, sunshine," she greeted me. "Let's enjoy our breakfast. And then…" She leaned in dramatically. "Let's take a walk out to the gazebo. I have some exciting news to tell you."

Interesting, I thought as I began to eat. "Did you know that you had a dream last night about your mother, I think?"

She smiled, her eyes radiating a sense of peacefulness. "It was more than a dream. That's what I want you to know."

So, we headed down to the gazebo, one of her favorite places. Once we were settled in the wicker rockers, she took a deep breath and began.

"You aren't going to believe this, Angela, but my mother was here last night! It was not just a dream! She came to see me and told me she loved me. I could feel her arms around me. Does that sound crazy?"

I breathed a huge sigh of relief. So, Angelique had come back, recharged and ready to be a part of our lives again...at least for a little while? At least until her business on earth is finished and she is ready to move on into the spirit world.

"Not at all," I assured her. "I'm so happy she finally found her way to you. I'm sure she waited until the time was right. I was afraid she'd already moved on. But she apparently wasn't ready to leave until she could come to you, Mother."

"She was here all right." My mother's eyes glowed with a mixture of happiness and delayed grief.

"You do feel much better after that, don't you?"

"I do. But I'm a little puzzled also. About some of the messages she sent me last night."

"What do you mean?"

"Well, she put some strange ideas into my head, some things she wanted me to think about. She almost seemed to have some sympathy for my evil father, as crazy as that sounds after what he did to her. She called him a 'tortured and tormented soul'—her words exactly. Something about him having already completed a life sentence in his private hell on earth. She told me that his soul has been set free from the insanity that haunted him here on earth. And that he would be held liable for his sins but would learn to be a better person and help others someday in the future. In another lifetime, I guess?"

"Wow, that's a lot to process," was all I could say in response.

"To top it all off, she told me to remember that forgiving others is one of the greatest gifts you can give yourself. It helps you heal and sets you free instead of wallowing in negative emotions."

"But how on earth can you forgive someone who murdered one of your loved ones?"

"That's it! You asked 'how on earth?' Well, maybe she was speaking from the perspective of someone who has been enlightened. Someone who has learned things in heaven that we humans don't quite understand."

"You amaze me, Mother." I patted her hand.

"It's not me, Angela. It's what Angelique put into my head."

"I think we need a little time to think this through. If Angelique actually feels we should forgive him, maybe we need to at least consider doing that...someday, perhaps. I'm certainly not ready yet. But for now, I have an urn of ashes that I really don't like sitting in my cabin."

"Didn't he ask that his ashes be scattered on Lake Superior?"

"He did. My friend Thomas...the one I told you about? Well, we are thinking of taking a boat ride and dumping them out there someplace, if that's okay with you? I was planning on tossing the urn into the lake and uttering a few cuss words, telling him to go to hell where he belongs."

Mother laughed. "I'm also tempted to do that, but maybe that's not what Angelique would want us to do? Maybe we can sprinkle his ashes in the lake and let them gently float away on the waves. We can maybe even wish him a safe journey along the Path of Souls to the other side of life. I think that's what she would want us to do."

"Did you say 'we'?"

"I did. I want to be there. I can handle this. After my mother's visit last night, I think I can handle most anything."

"You are amazing, Mother. So strong. So insightful, and even forgiving." I gained a new respect for the mother I really hadn't know very well in the past—not until some of our family secrets had come bubbling to the surface of our lives.

...

Thomas, Mother, and I decided to wait at least a few more weeks before giving Jonathan his burial at sea—a little more time to process all of this. But summer was already slipping away and we didn't want to wait too long. Lake Superior could be quite unpredictable in the fall. Once we settled on a date, we invited Sabrina in appreciation for all she'd done to help us solve this mystery. We also invited Mike from Kettle Falls, in case he was still interested in coming along. He was, and we were grateful to have a few special guests attending this informal send-off service.

Janet Kay

We met them at the marina in Grand Marais just before sunset on a beautiful late-summer day. Thomas had the boat ready to go. He helped my mother in and seated her. She clutched a bouquet of roses she hand-picked from her garden. I climbed in with a bottle of champagne and four glasses. Sabrina quietly took her place in the bow.

Mike boarded with a bottle of Jack Daniels. "Jonathan's favorite over all the years." He chuckled. "I thought I'd toss it out into Lake Superior along with his urn of ashes."

Then he grew serious. "Ya know, I hardly knew your grandfather." He directed his gaze at me. "For all those years, he was just a fixture who showed up every week to drink. He rarely talked to anyone. We knew nothing about this guy who later called himself Robert Andersen. He was obviously a troubled and unhappy man. Tormented by something he'd never speak of. I wondered if he'd been in a war and was suffering from PTSD. We felt sorry for him, although he could be a pain in the ass when he was drunk. Can't tell you how many times I had to put him up in the room by the fish house so he didn't get out on the lake and kill himself."

"And then that's exactly what he finally did," I lamented.

"Yeah. Maybe I should have done more, especially after he decided he was Robert Andersen and started talking about witches and going down with his ship in Lake Superior."

"Nobody could have done anything to change this outcome, Mike," Thomas assured him. "Your being here, and putting up with him all these years is what's important. Thank you, man."

Thomas pulled away from the dock and we headed out of the harbor toward a quiet bay where the waves rolled peacefully. The setting sun began casting reflections upon the water as the sky turned into subtle shades of pink and gold.

Thomas killed the engine. We floated a while in silence as I poured us each a glass of champagne. Mother nodded, taking control, lifting her glass in a toast. She put her glass down, retrieved a note from her purse and began to read.

"To Jonathan. May you rest in peace. May your soul heal and be restored. May you earn forgiveness for what you did, and gain insights on the other side of life that will help you to become a better person in the future."

220

We quietly drank our champagne, rocking on the waves, as the sun slipped beneath the horizon. Mother stood up with her bouquet of roses while Thomas steadied her. She tossed the roses into the lake. "For you, my troubled father," she whispered as tears filled her eyes.

I rose carefully, opened the urn of ashes, and gently scattered them upon the waves. As they drifted away, a chill swept through me and I felt Angelique wrap her invisible arms around me. *Forgiveness is the key to your happiness, my dear,* her spirit whispered into my mind.

"I am trying to learn to forgive you, Grandfather, if that is what my dear grandmother wants us to do," I whispered into the wind. "Dear God," I prayed silently, "please heal and restore this lost soul so he can make up for his past sins. So he can do better, do good things for others, in his next lifetime on this earth."

I glanced over at my mother who had a strange and wistful look upon her face, as if she too felt Angelique's presence.

"My turn?" Mike broke our reverie as he stepped to the edge of the boat and tossed the bottle of Jack Daniels into the midst of Jonathan's ashes. "Here's to you, Jonathan, a little reinforcement for your journey to the other side."

And so, it was done. Jonathan was buried at sea, sixty-six years after his ship had gone down without him.

CHAPTER FORTY-EIGHT

We all enjoyed a delicious fresh fish dinner on the deck of the Angry Trout Café after Jonathan's burial ceremony. Today was the first time Mother had met Thomas, and I was pleased that she seemed to like him and enjoyed his company. After dinner, Mike retreated to his room at the Shoreline Inn.

I walked Sabrina out to her car and gave her a big hug, thanking her for all she'd done to help us discover the truth about our past. Without her, and Justine's journals, we never would have known. We made plans to get together soon. For now, she needed to get back to Annette and the Gunflint Lodge.

Mother and I went to Thomas's place for the night. But instead of spending the night in his arms in the master bedroom, I slept in the spare bedroom with her.

It had been an exhausting yet almost comforting day in some respects. Tomorrow Thomas was taking Mike fishing. Mother and I would explore Grand Marais, stopping to visit the old Lake Superior Trading Post, art and antique galleries and other interesting sites. She'd always loved our summer trips to Grand Marais. Little did she know then that her roots and traumatic history actually began up here on the Gunflint Trail.

Before we turned in for the night, Thomas and I found a quiet moment alone to say good night. We fell into each other's arms, into a warm lingering kiss that would have to sustain us until we could be alone and together again.

I slipped into my bed quietly, trying not to wake my mother. But I heard her stirring in her bed.

"Angela? Tell me more about your *friend* Thomas." She emphasized the *friend* word, insinuating that he was probably more than a friend. She didn't miss much.

I sighed. "He's a wonderful man, Mother, and has helped me through all of this. He has held me together. Without him, we would not have solved this mystery."

"I'm not blind, my dear. It's obvious that you love each other. I can see it in your eyes, the way you interact together. If he makes you happy and is good to you, it would make me happy to see the two of you together."

"I know it hasn't been that long, but we do feel like we have known each other forever. We love each other and hope to marry someday soon."

"Congratulations, Angela, and I mean that sincerely. I have a lovely vintage wedding dress for you to wear, one that my lovely adoptive mother was married in about 1930. I wore it when I married your father. I didn't offer it to you when you married Jeff simply because I had a bad feeling about him. I always did. This is different. It would be an honor if you would wear it when you marry Thomas."

"Oh, Mother." I got up to give her a hug. This had been far too easy. And the very thought of wearing her dress on our special day was one of the greatest gifts she could have given me. "Thank you from the bottom of my heart."

She patted my hand. "And thank you, and Thomas also, for discovering the truth about our family history and putting my mind to rest after all these years. Now, it's time to get some sleep."

Mother and I meandered around Grand Marias the next day. We sat on a bench in the little park area overlooking the harbor watching boats coming and going, seagulls flittering around, and Canadian Geese beginning to gather. Fall was already in the air, and it wouldn't be long before they made their way south for the winter. That was always a sight to behold as hundreds of geese gathered into formation, honking loudly as they took to the sky and flew away. They'd be back next spring.

We returned to Thomas's place shortly before he and Mike arrived with their catch of lake trout. They'd bonded as they shared their "big fish" stories. Mike thanked us and invited us to come on back to Kettle Falls anytime. He would stay in touch.

As I was preparing to take Mother back to Duluth, my phone rang. It was Sabrina calling to tell me that an important package addressed to me had just been delivered to her at the lodge since nobody was home at my place. Fed Ex advised they could not leave the package without someone signing for it. The package was from a funeral home in Michigan.

"Angelique's ashes!" I inhaled. "We'll be there in another hour or so."

"Change of plans," I announced to Mother and Thomas. "Angelique's ashes are here. Mother, do you want to stay so we can have a little ceremony at the cabin?" She frowned.

We had already discussed a number of options ranging from burying them at the Duluth cemetery where Mother's adoptive parents were buried to burying them beside Angelique's parents at the Chippewa City cemetery just north of Grand Marais. Or simply scattering her ashes at Angelique's cabin on Gunflint Lake, my home now.

Mother had not been able to decide what she wanted to do. It was all too much for her, she said, until now when she suddenly blurted out, "I don't want to do anything yet. Something tells me the timing is not right. Not yet. I want to take her ashes home with me for a while. Later, I'll come up to scatter some of them at the cabin. Then we'll bury the urn at the Chippewa cemetery. I've decided to be buried there myself someday instead of Duluth."

"That's wonderful news, Mother. She, and you, someday, will be close to us. I love that idea. Maybe we'd better check into getting some cemetery lots there?"

She chuckled. "I'm one step ahead of you. I've already done that. I have several lots right next to Angelique's parents. For her, for me, and room for the two of you...and perhaps your children someday. You can bury four urns in each of my two lots."

What had happened to my meek and withdrawn mother? Once she'd moved beyond her initial shock and horror, she seemed to have thrived. She had more energy, more strength, more hope. Perhaps Angelique's visit to her helped? Whatever it was, I was grateful to see her taking charge of her life and enjoying it.

Thomas gave my mother a big hug. He'd been accepted into her family. "Thank you, Emily. You truly are amazing, just like your daughter, and I am honored that you are welcoming me into your family. We just may have a big day coming up before too long. Of course, I need to confirm that with my lovely Angela."

"Confirmed!" I beamed as I embraced the two of them together in a big hug.

Thomas dipped down in a gentlemanly bow and directed his gaze at my mother. "I promise you that I will love and honor your daughter for the rest of my life—and beyond."

With that, Mother and I made a quick trip out to the Gunflint Lodge to say hello to Sabrina and Annette, and to pick up Angelique's urn. Then I drove Mother back to Duluth. She was anxious to get home since she was hosting an important book club meeting at her place the next day. More importantly, she was determined to place her mother's ashes on the mantle over the fireplace in the library. They would remain there for now, until we buried them at the Chippewa cemetery in the fall.

I spent the night there before leaving for home early the next morning. She had a surprise for me before I left. She called me into her bedroom where I found a stunning cream-colored silk wedding dress hanging beside her bed. Truly vintage, it was slim fitting with simple clean lines, long tapered sleeves, and a lacy embroidered inset. A long veil hung behind it. It was incredibly beautiful.

Mother beamed. "Do you like it?"

"I love it!" I gently touched the silky dress, imagining myself wearing it beside my handsome husband-to-be on the deck of the lodge where we'd be married. I embraced my mother before she called out to Beth.

"Beth, we need your help altering our wedding dress. Angela, here, try it on."

Amazingly, the beautiful dress fit me perfectly after a few minor alterations. Perhaps a sign that this was meant to be.

CHAPTER FORTY-NINE

"So, is it time yet?" Thomas teased me as we hiked down one of the trails near my cabin. Fall was in the air and the forest was turning into fireworks of red and gold leaves amidst the dark green of the pine trees.

"Time for what?"

"Well, you know it's only been about a hundred and sixty years since we became betrothed to one another." He grinned that irresistible grin of his as he tousled my hair. "Long ago. Virginia City, Montana. Remember?" He sighed, flashing back in time to our last lifetime together.

"So, are you asking me to marry you, again?"

He grew serious and got down on one knee in a pile of fallen leaves. "Will you take my hand in marriage, my lovely?"

"I will, honey," I beamed, my heart so full of love for this man that I felt like it would burst.

With that, he retrieved a dazzling Edwardian diamond engagement ring from his pocket. The diamond was set in a scrolled silver band, typical of the 1800s when we had been engaged for the first time. He gently placed it on my finger. It fit perfectly.

I sat beside him and we fell into an embrace as falling leaves scattered around us. "And I will make it up to you for all you've done for me this time around. You know I could not have gotten through this without you. I promise to be there for you, forever, whatever the future may bring."

It was time to plan our wedding, and our future. We decided that for now, we would keep both of our homes but we'd live together at one or the other. We'd stay at his place in Grand Marais when he needed to be there for his boating excursions and sled dog adventures. While he was busy working, I'd have time to pursue my art and start work on my novel. I might also do some freelance writing for the local newspaper, just like Justine Kerfoot did. We'd get away to my cabin when we needed a break.

I couldn't wait to tell Sabrina, so I paid her a visit at the lodge the next day, flashing my ring when I found her stocking shelves in the gift shop.

After admiring my antique ring, she hugged me close. "Oh, Angela, I'm so happy for you! Of course, I'm not the least bit surprised. I've always known this would happen from the first time the two of you set eyes on each other. It was *so* obvious."

We giggled together like a couple of school girls, planning the wedding. Of course, Sabrina offered to cater the event at the lodge. And she accepted my invitation to be my maid of honor. I couldn't imagine having anyone else stand up for me.

We set a date of October first for a simple outdoor wedding on the deck of the Gunflint Lodge. Fall color should be at its peak. Sabrina would arrange the flowers and decorations, music, and a small dinner reception after the wedding. All we had to do was invite our guests and show up.

While Sabrina was planning for our big event, Mother and I had some unfinished business to attend to. It was time to put Angelique to rest, finally, after sixty-six long years. We made arrangements with the local funeral home to dig a small hole for the urn at the Chippewa cemetery where Angelique's parents were buried, and we ordered a headstone.

Beth drove Mother up to help with funeral arrangements including a visit to the Maple Hill Church in Grand Marais, the place where my mother had been left when she was a toddler. I worried a bit about visiting this church. What if it triggered difficult memories for her? However, she was adamant that we needed to engage the pastor there to officiate at the burial.

The three of us drove out to the little country church early the next morning after scheduling a visit with Pastor Jorgenson. We parked near the quaint little cemetery. I watched for any reaction from Mother as we walked to the church.

She stopped, a frown upon her face, deep in concentration. "For some reason this place looks vaguely familiar to me. Could it be? Is this where..."

"It is." I took her hand. I had, of course, told her that Angelique had left her at a country church before fleeing for her life.

She took a deep breath, closing her eyes, flashing back in time. "I was sad because Mommy wasn't here with me. I remember now. But they were very good to me. I used to play out here under the trees and have picnics with my new doll. It wasn't Susan...but she was still nice. I was okay, Angela. I'm still okay."

With that, she marched on into the church as I marveled over her newborn strength and ability to accept what had happened in her past. Her step was quicker and more confident than before.

We decided that Angelique's burial ceremony would be a simple one at the cemetery for immediate family only. Her urn of ashes would be buried there, after Mother had retrieved a packet of ashes that she planned to scatter over Gunflint Lake later, after she'd taken them to our wedding ceremony. This is what she wanted and felt she needed to do.

We arrived at the cemetery beside the historic St. Francis Xavier Church and made our way along the trail to the spirit house that hovered over her parents' graves. The pastor, who was also an accomplished violin player, played several hymns as we sang along. He then said a few words and offered a prayer before gently lowering the urn of ashes into the hole in the ground.

"May your journey back to the afterlife be a smooth one, now that you have completed your unfinished business upon this earth. And may you find your departed loved ones waiting for you there. Until we meet again, may God bless and keep you." The pastor concluded his remarks, crossing his heart. "Amen."

"Amen," we echoed his words, bowing our heads. Mother, Beth, Thomas and I then gathered around the site, scattering wild flowers we'd gathered in the woods over Angelique's grave as we said our tearful goodbyes.

"I'm sorry for doubting you, Mommy, for blaming you for leaving me behind," Mother whispered. "I'm sorry for all you went through. I love you and I always will." I held her close as our tears fell, as I whispered my own goodbyes to the grandmother I'd never met physically but had grown to know and love through our spiritual connection.

We huddled together, crossing our hearts, observing a moment of silence before hiking back out. A sense of closure and peace enveloped us as a comforting chill swept through us all. Angelique was there with us.

Once we returned to the car, Thomas asked, "It's not easy to understand how a spirit can cross back and forth to the afterlife over this Path of Souls, just because she has unfinished business here. Is this something the Ojibwe believe?"

"I think it's hard for humans to understand things like this—until they have died and crossed over into the heavens," I replied. "The Ojibwe believe the spirits of the deceased take a four-day journey along a Path of Souls that takes them into the afterlife. They believe that spirits travel this path of souls when they descend to earth to be born, and again when they return to heaven after they die. Sometimes, on a clear night, you can see that Path of Souls—the Milky Way."

"Does this mean that Angelique crossed that Path of Souls sixty-six years ago, and she has now crossed it again?" Thomas inquired.

"Not yet," Mother suddenly interrupted. "Not until we scatter her ashes over the lake she loved."

We both turned to find her standing firmly, arms crossed, beside her mother's grave. She was determined that it wasn't quite time for her mother to leave.

"Oh, well, okay," I mumbled. Turning back to Thomas, I continued, "To answer your question, it's still a mystery to try to understand how her spirit has been able to come back to visit us, but I understand this has happened to lots of others also."

"And sometimes," Mother added, "when the Northern Lights dance across the sky, it is actually the spirits of our ancestors rejoicing and dancing to celebrate the arrival of a loved one on the other side of life."

"Very interesting," Thomas said. "Maybe we need to keep our eyes open for the Milky Way or the Northern Lights tonight."

But they didn't come out that night, despite our efforts to monitor the sky.

CHAPTER FIFTY

Our long-awaited wedding day dawned clear and bright. The fall leaves were at full peak, shimmering in a light breeze as rays of sunshine filtered through the canopy of trees. Thomas and I, holding hands, strolled over to the lodge where Mother and Beth were staying.

We had a leisurely breakfast before sitting outside watching Sabrina and her crew decorating the deck overlooking the lake with beautiful bouquets of white flowers and an arch of roses. A small group of chairs had been arranged for our guests which included Sabrina's family and some of the friendly neighbors we'd met on the Gunflint Trail—including Karl, the former owner of our cabin. Some of Thomas's work associates and regular customers also attended.

It was time to leave Thomas behind while we three girls went back to the cabin to get ready for the wedding. Mother was adamant that it was bad luck for the groom to see his bride in her wedding dress before the ceremony. We gave in to her traditional beliefs.

I kissed him goodbye. He would hang out at the lodge with some of his friends and get into his suit before the ceremony. It wouldn't be long before we would finally be man and wife, just as we'd planned 160 years ago in another time, another place.

Mother and Beth helped me into the beautiful wedding dress. Beth did my hair and makeup. I felt like a princess and could hardly believe it was actually me when I looked into the full-length mirror.

We were ready to climb into the car and head back to the lodge. Mother clutched her purse containing the packet of Angelique's ashes that she'd retrieved from the urn. She wanted to be sure that Angelique attended the wedding of her granddaughter in one way or another. After all, it had been her granddaughter, Angela, who had solved the mystery of her disappearance!

Sabrina met us at the door of the lodge, oohing and aahing over my dress. She guided us to chairs inside overlooking the deck where we were to wait until it was time for my mother to escort me down the aisle to the deck. Peering out, I could see guests gathered around my Thomas who was looking extremely dapper in his dark suit. My heart leaped at the very sight of him.

Beth fixed my long veil before she went out to join the guests. A small band began to play the wedding march.

"It's time," Sabrina, my beloved maid of honor, beamed at me as she guided us out onto the lawn, handing me my bouquet of flowers and holding up my veil. "You look absolutely stunning, Angela. Thomas is one lucky man."

"And I am one lucky woman," I responded as my mother took my arm to give me away to my soulmate, the man of my dreams.

All heads turned our way as we began to slowly walk down the flower-strewn aisle toward the arch where Thomas waited, a huge smile upon his handsome face.

He took my hand and leaned in to whisper, "You are the most beautiful bride in this world, my lovely."

Pastor Jorgenson guided us through the usual wedding vows before we exchanged rings to the sound of loons wailing on the lake.

"You may kiss the bride." He smiled as Thomas scooped me into his arms and the band began to play again. After that we headed for the reception in the lodge, complete with champagne toasts, a delicious buffet and more photos taken by the photographer that Sabrina hired.

It was soon time for Thomas and I to depart on our honeymoon, actually just a quiet weekend at my cabin—something we craved after all the recent drama in our lives. We'd save our trip to Hawaii for another time.

As we walked out of the lodge to the beautifully decorated horse-drawn carriage that would take us home, our guests followed, cheering us on and congratulating us once again. I tossed my bouquet to the crowd. Beth caught it! Well, who knew? She may be in her sixties but perhaps it was never too late.

The horses whinnied as they clip-clopped along the road to our cabin and the setting sun turned the sky into brilliant shades of orange and gold.

Thomas carried me across the threshold, another old-fashioned tradition. But before we settled into honeymoon mode, there was one more piece of business to take care of. We needed to scatter Angelique's remaining ashes over the lake. My mother had insisted on taking them to the wedding first. Now she and Beth would stop over—for a short visit, she assured me—to participate in this ceremony.

Thomas and I changed into comfortable clothes before they arrived. It was dark by the time we hiked down to the lake with our flashlights. We made our way to our special bench, where we sat or stood in silence for a few minutes. Mother then retrieved the packet holding her mother's ashes and slowly walked the few remaining steps to the lake. We followed.

"To my beloved mother, Angelique. May you rest in peace, finally."

Thomas and I huddled together as my mother scattered the ashes over the lake. As she did, a familiar chill swept through us, that comforting sense of Angelique's presence. She was still here with us!

The sky darkened as billions of stars glittered from above, forming a stairway into heaven. They cast their reflections over Gunflint Lake, over Angelique's scattered ashes. We stood in awe as the Milky Way arched above us.

I felt a surreal hug that encompassed my entire being. I watched as my mother reacted in the same way, cherishing one more hug from her dear mother. Then, a transparent image that I immediately recognized as my beloved grandmother began to float across the sky.

Angelique's words swept into my mind. "Mission accomplished. My unfinished business on this earth is finally completed, thanks to you. Until we meet again, remember that I will always love you."

As she crossed over, the sky burst into brilliant shades of green and red swirling throughout the heavens. The spirits above were dancing, rejoicing, as their beloved Angelique joined them once again.

Mother sighed and wiped away a tear as I held her other hand. "My dear mother has finally crossed over. I love you, Mommy." She turned to us. "Someday we will see her again on the other side of life."

"Amen," I whispered.

THE END

Acknowledgements

This book would not be possible without the valuable feedback and assistance from a number of individuals, groups and resources.

I would like to thank my wonderful first readers and reviewers: Jim Bishop, Shane Jenson, Sue Kerfoot, Debra King, Judy Liautaud, Rodney Savary, Jean Swanson, and Mike Williams. Many thanks also to my awesome writers' group, The St. Croix Writers of Solon Springs, Wisconsin. And a special note of appreciation to Donna Soland for her relentless efforts to keep me on track!

I also wish to thank my amazing editor, Lisa Lickel; and my awesome cover designer Hannah Linder of Hannah Linder Designs.

In addition, I want to acknowledge Sue Kerfoot, her late husband Bruce, and late mother-in-law Justine Kerfoot. The Kerfoot family, longtime former owners of the Gunflint Lodge in Grand Marais, did so much for the Grand Marais, Minnesota, community for so many years. Justine and her books inspired me to set my novel in this area. While I have included "Justine" and some of her written works in my novel, please note that I have fictionalized any real people and places. I greatly appreciate Sue's assistance and review.

My friend, fellow author and historian Mike Williams also inspired me to include Kettle Falls and Voyageurs National Park. Mike grew up there and is a wealth of historical knowledge with incredible stories to tell. Thank you, my friend!

And last but not least, many thanks to my awesome children Shannon & Will Graber, Shane & Sandi Jenson, and Sherry Jenson; and my amazing grandchildren Derek Jenson, Madelaine & David Altman, Malachi & Jasmine Jenson, William Graber, Abigail Graber, Andrew Graber, Audrey McLochlin, Milton Jenson, Jared McLochlin and George Jenson. And the latest additions to my family: my darling great-grandchildren Kyler Jenson, Joe Jenson and Faith Jenson. Thank you all for your love and support, and for your understanding when I'm sometimes pre-occupied—lost in the world I've created for my characters! Love you all.

To my readers: a very special thank you! I love hearing from you and would greatly appreciate your posting reviews of my books on Goodreads, Amazon or other review sites. For more information, please check out my website at www.novelsbyjanetkay.com.

JANET KAY
www.novelsbyjanetkay.com

Janet Kay lives and writes on a lake in the woods of Northwest Wisconsin. Drawn to nature since she was a child, she sees it as a source of renewal, reflection and connection with something greater than oneself.

She has published five novels to date: WATERS OF THE DANCING SKY, and RAINY LAKE RENDEZVOUS, set on the wilderness islands of Rainy Lake along the Minnesota/Ontario international border; AMELIA 1868, which is set in the old western ghost town of Virginia City, Montana; THE SISTERS which is set on the historic, haunted Galveston Island in Texas; and her latest, UNFINISHED BUSINESS, set on the North Shore of Lake Superior including Isle Royale and Voyageurs National Parks.

Her novels blend thriller and mystery genres with historical fiction, romance, psychological suspense and the supernatural. Her mission is to make a difference in people's lives by expanding their horizons above and beyond the confines of this world and this lifetime.

Janet Kay's lifelong passions include creative writing, travel, photography, and spending time with family and friends. She frequently combines these interests as she explores new and exciting destinations to set her novels.

If you enjoyed one or more of her novels, she would greatly appreciate it if you would leave a review on Goodreads, Amazon.com or other sites of your choice.

For more information, check out her website at
www.novelsbyjanetkay.com; or her
Facebook page – www.facebook.com/Janet-Kay-Author.

www.ingramcontent.com/pod-product-compliance
Lightning Source LLC
Chambersburg PA
CBHW020623110726
47899CB00002B/626